BREWER

SKYE MCNEIL

ALSO BY SKYE MCNEIL

The Mobster Files

Appointed by Fate

Exonerated with Love

Credence

Atlas Series

Hearts Abroad

Oceans Away

Macha MC Series

Doc T

Kevlar

Rubble

Brewer

For information, contact the publisher, Hot Tree Publishing.

www.hottreepublishing.com

Editing: Hot Tree Editing

Cover Designer: BookSmith Design

E-book: 978-1-922679-17-8

Paperback: 978-1-922679-18-5

For those still searching for their Macha family.

PROLOGUE

A cool breeze slid across Alannah Stapleton's face as the motorcycle she rode hugged the curve of the highway outside of Snowshoe, Colorado. Beside her, RK—or Roadkill to Macha MC—grinned at her from the custom-made Harley he straddled. It was a perfect autumn evening to take a ride. They turned down the main drag into town. But they weren't merely out to feel the breeze on their skin. Something wasn't right at the club's bakery, and they needed to figure out why the register continuously lost money.

RK flipped on his blinker, taking them down a back road and away from the wandering eyes of the deputy sheriff parked on the right side of the road. As much as Macha appreciated the law, the club skirted the lines of legality on a daily basis.

The cell phone buzzed inside her leather jacket pocket. Alannah pulled it out and frowned.

Unknown: Leave the bakery alone or you'll regret it.

It was a duplicate of the message RK received earlier that morning and was the reason they were checking in with the bakery staff before the club got involved. They managed the store, so it was their responsibility to handle it first and ask the club for help only if the need arose.

Alannah shoved the phone back into her pocket and caught up to RK. They couldn't back down from a fight. It wasn't Macha's way. Neither she nor RK would let their club be brought down by fear. It was the same philosophy they instilled into their children.

A smile found her face at the thought of Brewer and Dorthea. RK conjured their names when they were born. Alannah had to give him credit where it was due. While their daughter opted for her nickname Dolly, Brewer fit like a glove. Their son had been obsessed with all things Macha since infancy, and his lust for Irish brews only increased over the years.

She looked over at RK, his ruddy face weathered beneath his bushy white beard. He grinned, revealing his slightly crooked front teeth. She couldn't imagine raising a family with anyone else. Their love story had blossomed in Ireland, and she'd never forget leaving that island to start a life with the man she'd die for.

Shivers raced down her spine, but not the good ones RK's kisses created. Alannah glanced over her shoulder and her pulse quickened. Three riders were quickly gaining on them. None wore cuts. Their leather jackets were as black as a moonless night, and their faces were disguised by skull masks.

RK saw them too, and he maneuvered behind her slightly. He'd have her back until the very end. Unfortunately, when she noticed a glimmer of silver, Alannah sensed it'd be sooner rather than later.

Drawing her gun simultaneously with RK, she braced for the unknown riders to reach them. It didn't take long. The rumble of motorcycles drowned out RK's yells. The first gunshot sliced through the front tire of her bike, causing her to struggle with the handlebars. She popped off a round, but the bullets missed the riders with hidden faces.

More gunshots peppered the air, the sunset haloing the scene accompanied by the screaming of tires and collision of metal. It all happened so fast. Alannah was upright in one moment and in the next, her legs were pinned beneath her bike.

In her peripheral, she saw RK go down hard. He managed to duck behind his bike and was shooting rounds toward the attackers. Alannah struggled to move the bike, blood oozing from the wound on her shoulder. If she could get to him, they'd be all right. He had more than enough extra bullets in his saddlebag to keep the rogue bikers at bay until help arrived. She searched her pocket and cursed when she came up empty. Glancing around, she spotted the phone lying precariously close to the road.

RK was crawling toward her when a bullet hit his leg. He grimaced at the pain but made it to her side nonetheless.

"Lannah, you okay?" he said breathlessly, searching her for injuries.

"I'll live." She took in his worry lines that were splattered with blood. "Who are they?"

RK pulled her free of the motorcycle, then peeked around it. "Not sure. Cutthroats, maybe. They haven't said a word, so I can't tell if they have accents."

"You think they're Macha?"

"It's possible." He fired again and hunkered down by her. "Who better than one of our own to get away with stealing from the club?"

Alannah gritted her teeth. He wasn't wrong, and

that royally pissed her off. A pause in the shots gave her a chance to quickly let off the round in her gun. Just as she turned, a bullet sped toward them. RK lunged in front of her. The shot hit him directly in his chest.

Crying out, she caught him as he fell. Blood drenched his cut, the slickness transferring onto her. Cradling him, Alannah shook her head, her tears falling on his face.

"Don't you dare die. We got too much to do. Too much to see." She kissed his lips as they moved, his words inaudible. Peering through her tears, she grabbed RK's gun and pulled the trigger. The bullet hit one of the approaching masked figures, felling him instantly.

RK gripped her arm, stealing her focus. "I've seen it all and done it all because of you. Now it's time to go."

She hugged him close. The light in his eyes waned with each passing second. "I'll see you soon." She kissed his forehead, and his eyes closed for the last time. It was their special phrase they said anytime, anywhere to express their love to each other.

Sniffling, she lifted her chin and met the dark gaze of the executioner. "You." She recognized him instantly. "How could you?"

The only answer she received was a bullet to the chest.

Alannah drifted quickly toward the warmth of the setting sun, but she managed to hear one of the men seal his fate.

"Pick up every shell. We can't leave any evidence. Macha will blame another MC."

Resting her head against RK's, she watched the sun dip below the horizon as their murderer rode toward Macha's clubhouse. "They'll find out who did this. Brewer and Dolly will make it right," she promised with her last breath.

CHAPTER 1
BREWER

Slinging a dish towel over his left shoulder, Brewer Stapleton waved at the group of tourists leaving the bar. If he wasn't already late for church, he'd have taken one or two of those blonde, tanned beauties to his room and shown them exactly how charming he could be.

He watched the last woman shut the side door, her miniskirt riding up her long legs. *Damn you, Rubble, for calling a meeting before happy hour.* Shaking his head, Brewer willed his blood to cool. He couldn't go to church with tight jeans. More than one nymph would release the pressure, but he didn't have time. Time to himself was something he rarely had.

"Be back in a bit," he called to the night manager before walking out the doors.

The crisp spring air bit at his face but less

intensely than it should, thanks to his bushy red beard. He zipped up his leather jacket with the Macha emblem stamped on the back and his name and role in the club on the front. For as long as he could remember, he'd been in Macha. His parents met thanks to the MC, and both he and his sister were conceived and delivered in Macha's clubhouse. Macha was in his blood. He'd never leave the club that was his family.

A stray snowflake fell on his head, and he smirked. Colorado's springtime was a daily game of roulette. After the brutal winter, he was ready for sunshine, beer, and riding his motorcycle until the stars burned out.

Brewer opened the door to the clubhouse, stepped inside, and inhaled the sweet scent of baked blueberry. He stopped by the kitchen and snatched a turnover cooling on the racks.

"Oy! Those are for later," Isa scolded, her Irish accent making him grin.

"Sorry, gotta run." He waved and headed in the other direction. No doubt Isa was rolling her eyes and cursing under her breath. She was his distant cousin, but even if she hadn't been, they'd still get along like siblings always teasing each other.

Brewer snuck passed two nymphs arguing in the den, his little sister patiently enacting her madam role despite the annoyed expression on her face. Dolly could handle her own. Hell, he'd witnessed her take out a biker twice her size and not break a sweat. She'd fix whatever problem her nymphs had.

Finally reaching the inner sanctum of Macha's clubhouse, Brewer pulled out a chair and plopped down between Kevlar and Hawk.

"I see you're stealing from my old lady again," Doc said with a knowing look from across the table.

Brewer stuffed the rest of the pastry in his mouth and shrugged. "Least that's all I'm stealing. I could've whisked her away last summer."

Hawk snickered and Doc glared at Hawk. "In your dreams."

Chuckling, Brewer sat back and swiveled his chair, ready for church to be over. The bar, Booze & Tattoos, was hosting a karaoke night in less than an hour, and he couldn't wait to hear the amateurs take the stage. *Plus, rein in a little action for later.*

Reaper, the club president, rapped the wooden gavel on the table, and the room went silent. "Thank you all for making it to this last-minute meeting. Brewer, I know the bar has a gig tonight, so we won't keep you long."

Several pairs of eyes landed on Brewer, and he nodded once. The bar staff could survive without him, but he appreciated the shout-out nevertheless.

Reaper glanced at the mountain of a man to his left. "It's time for me to step down as president."

A chorus of voices echoed in the room, but Reaper held up his hand and hushed them.

"I'm gettin' old, boys. You've all seen it over the last year." He pulled out his reading glasses and waved them. "Lord knows I can't see worth shit. Macha needs better for her president. You also need a VP. One who won't ever betray our family."

Doc clenched his hands to fists on the tabletop. Less than a year ago, the club had endured the worst kind of betrayal from their own vice president. It was more than time to put that scoundrel out of their minds.

But Brewer couldn't. Not after Kevlar and his old lady, Nikita, had mentioned seeing the last VP, Shovelhead, hanging around Diablos and the Greenback Cutthroats MCs.

"I've been president of this mighty club in Snowshoe for twenty-five years. I look forward to watching Macha grow during my retirement." He smiled sadly. "I won't be far away, so don't worry. You're not rid of me yet."

The club chuckled good-naturedly. Reaper and Queenie, his old lady, were family, and that's how they'd stay long after the new president took the seat.

"We'll vote on all cabinet roles before summer begins. If you'd like to toss your patch in the ring for president or vice president, come talk with me." Reaper looked around the room slowly. "Any one of you could handle these roles, but only two will be elected. Think it over." He nodded to Rubble, the club's sergeant at arms. "Anything you'd like to add?"

Rubble shook his head. Even though he'd be a kick-ass president, Brewer knew Rubble wouldn't want it. The onetime MMA fighter and former Marine was better behind the scenes and amid the action. A diplomacy position wasn't Rubble.

"In that case, may the goddess ride with you." Reaper pounded the gavel once. Members immediately started to chatter, milling about while they all discussed the impending presidency change. Several went up to Reaper, intent on making their interest clear.

Brewer cracked his neck from side to side. Politics wasn't one of his interests. Beer, women, fast bikes, and good food, on the other hand…. They were all on his daily checklist.

"What do you think of all this?" Hawk asked, pulling out a pack of cigarettes.

"Not sure yet. We all knew Reaper was getting up there." He looked to Prez and sighed. "But it's gonna be a shit show until the new president and vice president are elected."

Hawk lit a smoke and offered one to him. "So, you're not adding your name?"

"Hell no. You?" He took the cigarette but didn't light it, simply rolling it between his fingers and already tasting the addictive nicotine. He tried to stop years ago. It was nearly impossible when cigarette smoke was as available as air in the club.

"Please, God, no." Hawk blew out a billow of smoke and stood. "Hate making decisions that affect the whole club, ya know? Not sure I could do it longer than a week."

"Agreed. It'll be a sad day when Reaper steps down." Brewer followed suit and stood, pushing the rolling chair back under the table. He briefly made eye contact with Reaper. The man was a second father to him, especially after his own dad died. The same could be said about most the club members. Reaper was always there when somebody needed him. Without a doubt, that would remain true during Reaper's retirement, but Brewer wasn't looking forward to Macha's future without the old Irishman heading it.

"Brewsky, are you coming? Karaoke starts in five minutes. Don't wanna miss the first group."

Turning back to Hawk, he nodded, and they

made their way out of the room. "You offering some deals at the parlor tonight?" Brewer asked the other man.

Hawk pinched a nymph's ass as they walked past her. "Hell yeah. Twenty percent off any music-themed tatt. Should be fun."

"I'll get the bartenders to spread the word." They walked by the kitchen, where they each grabbed some fresh pastries before exiting through the side door and walking across the lot to the bar and tattoo parlor combination.

"Thanks." Hawk took one long drag, then snuffed out the cigarette in a melting pile of slush outside the tattoo shop entrance. "Any drink specials tonight?"

"Nah, just the usual." They stepped into the parlor, and he snapped his fingers. "Which reminds me—I need to grab some more pretzels from the basement. I have a feeling we'll go through a lot tonight."

Hawk nodded but was quickly distracted by a woman in a low-cut shirt waiting at his station.

Brewer paused at the saloon-style doors that separated the bar from the tattoo shop. Three artists were already hard at work, and two others were ready to go. It was what he liked to see on a Friday night.

Pushing open the doors, he grinned at the

onslaught coming from the bar. It was already filled nearly to capacity. Karaoke had been a good idea. He hurried to the basement, filling both arms with pretzel boxes before heading back upstairs to slide into his spot behind the bar. It was looking like another successful night. The first singer chose a Carrie Underwood ballad, and he rolled his eyes at the two ready to sing the duet. *Women. Who the hell has time for them for longer than an hour or two?* His only priorities were his club, the bar, and finding out who murdered his parents. Everything else was static in the background.

CHAPTER 2
DELPHI

"I can't believe you convinced me to do this."

Delphi Windsor grinned like a cat with a bowl of cream. "Aw, come on. Live a little, Jupiter. It's just a little Carrie and Miranda."

Jupiter Hardy bit her bottom lip. "I haven't sung in public since… well, college, probably, and I was drunk off my ass." She pointed to her torso. "I can't exactly get wasted in my condition."

Leaning down, Delphi patted the bump that had finally started to show on the lean woman. It was petite and adorable just like Jupiter. "Kick if you want your mama to sing some karaoke."

"That's not how it—" Jupiter's eyes bugged when the little one sent a flutter toward Delphi's hand.

"Ha! See, now you have to do it! Your baby commanded." Delphi stood upright and placed her hands on her hips. "Once this little MC cutie is born, you'll be up to your nose in diapers and bottles. The least you can do is give me some blackmail material."

The other woman sighed. "Fine. One song, but that's it." She glanced around the bar and waved at the incoming Macha bikers. "Oh, goody. Rubble's here to see us too."

Delphi downed a shot of whiskey and let out a breath. "All righty, girlfriend. We're up first."

"Wait, what?"

"I planned ahead." Delphi took another shot as a spotlight focused on the stage. "No pansying like you did with paintballing."

Jupiter gave her an incredulous glance. "I found out I was pregnant, and you wanted to go paintballing the next day. I'd hardly call that being a pansy."

"Okay, okay, you win." She slung her arm around Jupiter's neck. Since meeting her four months earlier, Delphi couldn't imagine a better friend than Jupiter. Between joining a bowling league together and their common love for food, it hadn't been hard to find a kindred spirit in each other.

Pushing her shoulder-length brown hair behind her ears, Delphi steered Jupiter toward a booth near the makeshift stage. Despite living in Snowshoe for

most of her life, it was her first time at Booze &
Tattoos. *Mostly because it's a biker joint.*

She glanced around and noticed that at least half
of the patrons were current or retired MC patches.
Yep, bikers, bikers, and more bikers.

A few of her friends from high school went for the
bad biker boys, but Delphi had sworn to steer clear of
them as much as possible. She had a plan for her life,
and no hunky guy would keep her from it.

"First up, the dynamic duo Delphi and Jupiter
singing 'Somethin' Bad,'" the DJ—another MC biker
—called from the stage.

"No turning back now," Delphi said, grabbing her
friend's hand and hauling her up front. The bright
spotlight heated her instantly. Looking to her right,
she saw Jupiter grab the other mic with an anxious
expression on her face. Delphi winked and the music
started.

After diving in on the first verse, Delphi grinned
over at Jupiter. By the time the chorus came, they
were both smiling and singing along with the music.
On the last note, they linked arms and bowed. Whis-
tles from the back of the bar accompanied the modest
claps from the audience.

"That'd be Rubble and the boys," Jupiter said,
pride evident in her voice.

Although she only knew part of their love story,

Delphi respected the hulking man Jupiter fell in love with. He'd protected Jupiter from a horrid past and gave her a future worthy of her. Delphi couldn't ask for more than that for her fast friend.

Following Jupiter through the crowd, Delphi approached the booth filled with men and women sporting Macha MC apparel.

"Great job, ladies," Rubble said, his mismatched eyes homed in on his wife. The first time Delphi saw him, she did a double take at his one blue eye and one green eye combination. It wasn't a trait she'd ever come across before.

"Thanks." Jupiter propped herself on Rubble's knee and kissed him lightly. "But it was Delphi who led the vocals." She stuck out her tongue at her. "I was up there under duress."

"Who's getting under a dress?" someone teased while bringing a round of beers to the large booth.

Delphi glanced over at the tall man who had curly red hair and a beard to match. He passed out the Guinness, making jokes as he chatted.

"You wish," said a man with the name Cueball on his vest.

"Oh, believe me, brother, I'll be getting under some lucky lady's dress." He caught Delphi's gaze and slowly eyed her from head to toe, then back up to her face. "Maybe even yours, if you'd like."

"She wouldn't," Jupiter jumped in, playfully swatting the man.

Delphi gave him a onceover and shrugged. "Meh, if this is the bottom of the Macha barrel, I guess you'll do."

A round of *"Oohs"* echoed around the table and she smirked. She wasn't expecting the equally jovial expression from the man she recently dissed.

He took a step closer, his black T-shirt showing only the name of the bar on the left breast pocket. "I don't think I've seen you around the bar before."

"That's because it's my first time here."

"Brewsky likes the first-timers," Cueball snickered, sipping his beer.

Ignoring him, Brewer held her gaze. "What's your name, sweetheart?"

"I'm no one's sweetheart, but you can call me Delphi," she said, lifting her brows, a smile playing on her lips.

"Delphi." He nodded. "I like it. Sounds exotic. Got a last name to go with it?"

"None I'm willing to share." She smirked. "Is Brewsky actually your name, or is it a nickname?"

"Both. Name's Brewer." His blue eyes danced. "My parents were pretty unique."

"Yo, Brewer, you flirting or slinging drinks?"

Delphi looked over her shoulder at the petite

blonde who was gesturing with her hands in the air, clearly overwhelmed.

"Better get back before thirsty customers take over the bar." Brewer grabbed the empty tray. "Catch you later, Delphi."

"Doubtful," she flirted back. "Nobody catches me."

"Slippery, huh? Or just wet?" Brewer leaned over and whispered, "I can handle it either way, sweetheart."

Taken back by his brazen words, Delphi's mouth dropped open. He chuckled, chucked her under the chin, then walked back to the bar.

"What the hell just happened?"

Jupiter sipped water through a straw. "Brewer happened." She nudged Rubble to get him to make room for Delphi. "Have a seat. I'll explain the havoc of Macha's men."

Delphi shook her head. Her mind was too fuzzy. "I better not. Gotta get up early and make a fresh batch of baguettes."

Her friend saw straight through the fib but didn't let on. "You sure? Hawk can tell Brewer stories until last call."

"Yeah, I haven't hired a new baker, so it's all on me." She laughed. "That's what happens when you own a French bistro. People want authentic food, and

I'm the only one who can give that to them right now."

Jupiter rose quickly and gave her a hug. "Don't let Brewer fool ya. He's got a heart of gold. All of Macha's men do. Just takes a while to see that, with some of them."

Delphi didn't want to break it to her that she'd never mine long enough to find Brewer's gold. The time for bad-boy projects was long over. She had her café and her tabby cat, Fiona, waiting for her at home. She didn't need a man. *Well, except every now and then.*

"I'll stop by the bakery in the morning," she promised, mouth already salivating at the thought of whatever pastry concoctions Jupiter and Yasmina would have waiting.

"Only if you bring a baguette or two."

"Deal." Delphi waved goodbye to the bikers, but only Rubble acknowledged her before she made a hasty escape to the side exit.

"Leaving so soon? Hope I didn't scare you off."

Brewer's low voice made her gasp. It wasn't easy and teasing like it had been a few minutes earlier. It was concerned. Soft, even.

Turning toward him, she shook her head. "Not at all. I have to get up early for work."

"Where do you work? Maybe I can talk to your

boss so you can stay out for a while." His gaze dipped to her mouth. "I make one mean Irish car bomb."

There was that teasing tone she'd grown to both adore and loathe within moments of meeting him.

"Thanks, but I'm my own boss, so no chance there." She grabbed the handle and pushed the door open.

"If you change your mind, I'll be here until last call." His blue eyes turned a shade darker. "Then in my room at the clubhouse if you'd rather take the party elsewhere."

Rolling her eyes, she flipped him her middle finger. "Keep dreaming, Macha man. I don't have the energy to deal with a flirtatious dick."

"You sure about that?" He straddled the threshold, wiggling his brows mischievously. "You haven't tried mine yet. I've heard it's pretty fabulous."

Seeing that her off-putting attitude wasn't getting her anywhere with this guy, Delphi turned the tables. She closed the small distance between them and pressed herself against his chest. "You honestly think you can handle this, darling?"

She nuzzled his nose before licking his top lip. His body stiffened, and she felt the telltale signs of his arousal against her stomach. If she wasn't turned off by his biker arrogance, she thought she'd rather like the idea of having a tattooed guy on her arm.

"You think you're any match for my prowess?"

She smirked when he tried to kiss her. The look in his eyes was a mixture of thrilled and exasperated. "Please, *sweetheart*. Don't make me laugh." She reached down and cupped the sizeable package in his jeans. Once again, her desire to feel him inside her nearly outweighed her determination to serve him a slice of humility.

Delphi then placed a small kiss on the side of his neck and said, "I don't date bikers, so get it out of your mind, Brewer."

He didn't move. His lust-glazed eyes stayed focused on her. She could almost see the words trying to form within that fevered brain under his mop of red curls. "Delphi— "

She put a finger over his lips. "Not happening. End of story."

With that, she turned on her toes and escaped into the night air, heading toward her blue Ford SUV. Only when she reached her car did she let out the breath she'd been holding. Her heart pounded in her chest, a familiar warmth spreading between her legs. *No, I can't get involved with him.* It'd been years since she felt anything remotely like sexual attraction for anyone, much less a patched Macha member.

She climbed in and started the engine. The girls' night out she'd planned on having quickly morphed into hungering for a type of man she promised herself to never fall for again.

"Shake it off, Delphi. There are other men in Snowshoe who'll make you feel alive." She put the car in gear and hoped to God she was right.

CHAPTER 3
BREWER

That girl is crazy. Brewer linked his arm around the brown-haired nymph who'd been dancing seductively near the bar. Instead of staying until last call, he snagged one of the prospects to take over while he led her to the basement. Nothing but boxes and crates filled the space which was more for storage than anything else.

"How do you want it?" the nymph asked with a smile.

Pointing to the ground, Brewer unzipped his pants and let his belt hang loose. The nymph knelt and rolled a condom over his dick. She immediately got to work on the hard-on that just wouldn't go away after his interaction with Delphi. *Hell, I don't even know her last name, and she won't stop tormenting me.*

He cupped the back of the nymph's head, urging her closer. He wasn't seeing the nymph on her knees. He was imagining Delphi instead. Her pouty red lips wrapped around his dick and her clear blue eyes locked with his while she sucked him deep.

Brewer gripped the handrail, his cock thrusting into the nymph's mouth. This was one of the most popular perks of club life, but it was one he didn't take advantage of as often as others did.

He wrapped the nymph's hair around his hand. Sharing was one thing he couldn't do. Not like the other men in the club. A blow job here or there, sure, but sex was almost off-limits. The act itself was satisfying, but he didn't want his brothers to know everything about his sex life. This was partially why he chanced it and picked up girls from the bar. He also liked knowing the girl wasn't getting paid to sleep with him. *But not tonight. Tonight, I need a fast release.*

The nymph increased her pressure, and her free hand gently massaged his balls. Normally, he'd last longer. *But shit, that girl mind fucked me tonight.* Her quick switch from sweet to tough was the biggest turn on.

Brewer pictured Delphi, her hair swishing softly in the night air and her eyes alight with playful pleasure. He'd seen the desire in her face. She wanted him even as she snarled the opposite. It might take longer with her than his usual conquests, but he sensed she was worth it.

Thrusting faster, he let out a strangled grunt as he came. Once he finished, the nymph carefully pulled the full condom off. He gently cupped her face, tracing her bottom lip before helping her to her feet and swatting her ass.

"Do you want anything else?" she asked, gazing at him with her brown eyes, ready to please.

Zipping up his jeans, he shook his head. "That's all, thanks."

By the time he buckled, the girl was gone, and he was alone in the basement. Sighing, he leaned against a tall stack of boxes. This was the part he wasn't fond of. Right after. That awkward sensation of loneliness he always felt no matter who he had been with.

He rubbed the back of his neck, his dick still pulsing. Even after an epic BJ, he wasn't satisfied. Something was missing. *Or maybe it's someone.* He shook his head.

His phone buzzed in his pocket. He pulled it out and checked the messages. One was from Boulder, wondering where he ran off to, but the other was from Rubble.

Rubble: Need an update tomorrow.

Brewer cringed. Since volunteering to hunt down Shovelhead, he and Dolly had come up empty. The few leads they found went nowhere other than veering off onto more paths to chase down.

After sending a message to his sister, he trudged up the stairs and flipped off the light at the top. Reorganizing the mess down there could wait. For now, he needed a cold Guinness and ten hours of sleep before finding his sister and hoping she had some intel they could present to the club.

A few hours later, he went next door with beers in tow. Hawk and two other artists were finishing up their tattoos.

"Hey, man, you wanna grab a drink?" Hawk called, wiping off his station. He collected the cash from his customer and patted the man on the back. "All done for the night, and I'm itching for a brewsky."

"Already ahead of you." Brewer pulled a case out from behind his back and set it on the floor.

"You're my hero." Hawk grabbed one and pulled off the top. "Fuck yeah, this is the stuff." He drained half the bottle before coming up for air.

"Rough night?" Brewer leaned against the wall, cracked open his, and swigged. The speakers overhead pumped out rock music, a familiar guitar riff filling the room.

"Just busy as hell. One chick was all pissy 'cause the sparrow I drew didn't look evil enough or some shit, then a guy had a cover-up that took so much longer than I anticipated. Had to reschedule the appointment after him." Hawk eyed him. "What about you? Karaoke night go well?"

"Oh, yeah. It was fine." He drank more, trying to keep his mind off Delphi. His gaze drifted to the woman wincing in pain over the butterfly tattoo Snoopy was inking on her lower back.

"Dude, you okay? You're looking all serious and shit." Hawk kicked him. "That's not you."

Brewer chugged the rest of his beer. "No, it's not." He shook his head. "Struck out on a girl, is all."

Hawk swiveled his chair in a full circle. "Hold up. A girl resisted your charm? Whoa. Was she not drunk enough or something?"

"That wasn't it." He swept his fingers through his hair. "She doesn't date bikers."

"Ah." He shrugged. "Guess there's nothing you can do. Girls like that won't change their minds, bro."

"Nikita did."

Hawk gave him a pointed look. "Nikita was born into a club. She's different."

Brewer grabbed two more beers and opened them. "Yeah, maybe. But then there's Jupiter."

"Did she actually swear off bikers?"

They both wracked their brains for the answer.

"Nah, don't think so," Brewer finally admitted. "It sucks. This girl's a real looker too. Got one plump ass." He took a long drink. "But it's her fire that pulled me in. She gave it back to me just as easily as she took it."

"So, a spitfire with sass?" Hawk chuckled behind his bottle. "Perfect."

Brewer sank into a chair opposite Hawk. "I'll win her over. You'll see." He sipped the beer, setting his very soul at ease. "She'll see too. Delphi is meant to be mine."

"The fuck kind of shit you spewing?" Hawk slugged him good-naturedly. "You're sounding more and more like Doc and Kevlar. Don't get pussy-whipped like the others."

Brewer laughed and clinked his bottle against Hawk's. "No worries that'll happen. No woman can handle me for more than a week anyhow."

Three nymphs walked into the parlor, stealing the attention away from the conversation at hand, and Brewer had never been more grateful. Even though he had said what he hoped would be true, he couldn't believe it himself.

Maybe Delphi is what I've been missing in my life. He

tipped up his beer and smirked as he drank. Hawk was right. He needed to get laid. Once he did, Delphi would be out of his thoughts for good.

CHAPTER 4

DELPHI

Tossing the last baking sheet in the oven, Delphi swept a hand over her forehead and blew out a breath. The clock above the wall illuminated the time, which showed that it was still hours away from opening time for the bistro. She leaned against the counter and rolled her shoulders. Working both opening and closing was harder with each passing day. *The sooner I hire a pastry chef, the better.*

Her phone vibrated on the quartz countertop, and she smiled at the message from Jupiter.

Jupiter: Meet me in thirty minutes or I'm gonna eat all the cinnamon buns.

Delphi chuckled and quickly sent a reply, disregarding her floury thumbs.

Delphi: Not if I beat you there.

She didn't have to wait long to see a plethora of emojis texted back from her friend. Putting the phone down, Delphi surveyed the kitchen. It was neat, clean, and just the right size for the small restaurant. With only eight months of business ownership under her belt, she hoped the economy would continue to support local restaurants.

That had been her father's biggest concern when she showed interest in culinary arts.

"Boss lady, you here?"

Frowning, Delphi made her way to the side entrance. Her maître d' stood just inside the door.

"Peter, everything all right? I wasn't expecting you until three this afternoon."

Peter took off his beanie, which made his dark black hair stick up every which way. "It's my mother. The hospice worker called. She isn't going to make it much longer."

"Oh, God." Delphi closed the distance between them and hugged the man she viewed as an uncle. "I'm so sorry. Please, take all the time you need."

Peter sniffed, wiping the tears on his cheeks. "You're sure? It's been so busy here. I don't want to make it worse for you."

She patted his shoulder. "I'll cope, don't worry."

"Thank you, Delphi." He managed a small smile. "You're truly the best boss I've had in years."

"Let me know if there's anything I can do to help."

He waved, then slipped out the door as quietly as he arrived. Delphi sighed. She felt for him. She'd lost her father a year earlier, and the pain resonated just as harshly even now.

"Okay, you can do this." She looked at her watch and chewed her bottom lip. She had just enough time to grab the loaf out of the oven, then head to the bakery to meet Jupiter. "Maybe Jillian can man the front. Or I will." She winced at the thought but couldn't afford to hire anyone, even temporarily. "I'll get through this. A little hiccup, is all."

She walked back to the kitchen, praying she was right. It'd been problem after problem ever since she'd opened the bistro. She smiled at the picture of her with her parents on her graduation day. "Don't worry, Dad. I'll manage. I always do."

The scent of fresh bread wafted to her, and she hurried to take the bread out before it burned. The timer had four minutes left, but she knew from years of training that her nose was always the best judge. *Except when it comes to men.*

She placed the loaf on the cooling rack, determined to keep the redheaded Macha bartender out of her thoughts. It would've been easier if his scent didn't linger on her jacket. She couldn't help but put it on before walking down the stairs to the bistro hours earlier. Inhaling deeply, Delphi closed her eyes and let out a curse. Spicy cologne mixed with Guinness and a hint of mahogany sent her heart racing.

"Stop it." She shook her head and quickly put the dirty dishes in the sink since the dishwasher was still running before locking the door behind herself and walking down the snowy street. There'd be no more thoughts of Brewer or his mesmerizing eyes. She rounded the corner and groaned as the very man she meant to forget came into focus as he entered the bakery.

For a split second, she considered bailing, but the better half of her dissuaded it. Jupiter would miss her and vice versa. Delphi straightened her shoulders and trudged forward. She could handle one Macha man. *How hard could it be?*

***

Entering Heaven's Treats, Delphi decided to make a point of avoiding eye contact with Brewer. He didn't even give her the chance. He stood to the left of the line at the counter, bending down looking at the goodies in the display case. From her viewpoint, he looked like the most delicious treat. Wearing dark-wash jeans and a blue hooded sweatshirt with his Macha cut overtop, Brewer had caught more than one woman's eye in the shop.

"Delphi, you made it."

Glancing away from the finest male specimen in the small space, Delphi walked up to the right of the line where Jupiter stood with an apron loosely tied around her waist.

"Of course, I wouldn't miss our breakfast date." She jutted her chin at the crowd. "And I'm glad I made it when I did. You guys are busy."

Jupiter ran her fingers through her hair. "When I got here, Yasmina looked about ready to fall over. The nymph we hired called in sick, so I hurried in to help."

"Good thing you did, too, or I'd never leave," Yasmina said in her thick Eastern European accent. She waved at them as she rang up the next sale, and then she focused on the next customer.

"Let me get caught up, then we'll have breakfast," Jupiter promised, heading back to the register.

Moving to the front of the store, Delphi sat in one of the tall chairs at a long table facing the window, ideal for sitting and watching Snowshoe's streets come to life. Light snowflakes fluttered onto passing cars. With the sun cresting the buildings, the pastry shop would slow down once people made it to work and school.

"It really is a great view."

Delphi suddenly wished she'd bought a cup of coffee, if only to calm her nerves by sipping on it. The sound of his voice sent shivers to the tips of her fingers in the best way.

"Mind if I sit?" Brewer took the seat next to her before she could answer. A woodsy scent clung to his sweatshirt. It overwhelmed her on the first inhale and made her stomach swirl.

"What's a bartending biker guy like you doing up this early?" She swiveled toward him, her left brow lifted in question. "Shouldn't you be banging some club bunny or sleeping it off?"

"Zing! You got me again, girl," Brewer teased, clutching his chest. He reached over and bopped the tip of her nose. "Why so growly? Is it 'cause nobody's banging you?"

Delphi's body went hot. "You son of a— "

"Save it, sweetheart." He sat back and chuckled. "I just like getting a rise out of ya. Don't mean no harm. You're fun to tease." He pointed to her. "You're beautiful when you're pissed. You get all red and your eyes flash blue fire."

Not fully immune to his form of flattery, she slowly felt herself calm. Any other guy, she'd tell him to get lost. Brewer's kind of attention meant trouble. Yet she found herself leaning closer toward him instead of the opposite.

"Look, I'm sorry." He pulled off his black stocking hat, and the shock of red hair made her smirk. Static clung to his curly locks, making them fly in every direction but down. "Can I buy you a coffee or something while you wait?"

"I suppose." She unzipped her jacket. "Jupiter knows how I like it."

In one swift move, he stood and walked soundlessly to the line. She watched him apprehensive. He made small chat with the guy in front of him and complimented the little old lady behind him. By the time he made it to the front of the line, the entire shop was eating out of the palms of his hands. *Very rugged ones, I bet.*

Letting out a slow breath, Delphi closed her eyes and did her best to keep her attraction under lock and key.

"Here ya go." Brewer placed the large purple mug on the table just as she opened her eyes. "Smells pretty fancy to me. What is it?"

Picking it up, she licked the whipped cream and took a timid sip. "Vanilla bean latte with an extra shot of espresso."

"Vanilla?" He shook his head. "You're anything

but vanilla."

Delphi wrapped both her hands around the large mug. "How do you know?"

He leaned close, blue eyes sparkling. "It's in your smile."

She laughed. "My smile?"

"Yep. You've got this naughty quality about you."

Rolling her eyes, Delphi offered him a cheesy smile. "Nope. I'm as vanilla as they come."

He searched her face. "I don't believe that for a second."

She shrugged. "Think what you want. I'll be enjoying this cup of heaven while you scurry back to whatever hole you crawled out of."

Brewer licked his top lip, the smile never leaving his face. He wasn't backing down and neither was she. It both frightened and bewitched her. "I'd like to tame that tongue of yours, but it'd be a waste." He stood, replacing the beanie to his head. Almost instantly, she missed the mussed hair.

"Why's that?"

Placing one hand on the table and the other on the back of her chair, Brewer trapped her in the seat. He rubbed his lips together and let out a low sigh. "Because I'd rather let it roam free against mine instead." He moved closer, his nose brushing against hers.

Delphi couldn't breathe. He was close enough to kiss, and she desperately wanted to bite the lip hidden beneath his bushy beard.

"Keep looking at me like that, and I won't be able to control myself." He pressed a feathery light kiss to her cheek. "And if that happens, I'll want to see how vanilla you truly are behind that fiery façade."

She held onto the cup of coffee as if her life depended on it. His mere presence sent her blood pumping, and the wetness between her legs couldn't be ignored. She wanted him. She shouldn't. He was the absolute worst bad boy of the kind she'd sworn off. *And yet....*

Brewer flashed her a bright smile and left her sitting there in the next moment. Delphi swallowed hard. She couldn't move let alone watch him leave. And she wanted to see his tight ass sway out of the small shop.

Craning her neck, Delphi managed to see the tail end of Macha's bartender as he rounded the corner. She rubbed her lips together, hoping he'd turn around and give her one last look.

"What are you doing?"

Startled, she yelped and spilled coffee on her pants. "Shit, you scared me."

Jupiter handed her a napkin. "What were you looking at that had you so engrossed?"

Delphi dabbed at her leggings. "Oh, nothing."

"You sure?" Jupiter wiggled her eyebrows. "Not watching a certain Macha biker walk away, were you?"

"Ha, no." She met Jupiter's questioning eyes. "What? I wasn't. There was a… bird."

"Mm-hmm, a bird." Her friend rolled her eyes. "We'll circle back to Brewer Stapleton later. For now, I brought these cinnamon buns over, and I'm starving." She handed Delphi a plate. "Dive in."

Staring at the rolls slathered in icing, Delphi couldn't decide which looked more scrumptious: the cinnamon buns or Brewer. Her stomach said the first one, but the rest of her body was overwhelmed with the truth.

"Have you found out the thing you need to know about that certain person?" Jupiter asked, and Delphi couldn't help but laugh around the roll.

Wiping her mouth, she shook her head. "About my biological father? No." She picked up a fork and scraped icing off the plate. "I think I'm getting close, but nothing ever pans out. It's like the guy wants to be a ghost forever."

Jupiter finished off the roll on her plate and grabbed another one. "But you think he's an MC member, right?"

"Yeah. That's what my dad said before he died."

She sipped her coffee. "Maybe I should give up. If he doesn't want to be found so, be it."

Jupiter placed a hand on Delphi's arm. "Macha can help, you know."

"No, I—"

"Seriously, Delphi. Between Nikita's FBI connections and the guys themselves, Macha can make this process go a bit faster."

Delphi stared at the woman she could no longer imagine her life without. "Thanks, but I don't think I'm there yet." Jupiter opened her mouth, but before she could argue, Delphi continued, "But if I do, I'll ask for help."

"You better." Jupiter poked Delphi's side. "Macha's better than you think. Give the guys a chance. I know I'm glad I did."

Nodding, Delphi took another drink and glanced out the window. If she trusted another MC, would it be a mistake or the best thing to happen to her? She just wasn't sure.

CHAPTER 5
BREWER

Fire. That girl spit fire. But hell, if he didn't want to consume her whole, burns be damned. His entire body buzzed from their recent interaction.

Brewer finished polishing his motorcycle and tossed the rag onto the pavement of the parking lot outside the clubhouse. His beauty gleamed from wheel to wheel and everywhere in between. With the weather cooperating more and more each day, the entire club was itching to get out on the roads with their motorcycles.

"We're heading to Waverley," Cueball said in passing with Boulder at his side. "Wanna come?"

Standing up, he shook his head. "Nah, I'm good. Gotta take inventory and do some shit around the bar. Next time."

He watched the duo grab the keys to one of the

trucks and the puff of diesel smoke escape as they left the parking lot.

"I finally heard back from one of the Cutthroat dolls."

Turning, Brewer spotted Dolly approaching as she spoke. In true Dolly form, she wore a black cut-off shirt, her tattooed arms displayed proudly while jeggings, a high ponytail, and dark eye makeup completed her signature look.

"Yeah? What'd she say?"

"She saw a guy fitting Shovelhead's description about six months ago." Dolly shrugged on a leather jacket that had Macha's emblem embroidered on the back. Only club members were patched, but Dolly was as good as joined. She ran the nymph side of the club business. If she asked, they'd induct her, but she never would. His sister preferred to be behind the scenes.

"Great. So, we're six months too late." He leaned against the bike. "I know it was him, Dolly. I feel it in my bones. He's the one who killed our parents."

"Me too, but we gotta be cautious. Can't be running around like crazy kids anymore."

Thinking back to when they'd done exactly that in their childhood, Brewer smiled. They'd gotten into more trouble than their parents deserved to deal with from their kids. It never failed; Macha would take care of any monetary indiscretions they caused, and their parents would give them god-awful chores for a month.

"They'd want us to find the bastard and make him pay."

Dolly laid a hand on his shoulder. "But they wouldn't want us dying in the process. We both have futures to look forward to."

"Futures?" He snorted. "What else is there other than the club? Macha is our lives."

"But what if it isn't?"

He narrowed his eyes. "What're you talking about?"

Dolly examined the row of motorcycles as she weaved between them. "I've been thinking of retiring."

"Retiring? You're not even forty. Hell, I should retire, then, considering I'm two years older than you."

"As the club madam."

His brows rose. "Oh, shit. Seriously?"

She nodded. "I never imagined I'd even be considering it, but after seeing what Doc, Kevlar, and even Rubble went through over the last year, I'm not sure I want the same fate."

Something didn't feel right. His sister was born

and raised in Macha. No way in hell would she abandon the club. *Unless there's a good motivation.*

"What's the real reason, Dolly? Don't fuck with me." He crossed his arms over his chest and did his best big brother stare.

"You know that doesn't look menacing, right?" She chuckled and her booted heels stopped in front of him. "It's pretty funny, though. You think you're all big and bad when really, you're just my goofy brother."

He furrowed his brows, trying to give her a more intimidating glare like he'd seen on Rubble's face, but couldn't hold it. He burst out laughing at the same time Dolly did.

"But honestly, what's going on? You bleed Macha."

"I met someone."

He rolled his eyes. "Whose ass do I have to kick this time?"

"Don't you dare." She shoved him good-naturedly and started walking toward the clubhouse.

Following her, Brewer didn't let the subject drop. "Lay it on me. I can handle whatever you throw my way."

Dolly paused at the door, her hand lingering on the handle. "It's Yasmina."

"The girl Nikita saved?"

"Yeah."

He scratched his chin, reminding himself to trim his beard before he saw Delphi again. "I wasn't aware you even interacted with her."

Opening the door, Dolly smiled. "More happens around here than you know, Brewer."

"Do I want to ask?"

Her smile turned secretive. "Not unless you wanna hear a lot of sexy stories."

Brewer led them into the clubhouse kitchen and grabbed the whiskey bottle from the cabinet. Dolly hopped on one of the barstools at the large counter between the kitchen and dining area. It was one of his favorite spots in the clubhouse, giving him the ideal view into the kitchen while still being comfortable on the other side of the counter. Cooking wasn't his forte. Eating, on the other hand, was. After pouring two fingers into glasses, he sat next to her. "So, you and Yasmina. When did that happen?"

"Not long after she arrived. I volunteered to help show her around Snowshoe." Dolly stared into the whiskey, and then sipped it. "She's so quiet and shy. I like that about her. She's not like any of the nymphs." A wistful smile crossed her face. "Hearing her laugh is my favorite part of my day."

He understood now. "And you're afraid something bad will happen if she stays with Macha."

"She's already been through so much." Dolly's bright eyes faded slightly. "The trafficking ring was only part of her history. She deserves better than violence at every turn."

He finished off his whiskey in one long swig. It was the same thought he'd had after any one of his brothers had an unpleasant situation while wearing Macha's cut.

"This is club life, Dolly. We were raised in it. Our parents met because of the club." He reached over and rubbed her hand. "Bullets, booze, and babes are the epitome of any biker club. I thought you loved it."

"I do." Her blue eyes met his and he noticed the unshed tears. "But I'm afraid I love her more."

"Shit, Dolly." He pulled her into a giant hug. "I'm happy for you. I never thought I'd see the day where anyone—man or woman—got those words out of you."

She pinched his side. "Well, she hasn't heard them yet."

He tugged on her ponytail. "What're you waiting for?"

"The right time, I guess." Dolly grabbed the bottle of whiskey and refilled their glasses. "I want to put the whole Shovelhead business to bed. If he did murder Mom and Dad—"

"I *know* he did."

"Then I want to see him brought to justice."

"Who's justice? Macha's or the law's?" He sipped the whiskey, savoring the familiar burn he'd always loved.

"Doesn't matter to me. I'm good either way." She nudged him. "Then and only then will I act on my feelings for Yasmina. Don't worry—you won't lose me. Not completely."

"Fuck, I better never lose you." He kissed the top of her head. "You're my baby sis. I'd die before I let anything happen to you."

"I know." She gently elbowed him. "I'd do the same for you."

He sighed. "Rubble wants an update."

"I heard." She took a slow drink. "Think he'll let us keep looking into it?"

"Don't know why he wouldn't. As long as we're not getting into trouble, it should be fine."

Just then, Yasmina walked down the hall and into the kitchen. It shouldn't have, but it stunned him to see the change in Dolly. She went from moping to energetic, all thanks to the dark-haired, shy beauty.

"Hey, Dolly. Hey, Brewer." She opened the fridge and grabbed a bottle of water. "I'm going over to Delphi's restaurant in a bit. Do you want to come?"

"Absolutely," Dolly said without missing a beat.

"Delphi's, huh?"

Dolly shot him a look that could kill.

He chuckled and shook his head. "You girls go ahead. I need to check in at the bar." He stood and noticed neither one paid him any attention. "Have fun, you two. But not too much fun."

Dolly subtly flipped him the bird, her gaze glued to Yasmina.

Brewer walked through the clubhouse, waving at the boys playing pool. He couldn't be happier for his sister. She'd always been alone by choice, even though Dolly had her pick of men and women around the club. He wasn't in the dark about her bisexuality. Hell, even their parents had known long before he did. She was one of a kind and needed someone who accepted every inch of her. If Yasmina could give that to his sister, Brewer wholly approved.

Reaching the den, he eyed Hawk getting a blow job from one of the nymphs while he watched a sitcom rerun.

"Heard you had a run-in with that Delphi chick."

Brewer sat on the couch, his ability to ignore the nymph's actions second nature to him after all his years in the club. He was all but immune to seeing any level of sexual activity going on out in the open.

"I meant to just say hello, but she's a cauldron of fire." He snatched the remote and flipped through channels. "She likes me. I know she does. I saw that lust in her gorgeous eyes, and shit, I wanted to toss her over my shoulder and lock her in a closet with me." He found a cooking show and tuned in. "But she's fighting it."

Hawk rested a hand on the nymph's head, urging her to take him deeper. "You going to let off a bit or keep hitting her up hard?"

"Not sure. She's from Snowshoe, so she knows all about Macha. Not like Isa or Jupiter. Her parents probably warned her to steer clear of bikers."

"Girls love a bad boy."

"Usually, yeah, but I'm not really a bad boy." Brewer leaned back and rested his head against the cushion. "I'm more of the guy who will tease the panties right off a girl."

"Hey, whatever gets your rocks off." Hawk's voice hitched, and Brewer kept his eyes locked on the screen.

The scent of sautéed chicken and onions from the kitchen made his stomach growl. He'd missed breakfast, too excited at the possibility of seeing Delphi at the bakery. *No disappointment there.* Jeans tightening, he had to disagree slightly. His stomach and dick hungered for more of Delphi. He'd feast on her body the first chance he got.

The nymph stood and left the room. The familiar

zip of jeans met his ears, and he glanced over at Hawk. "Afternoon delight?"

"Not even lunchtime yet, brother." Hawk grinned. "But don't worry, I'll be getting some of that after I eat." He stretched lazily. "One of my favorite perks of the brotherhood. Unlimited pussy."

"It has its advantages." Brewer propped his boots on the coffee table. "But there's something about a non-club girl that just gets to me more."

"You're aiming for the restaurant chick, then?"

"Heart wants what it wants."

"Bullshit." Hawk shook his head. "Dick wants what it wants. And a good choice at that." He whistled. "Delphi has one fine ass, and those tits…. Yeah, I could get lost in those."

For the first time ever, Brewer felt a pang of jealousy ripple through him. Hearing Hawk undress Delphi so easily made his stomach drop. It was wrong on so many levels. She wasn't a club girl. She didn't even like Macha. *And even worse, she doesn't like me.* He brushed a hand over his beard, ignoring the sexual innuendos Hawk spewed. If he listened, he may not be able to control his reaction. If Hawk found out he seriously liked a girl, it'd be a mess for both him and Delphi. Hawk tended to try and steal girls from his brothers, and Brewer wasn't about to let that happen.

"Let me know how she is," Hawk said, standing. "Maybe she'd like having two Macha men at the same time. A lot of the Snowshoe girls do. Some kind of taboo shit." He chuckled. "I'm grabbing a beer. Want one?"

He nodded. He was in dire need of a pack of Guinness plus a bottle of whiskey. Sharing women was common in Macha, but he'd never done it. While some men enjoyed the thrill, he was never one to share at the same time. If he was with a woman, he wanted to be the only one.

Closing his eyes, Brewer groaned. His dick ached and his heart burned to see the spark in Delphi's eyes once more. He couldn't let her slip through his grasp. Sitting up, he slapped his knees. He'd make Delphi realize that Macha wasn't all dark and scary like the stories the citizens of Snowshoe liked to tell about them around the campfire.

"Better get your sleep, Delphi, because you'll only get a wink once you're mine."

He walked over to the pool table and racked the balls before he grabbed a cue stick. He had to get his mind off Delphi for a little bit at least. With music pumping through the clubhouse and nymphs passing beer around, it wasn't likely, but he had to try.

He waved at one of the prospects and let the

shorter man take the break. Stomach growling, Brewer watched the prospect sink three balls before giving him a turn. He'd need to eat eventually. *Something French, perhaps.*

Brewer hit four balls into the pockets and grinned. He knew just the place to stop at to satisfy his appetite. He'd just have to take the chance—every day if necessary—that the gorgeous chef would let him in the door.

CHAPTER 6
DELPHI

The afternoon rush at the restaurant made the day fly by. Before she knew it, the sun had dipped behind the skyline, casting an orange glow over the valley. Delphi paused at the window after seating a couple with a new baby and merely gazed out at the colorful streaks in the clouds. The rising and setting of the sun were her favorite parts of the day. She always saw both when time permitted. Missing either wouldn't feel right. Her parents used to sit out on their wraparound porch with a warm drink and watch each one. She had fond memories of enjoying that ritual all through her childhood to the day she left for Paris.

"Delphi, there's someone at the front, asking for you."

Snapping out of her trance, she peeked toward

the small waiting area, but couldn't see beyond the pillars situated midway through the bistro. "Thanks, Cindy." She smiled at the waitress and swiftly moved to the front.

Reaching the desk where she kept the restaurant's reservations book, Delphi frowned at the lack of new patrons. The three couples and one family were still waiting for their tables to open, but no one else was sitting on the bench along the wall.

She shook her concerns aside and skimmed the waiting list. A bachelorette party was scheduled to arrive in the next few minutes, and she chewed on her bottom lip. The shortness of staff wouldn't be a problem so long as the current customers didn't linger at the tables she planned to push together to seat the twenty women who were sure to be rambunctious guests.

"Delphi Windsor?"

The voice made her cringe. Pasting on a smile, she looked up. "Andrea. Nice to see you."

"Oh my God, do you work here?" the brunette with perfectly straight hair asked, judgment evident in her tone. A giant diamond ring sat on her third finger, and when Delphi saw it, she immediately realized who the bachelorette party was for.

"Actually, I own it." Anxiety bubbled in her gut as she watched the entryway fill with women she knew from high school. Most of them looked the same, but a few had deteriorated over the years. It was the one small victory, since these women had tormented her during her years at Snowshoe High.

Andrea cast doubtful eyes around the bistro. "How… quaint. We all wondered what happened to you. I mean, after that biker broke your heart, you kind of went AWOL on us."

She gritted her teeth. "I was never one of you, Andrea."

"By proxy you were."

Delphi tried to keep her composure as best she could. After all these years, the preppy girl shouldn't still get to her, but she did. High school was rough on everyone, but it had been especially bad for the formerly chubby Delphi and her love of all things food related. The only reason she attended the same parties as the popular girls was because of her boyfriend at the time. It wasn't until he broke up with her that she learned he'd dated her as part of the Greenback Cutthroats MC club initiation.

"Is this the rest of your party?"

Andrea flipped her hair. "Not yet, but you can seat us, right? I hate waiting in the lobby." She crinkled her nose. "There's a draft from your flimsy doors. I'll catch a cold for sure if I stay here very long."

For the second time that evening, Delphi fought back the urge to walk into the kitchen and toss pots and pans around until she had her fill. But she wouldn't. She was a dignified business owner whether her high school bully would ever admit it or not. Stooping to their level wasn't who she was.

"I'll go check on your table." She didn't wait for a response. It'd be a bitchy one, and she really wasn't in the mood to hear any more.

Making it to the kitchen, she spotted her favorite waitress chatting up the line cook while she waited for the rest of her table's order. "Hey, Tessa, the bachelorette party is here early. Do you think we can move a few tables to the far corner and get them out of the way?"

Tessa piled plates onto a tray, the food steaming. "You bet. Give me a quick second, and I'll grab one of the busboys to help."

"Thanks." Delphi walked around the kitchen, making sure the food was plated correctly. She stopped and stirred the Mornay sauce and sampled it with a spoon before adding a pinch more salt. Her stomach rumbled, reminding her that the last meal she ate was earlier in the day with Jupiter. The energy from the three cinnamon buns had waned with the passing hours.

Making a mental note to make something of

substance later, she bit into a slice of warm baguette and hurried back to the front. The phone rang on the reception table, and she answered it.

A large body blocked her peripheral view of the bachelorette party impatiently waiting on their table.

"I have you down for six tomorrow evening for a party of four. We'll see you then. Thank you!" She hung up and wrote down the reservation.

"Sounds like you're booked up."

Brewer. Delphi's pen paused on the reservation book. She glanced up and met his stunning blue eyes. *What the hell is he doing here?* Looking back down to finish up the note, she then flipped the page back to that day. "We are, actually. Are you here to pick up an online or phone order?"

He rested his hands on the edge of the table. Outfitted in all Macha gear, Brewer was even more breathtaking. His beard was smoothed and his red curls recently washed, if the scent of strawberry shampoo told her anything. She bit back a smile, thinking about the manly biker using fruity bath essentials.

"Not tonight. I hadn't stopped by to see this place yet. Jupiter raves about it, so I thought I'd pop in and see what all the fuss is about." He scanned the area. "It looks very nice. Not too upscale but fancy enough that you could have a birthday party or anniversary dinner here."

"Thanks." She shifted her weight, fully aware that the bachelorettes had their gazes pinned on Macha's bartender. "I'm afraid I don't have any open seatings tonight, but I can get you something to go."

Brewer shook his head. "That's okay. I'll come by another time when you're not so busy."

He swiveled to walk away, and Delphi couldn't help herself. "Brewer, wait." She moved around the tall table and lowered her voice. "If you don't mind sitting in the kitchen, Edgar makes a delicious beef bourguignon."

"Well, that depends." His gaze dipped to her lips, then back to her eyes. "Will you be there?"

The thought of spending more time with him made it nearly impossible to hide her smile. She quickly tamped down the desire she felt. Bikers were bad news. "I'll be in and out, but I can visit with you for a few minutes."

Brewer seemed to mull it over for a hot second before he grinned. "I'll take what I can get."

A tiny part of her jumped with glee. "Follow me." She tossed a glance at the women waiting to be seated. Each one had audacious expressions on her face, eyes conveying their eagerness to lap up the gossip. It wouldn't be the first time she'd been swayed by a biker. *But this is different. I'm not a dumb kid.*

Brewer followed closely, the heat of his body warming her. They passed through the double doors into the kitchen, and she led him to a small table and chair the staff used for breaks. "It isn't much."

He lightly touched her arm. "It's great. Thanks, Delphi."

The way he said her name sent delirious shivers down her spine. She didn't know why she was being nice to him. The man was everything bad. *And yet, I can't stay away from him.*

"Give me a minute. I need to seat a party, then I'll be back."

Brewer overtook the small space; his wide shoulders were bigger than she thought. "No worries. I'll be here."

Delphi offered him a small smile and headed toward the door, all the while feeling his hot gaze on her ass. *Don't give in so easily. He'll only break your heart.* She hoped she was wrong, but she knew better. Or at least she should know better by thirty-four years old.

CHAPTER 7
BREWER

The trophy wife wannabes weren't hard to peg the moment Brewer stepped into the small foyer. He'd come to see Delphi but unknowingly witnessed an exchange he couldn't ignore. When the waitress left to get the bistro's owner, he'd poked his nose around the front entry, finding the door to the kitchen, restrooms, and a coat closet. He waited until Delphi left to emerge from the restroom. It took a whole ten seconds before the woman she called Andrea made a move.

"You're a Macha biker, right?" the woman purred, her eyes alight with lust.

"Last I checked." He took a few steps away, but she followed him, as did all nine of her friends. If they ever stepped foot in the clubhouse, they'd jump on the first dick they saw. Club hoppers were what the bikers called that breed of women. It was a common term around the prospects since they looked for pussy wherever they could get it.

Andrea snuck her hand up his leather cut, the touch singeing him in the worst way. "It's my bachelorette party tonight. We're headed to Booze & Tattoos after this. Maybe you can meet us there and give us a private tour."

Her friends nodded in agreement, and Brewer could smell the tequila lingering on Andrea's breath. If he was in the mood, maybe he'd have said yes, but after he saw how this woman treated Delphi, there was no way in hell he'd lay a finger on the broad.

"Actually, I can't tonight. If you're heading to the bar, there are plenty of prospects and patched members who will take you up on that offer, though." He stepped backward out of her grasp.

Anger flashed in her eyes. "Fine. You're probably a shitty lay anyways."

Not one to let any person—man or woman—get away with damaging his reputation, Brewer chuckled. "Honey, you couldn't handle me." He nodded at her friends. "None of you could."

"A bit cocky, aren't you?" Andrea moved in again. "I can work with that."

Delphi's high ponytail came into view, and an idea popped into his mind. "Look, lady, I'm sure you're great and all, but I prefer my women with gumption and fire. Not groping the first man who catches her eye, even if it is her bachelorette party."

His gaze locked on Delphi, and he was grateful she hadn't seen him yet.

The other woman instantly scoffed. "Seriously? Her?"

Brewer nodded. "Only her."

Delphi answered the phone, oblivious to his presence. He rather liked watching her in her natural element. The fact that he barely knew her didn't matter. This was where she'd always dreamt of working. Somehow, he just knew it.

She smiled as she spoke to the caller and his chest clenched. To be on the receiving end of that beam of sunshine might turn him into a believer of true love.

The bachelorette hurried back to her posse of girls. He smothered the grin he desperately wanted to give the vultures. Delphi's history with these women was a story he wanted to hear, but from her lips. She'd tell the full truth and not the half lies the other woman would undoubtedly spew.

Now, as he sat in the kitchen, savory scents wafting around him, Brewer wouldn't trade this for even a possibility of the orgy the bachelorette had promised. Edgar outdid himself, though. It was the first time Brewer had French cuisine other than fries. *Not sure those are even French.*

Swiping the last bit of beef through the sauce, he ate it, licked the fork clean, and sat back. Delphi had yet to pop back in and check on him. Part of him was disappointed. Hell, he'd shown up unannounced. She should've booted his ass out onto the slushy potholes. *But she didn't.*

"How was the food?" Edgar asked, stealing the plate away from the table.

Brewer patted his stomach. "Amazing. Where'd you learn to cook like that?"

The man old enough to be his grandfather smiled. "Italy. I went to culinary school there for a year."

"Why didn't you stay?"

"My family asked me to come home." He shrugged. "So, I did. Family is everything to me."

"Me too."

Edgar grinned. "If boss lady comes back, tell her I'm taking a quick smoke break."

Brewer's phone chimed and he checked the screen. Dolly sent a grainy photo of what her Cutthroat contact had produced. He zoomed in on the man in a leather cut. It looked like Shovelhead, but he couldn't be sure. The lighting and poor quality made it impossible to confirm his identity. He forwarded it to Rubble nevertheless. *It might take a while, Pops, but we'll get the asshole.*

"Everything satisfactory?" Delphi asked as she slipped through the swinging door, her apron sporting a splash of red sauce.

"You don't have to be all professional with me," he said with a smirk. "Edgar is an amazing chef. It was delicious."

"Good." She pulled off the apron and tossed it in a bin labeled "Laundry" before finding a new one neatly folded on a rack beside it.

"Somebody spill, or are you just klutzy?"

Delphi lifted her middle finger, and he had to stifle a laugh. "No, asswipe. A kid spilled on me." She let out a breath. "I'll be glad when the night's over. I could use a glass—no, a bottle of wine. Seems like I'm always short-staffed, and we're consistently at capacity."

"If you want, I can ask one of the nymphs to lend a hand." He stood up, walked over to her, and tied the apron around her waist. The scent of her shampoo hit him hard. The clean yet fruity smell instantly made him crave dessert. "A lot of them have worked in food service before, so it wouldn't be a big deal."

She stepped away, and he immediately missed

her. "One of the *special* club girls? Not in a million years."

"What do you have against them?"

"Other than the obvious?"

He set his jaw. "Mm-hmm."

Leaning against the counter, she massaged the back of her neck. "That's it. Just the fact that they're biker playthings."

"Damn, I didn't take you as a stuck-up bitch like that girl up front."

"I'm not. I just…. I don't need your help." Her eyes narrowed. "Andrea chatted you up, I take it."

Brewer noticed the jealousy permeating her words. "She offered to do more than that."

"Shocking." Her ponytail swished in his face, and he reached out, grabbing a fistful of it.

He pulled her against him, and Delphi gasped. The sound sent a shudder through his body and settled in his groin. He was getting hard merely holding her. He couldn't imagine what would happen if she felt sensations reciprocating the ones coursing through his veins. "Don't make me regret sticking up for you."

"You did?" Her blue eyes flashed. "Why?"

Brewer studied her face, memorizing the lines of her frown and hoping he'd never see them again. "Because I like you, dammit."

"You what?"

Her bottom lip trembled, and he gently traced it with his thumb. "You heard me, woman. I like you. I like that fire in your eyes and the venom on your tongue." His hand slid to her neck, the backs of his fingers lightly caressing her skin.

She inhaled at the touch, gripping the lapels of his jacket. "You're a dick," she said, but her eyes didn't mirror the sentiment.

Nodding, he nudged her thighs open with his leg and was pleasantly surprised when her breathing increased, and her breasts pressed into him more. "I'll take you right now if you say the word. I don't give a damn where we are."

Delphi licked her lips, tempting him even further. If she uttered the word he needed to hear, he'd be inside her so fast the room would spin. His dick pulsed at the mere notion.

Her eyes drifted down the front of him, then back up to his face. "I have to get back to work." But she sighed, and he could plainly hear her inner struggle in the sound.

"But you want me too," he insisted.

She shoved at him, face flushed with both anger and lust. He'd hash them out later when she was fully sated on his bed.

"I want a bottle of wine and a comfy bed, Brewer." She didn't try to move away, but simply stayed with her back to the wall, her chest still touching his. "That's all."

Slowly releasing his hold on her hair, he took a step backward. Forcing a woman to do anything was against his moral compass.

"I'll wait for it."

She arched her brow. "Wait for what?"

"The moment you want me, I'll be here." He cupped the side of her face, her cheek a beautiful shade of pink. "And you will want me sooner than you think, Delphi."

"You're so confident, aren't you?"

"I know what I want. And what you want too." He brushed his lips over hers and smiled when she clung to his jacket, her lips moving closer. "But not until you say the words."

She let out a shaky breath, and he took a step backward. She wasn't ready, but she would be soon. He'd give her space and time to think about him. Time to think about all the dirty things she wanted him to do to her.

"I better let you get back to work. You've got a restaurant full of people eager for your food."

Delphi nodded. "I'm surprised nobody came looking for me."

"I bribed one of the waitresses to give us a couple minutes."

"What?" Delphi's eyes widened, and he chuckled.

"I'm kidding. I wouldn't do that." He moved toward the door as he said, "Tonight."

Opening the kitchen doors, he looked back and winked. That caused another flush of red to flood her cheeks. He was slowly throwing firewood on the embers in her eyes. *And I can't wait until it's a full-fledged fire.* No matter the burn, she was worth the pain.

CHAPTER 8
DELPHI

Delphi was woken by sunlight streaming through the open curtain. She winced at the brightness, the night before flashing through her mind. She'd met Jupiter at the bakery for a late-night espresso for her and tea for the expectant mama. Spending time with her friend had gotten her mind off the restaurant and, more importantly, Brewer.

Rolling over, she sighed at the time displayed on the digital clock she'd had since junior high. It was one of those clocks that showed international time too, a gift from her grandmother who'd been an avid traveler.

A heavy weight kept her from tugging the quilt over her face. She looked to her left and saw Fiona, her tabby cat, purring next to her. "It's too early, Fi."

The cat meowed once, then closed her green eyes.

Clearly, she agreed. Delphi laid an arm over her face, trying to nab another few minutes before starting the one day she had off each week. Mondays were as close to a holiday as she got.

Just as she started to drift back into a dreamless state, a loud song startled her awake. Groaning, Delphi blindly batted her left arm at the side table. She finally found her cell phone when the song made it to the chorus.

"What do you want?" she answered, eyes still closed.

"My, my, don't you have a sexy morning voice?"

Delphi's eyelids snapped open. "Brewer?" She sat up and glanced around the room as if she'd spot him waiting on her to wake up. "How'd you get this number?"

"Eh, called the restaurant last night and Edgar gave it to me."

"Dammit, Edgar." She flung the quilt aside and stood, sliding into her fuzzy pink slippers. "So, you going to tell me why you woke me up, or leave me guessing?"

She made it to the kitchen and opened the cupboard to find the coffee beans.

"Wow, you're not a morning person, are you?"

"Only after I drink coffee." She dumped three scoopfuls of beans into the grinder.

"Ah, good to—"

Delphi smirked when she flipped on the grinder, the rest of Brewer's statement lost to the noise. It was bold of him not only to get her personal number but also call instead of text like everyone else. The audacity of the man sent a jolt of adrenaline through her.

"Oops, sorry," she said, stopping the grinder and pouring the contents into the coffee maker.

"It's okay. I was talking dirty to you anyways."

She cocked her brow at his teasing. "Too bad for you I don't like dirty talk."

He chuckled. "You say that now, but I guarantee if I were there, your body would be giving off another vibe."

"Whatever." She pressed the On button and willed the machine to hurry up.

"Anyways, I was calling to see if you'd like to come on a ride with me today."

"A ride? What kind?"

"Not the kind you're thinking, but we can circle back to that one later." He cleared his throat. "I'm heading to Waverley on business and could use somebody riding bitch."

Finding a clean mug, she poured sugar-free vanilla creamer into it. "So, I'm purely a warm body behind you?" She shook her head. "I'm not buying it.

What's the real reason? Make an old girlfriend jealous?"

"I wouldn't do something like that. I have more respect for you."

For a split second, she considered badgering him about that statement. He barely knew her. "All right, keep your secrets then."

"Don't go quoting *Lord of the Rings* to me, girl. You're sorely outmatched."

Delphi laughed, silently complimenting his knowledge of classic fantasy novels, albeit one that had been turned into a hit movie series. "Fine. Give me one good reason to agree to go on some crazy bike ride with you."

Brewer hummed, the sound of music droning in the background. "How about—you have the day off, and if you don't come with me, you'll be stressing about your bistro?"

He wasn't wrong. She'd planned on doing exactly that after munching on cocoa cereal and three cups of caffeine. She poured coffee into the mug and blew on it. The sensible part of her brain warned her that Brewer Stapleton was bad news all around. Sitting down at the small kitchen table, Delphi wrapped her hands around the cup. The reckless side of her urged her to live a little.

"I'll agree under two conditions."

"Name them."

She took a sip, the fresh brew warming her instantly. "One: you have to buy the food. Two: you never call me before eight in the morning again unless you have a cup of coffee waiting on my doorstep."

"Deal."

She could practically hear the smile in his voice. She crossed her legs at the automatic flurry of desire.

"I'll pick you up in an hour."

Delphi glanced at the clock above the stove. "An hour? That's not enough time to get ready. I have nothing to wear that's biker chick."

"Don't worry. You'll look great no matter what you wear. See you soon."

"Wait, do you even know where I live?"

The call disconnected before he could answer. Admitting defeat wasn't in her nature, but she also wouldn't let him show up and see her makeup free and grungy.

A text message popped up the next moment.

Brewer: Just realized I don't have your address. Mind giving it to me?

Her thumbs hovered over the keyboard.

Brewer: Don't make me ask Jupiter.

Resigning herself to the fact that he'd do exactly that, Delphi sent him the address and hurried down the hallway to the bathroom. If she was going to do this, she sure as hell would make it a day to remember. *After all, it's just a ride. Nothing more.*

CHAPTER 9
BREWER

All morning, Brewer had tossed around the idea of inviting Delphi to go to Waverley with him. He was going on club business, hoping to catch a glimpse of the man Dolly's contact said was back in town. If it was Shovelhead, he needed to snap a decent photo to present to the club. They wouldn't act on a hunch if they could help it. Necessary proof was how Macha ran the lawless side of their club dealings.

Now, as he sat in front of the bistro, he had to give Delphi props. He'd stepped over a line to get her number, but she hadn't shot him down. In fact, she agreed to go. It sent a shiver of happiness through him.

A side door opened, and Brewer had to physically keep his jaw from dropping open at the sight. If anyone said she wasn't knockout gorgeous, he'd flatten them with one punch. The knee-high black boots with no heel she was wearing were perfect for riding bitch on his Harley. Skinny blue jeans and a comfortable-looking green hooded sweatshirt rounded out the rest of her outfit.

She walked closer, her face becoming clearer with every step. *Hot damn.* Her eyes made his dick jump in his pants. With her smoky dark eye shadow and perfectly lined eyes, Delphi was the very reason he jerked off twice before driving to her place.

"You look… amazing." He licked his lips and willed himself to stop ogling her.

Delphi smirked. "Thanks. You don't look so bad yourself."

He shrugged, the typical jeans and sweatshirt he wore nothing to brag about, in his opinion. "Comfy gear is the way I roll." He grabbed the spare helmet he had with him and held it out to her. "Ready for the ride of your life?"

She snorted and carefully pulled the hair back from her face and fastened it with a hair tie before she placed the helmet on her slightly springy curls.

"I'm ready for something." She clicked the strap and knocked on the helmet. "My dad would freak if he saw me on the back of one of these again." She circled his motorcycle, taking it all in. "I haven't ridden one of these in years."

"You had one?"

"No, an ex of mine did." Her face clouded beneath the sunny sky. "It's high time I got back on the horse, so to speak. I used to love riding around town on the back."

A zing of jealousy simmered through Brewer's blood. "You dated a MC man?"

"Why we headed to Waverley?"

Pushing down the urge to investigate the easy way she shrugged his question aside, Brewer started the engine. "Doing a little recon for the club."

Delphi swung her left leg across the bike and settled on the seat behind him. Her warmth was already tempting him to reach back and run his hand up her thigh. "You're not going to put me in any sort of trouble, are you?"

"I wouldn't dream of it." He flipped up the kick-stand and rolled away from the bistro. Her hands lightly gripped his waist, and he clenched his jaw. Suddenly, having her directly behind him, tempting him all day, didn't seem like such a stellar idea.

They drove slowly through town. He didn't want to scare her off before they crossed city limits.

"You want to tell me what we're looking for, or should I figure it out on my own?"

She asked when they stopped at a stoplight. He craned his neck to look at her. "The club's been searching for somebody who betrayed us. One of the Cutthroat dolls thinks the guy is in Waverley."

"Shovelhead?"

Brewer swiveled his torso completely, his eyes pinned to her. "How do you know about that?"

"Please," she scoffed. "Everyone in Snowshoe knows what Shovelhead did."

"Seriously?"

"No." She laughed and pointed to the streetlight. "It's green."

Releasing his hand, Brewer let the motorcycle glide through the intersection. "How did you find out, then? Macha keeps club business pretty quiet."

Delphi wrapped her arms around his waist as they picked up speed. "Because I used to date a Cutthroat," she said over the engine's hum.

THE FACT THAT HE DIDN'T ADDRESS HER STATEMENT FOR the rest of the drive to Waverley gnawed at Brewer's gut until he swore it was giving him an ulcer. If he heard her correctly, there was a very likely chance they'd crossed paths before her visit to the bar. *But she said it was her first time there.*

He shifted gears and hugged the curve of the mountain pass. Delphi's grip around his waist tightened, sending shots of desire to his groin. Having a woman ride bitch meant something to him. He didn't let any random girl hop on the back of his motorcycle. *But Delphi isn't somebody random.*

The city of Waverley came into view on the horizon. He downshifted with his foot, and Delphi loosened her hold. He'd purposefully worn casual clothes, his Macha cut safely stowed away in his closet at the clubhouse. The last thing the club needed was trouble with the Greenback Cutthroats, the biker club in Waverley. They'd had their fair share of conflict with them in the last year. Rubble would kick his ass all the way to Thursday if he stirred up shit today.

"You ever come here?" he asked, rolling to a stop at a traffic light.

"Oh, yeah. It used to be my go-to place back in the day."

The light turned green, and he swallowed his automatic response. The city was laid out similarly to Snowshoe, the buildings more antique than updated. Every few years, the two neighbors would get together for a community project. The mayors thought it'd keep the peace between the opposing clubs. The two played along, but the peace both cities craved wasn't possible at the moment. The Cutthroats were weeks away from appointing a new president even though the FBI had infiltrated their trafficking ring. Macha stayed out of it. Unless provoked, they'd keep their distance, and vice versa.

Spotting the Cutthroats' bar, Brewer pulled into the parking lot and shut off the engine. It was too early for hardcore shenanigans, which meant it was the ideal time for him to snoop around under false pretenses. A meal with a sizzling hot chef fit the bill.

"Why are we stopping here?" She pulled off the helmet, eyes covered by sunglasses she must've snuck on somewhere between towns.

"Thought we could grab a bite to eat. Their breakfast burrito is delicious." He unclicked his helmet and stowed them on the handlebars. "Plus, unlimited chips and dip is one of my favorite appetizers no matter the time of day."

"Hmm, I guess I can handle that." Delphi pushed up her sunglasses. "It's almost lunchtime anyhow, and I only got a small bowl of cocoa cereal this morning since I had to do my hair.

"Which is cute, by the way. Curls are sexy." He smirked. "Plus, anytime is a good time for food."

"Agreed." She walked around the bike and nodded. "So, you're here to try and get intel about the Cutthroats on the down low." She said it so matter-of-factly that he knew he couldn't convince her otherwise.

"Yep." They walked to the front door, and he held it open. "You hungry?"

"Always."

The mariachi band over the speakers would have drowned out his immediate response to seeing her ass if he wasn't already resisting the urge to comment on it. After finding a booth near the back, a waitress brought over two bowls, one filled with salsa and the other with homemade tortilla chips. Once she left, Brewer voiced the question that had been burning in his stomach since leaving Snowshoe.

"So, you dated a Cutthroat, huh?" He dipped a chip into the salsa and took a bite. "Want to go into more detail on that?"

She shrugged and broke a chip in half. "Not really, no."

"Aw, come on, Delphi. You can't drop a bombshell like that then act like it's no big deal."

"It's not. I was young and dumb." She popped the chip into her mouth. "Who wasn't?"

He looked over the top of the laminated menu and pointed a chip toward her. "You knew about Shovelhead. That means you dated a Cutthroat recently. Spill, girly."

Delphi set down the other half of the chip and

leaned over the table. Brewer did the same, eager to hear the juicy tale. "Leave it alone, Brewer. You don't want to hear."

"I wouldn't have asked if I didn't." He searched her blue eyes, not letting the subject drop.

The waitress came back with glasses of water and impatiently tapped her pen against her little notepad. They paused and gave her their orders, both grateful for the return of privacy when she left.

"You were saying?"

Taking a sip of water, Delphi cleared her throat. "In high school, I dated a Cutthroat prospect. Last summer, I was dumb enough to get back with him for a month."

"Who was it?"

"Doesn't matter."

It sure as hell mattered to him. He grew up in the club. If someone were dating a Snowshoe resident, he'd have known. MC men, especially prospects, didn't keep their mouths shut very often when it came to the women they were banging.

"I don't remember any of the guys mentioning dating a townie."

"That's because he never told anyone." She scooped salsa onto her chip, half of it splattering on the table before it reached her mouth. She dabbed at it with her napkin, only spreading the mess. "At least not right away."

"I guess I can buy that."

"Anyways, he was one of the cool kids in my high school. I loved him. Or I thought I did." She licked her lips. "But then one night at a party, it came out that it was all part of his initiation into the Greenback Cutthroats."

"What was?"

"Grant dating me. Andrea—the girl you met at the bistro the other night and Miss Popular all throughout high school—used to be his girlfriend." She shook her head. "His club president thought it'd be funny, so Grant started pursuing me. I resisted for a while. I mean, after all, my parents always warned me about dating a biker."

"Yeah, we're dickheads sometimes." Brewer polished off another chip. "How'd you find out?"

"I got invited to a party and overheard him bragging to all his friends and MC buddies." She rubbed her lips together nervously. "They ate up every nitty gritty detail he gave them. Some of it was true, the other stuff wasn't. It was probably one of the worst days of my life. I swore off club guys after that."

Brewer leaned back, the memories of his own high school coming back to him in waves. "Clearly, it didn't stick."

She smirked. "No. Bikers are the definition of bad boys. And a Snowshoe girl like me can't resist for very long. When I came home last spring, I came to this bar, and one thing led to another." She looked around the cantina. "My parents had just died, I was lonely, and Grant seemed like a good way to numb the pain. Obviously, I was wrong because he's even more of a dick now than in high school."

"Shit, I'm sorry, Delphi." He reached out and placed a hand on hers. He understood that pain well. "How'd they die?"

"Car accident. My mom died on impact and my dad a few days later from a heart attack." She let out a strangled chuckle. "Ironic, isn't it? He survived only long enough to die of natural causes."

Brewer waved his hand at the bartender and was grateful when the man brought over a round of beer.

"Damn, that sucks."

"It really did." She took a swig of the bottled beer. "So, I went out with Grant for a few weeks."

"Did it help you forget?"

Her eyes shadowed. "At first, yes. I'm not a party girl, never have been, but I couldn't face what happened. My dad told me some pretty heavy stuff right before he died, and I thought I could find answers here."

This got Brewer's attention. "Like what kind of stuff?"

She chewed her bottom lip. "About paternity."

Before he could compute the words, she went on. "One night, Grant got a little too physical."

Brewer's hands curled into fists. It wasn't uncommon in the club world, but Macha's men would never do such a thing. It was against everything they stood for. Women were revered, not abused in their club.

"Did he hurt you?"

She shook her head and ate another chip. "No, thank goodness. An older guy, the club treasurer I think, pulled him off me and I escaped. Haven't had anything to do with MCs since. Until Jupiter and Rubble came into my restaurant."

Brewer put aside the need to smack this Grant guy's dumbass face in for the moment. He'd find out more when the time was right. "How does Shovelhead fit into this?"

Delphi took a breath. "Before I left the cantina that night, I overheard a group of bikers talking about taking over a local club. They didn't mention which one, but I saw who was talking. His cut said Shovelhead."

The pieces fell into place for Brewer. If Shovelhead was talking with the Cutthroats about anarchy against Macha last summer, the rest of the year made perfect sense. Shovelhead was behind Isa's abduction, albeit with the help of an Irish biker club, and he had an easy fallback club, the Cutthroats, when his plan failed. *Then he tried again.*

The chips in his mouth tasted like ash, the salsa souring his stomach. He never expected the depravity to go so deep so fast. Without a doubt, Shovelhead had tried time and time again to rid Macha of their president so he could seize the club in a hostile takeover.

Meeting Delphi's uneasy eyes, he reached over and gently grasped her hand. "I'm sorry that happened to you. If I'd known, I never would've brought you here, I swear."

She nodded, but the fear wasn't gone from her gorgeous face. It killed him to see his normally feisty girl so shaken. "Thanks. I'm just glad I made it out."

"Well, if you ever—and I mean ever—see the guy who tried to hurt you, call me. I don't care what time it is, or even if you're in Hong Kong." He squeezed her hand. "Call me, and I'll come beat the shit out of him. All of Macha will."

A smile spread across her face, making her look five years younger in an instant. "Thanks, Brewer. That's really sweet of you."

He pulled back as the waitress approached with

their food. "Wasn't meaning for it to be sweet, girl. Nobody goes after a woman from our town without consequences."

The waitress placed their food in front of them before hurrying to the next table. They both dug into their plates. Brewer was grateful that she confided in him, even if only a little. It was a start, and he could work with that. Delphi was one of a kind and exactly what he needed more of. *Now the hard part. Convincing her that I'm what she needs too.*

CHAPTER 10
DELPHI

The Rusty Cantina brought back a flood of memories the instant she stepped foot in the establishment. Delphi wasn't sure why she expected to go somewhere other than another club's bar. Her apprehension didn't last long. Brewer had a way of making her feel safe that was brand-new for her. It scared the hell out of her. *Of all men to give you the warm fuzzies, you had to choose this one.*

She wiped up the small mess on the table her enchilada had made. Eating always resulted in messiness. It was the one thing she could count on in life.

"I'm going to chat with the bartender." Brewer stood and placed enough cash to cover the bill on the table. "Will you be all right here?"

Delphi pressed her lips into a thin line. "I can take care of myself."

He leaned over and tucked her hair behind her left ear. "Just because you can doesn't mean I won't worry about you."

She opened her mouth to argue, but he shook his head. "Not here, spitfire." He glanced around the bar that was slowly filling with Greenback Cutthroats. "If they think you're alone, they won't hesitate to come over here."

"Pretending I'm with you will protect me?" she scoffed, hoping he heard the sarcasm dripping from her words.

"You *are* with me today, Delphi." Brewer wiggled his brows. "Unless you beg for more time."

She ignored his last tease, and Brewer walked away. Delphi couldn't stop her eyes from following his fine ass as he made his way to the bar. The bartender, a man in his late forties, jutted his chin toward Brewer. He cast one last blue-eyed look at her, making sure she was safe before ducking behind the bar and following the other man.

She pulled out her phone and checked for any new messages. Peter had texted, updating her about his mother's condition and saying he'd be in as soon as he could. Worry filled her stomach. Running her own business was a struggle this month.

One minute blurred into ten. The speakers pumped

out music compatible with the cantina, but it was louder now than it had been when they arrived. She glanced over to where Brewer had disappeared again, tempted to retrace his footsteps and see exactly where he went.

Telling him about her club past was easier than she anticipated. Something about Brewer made her want to tell him everything, even if it hurt. *It's his eyes. It has to be.* They were sky blue, their depths digging into her soul with every glance.

"Can I get you anything else, hon?" the waitress asked, removing the plates from the table and stuffing the cash in her apron pocket.

"I'm good, thanks."

"Your man coming back, or did he leave you to fend for yourself?"

The way the woman said the words sent a cold shiver down Delphi's spine. Looking around the cantina, she recognized more leather cuts and fewer city residents who were merely popping in for lunch. She could've sworn the lighting had dimmed since they arrived.

"He'll be back. Just had to check on something." She scrolled on her phone, thumbs hovering over the dial pad. If worse came to worse, she could call for help, but it'd be too late by the time local law enforcement showed up. Until Brewer returned, she was on her own. *In a biker bar.* She held her breath. *You make wonderful life decisions, Delphi Windsor.*

"Sure, honey." The woman chuckled. "I saw them go to the back." She lowered her voice when a couple walked past them. "That's where the dolls stay during their breaks."

Delphi had heard about the Cutthroat dolls and had even seen a few in the past. They had a designated place for playing their role in the MC. It was a dollhouse not far from here, making it easy for them to come and go as they pleased with the club men.

"I wouldn't sleep with him if I were you."

A loud bark of laughter escaped her before she could stop it. Even if her body knew the opposite, she felt compelled to say, "Believe me, I wouldn't touch him with a ten-foot pole."

"Who has a ten-foot pole?"

Delphi and the waitress looked up, surprised to see Brewer back from his errand.

"Uh, nobody."

He held out his hand, and Delphi willingly took it. "Let's hit the road, sweet cheeks. Got a lot of miles to put under us." Brewer wrapped an arm around her waist as she rose from her seat. "If you value your life or mine at all, for the love of Macha, don't fight it," he said in a low tone of voice before she could react.

Looking behind them, Delphi held in a gasp. A group of Cutthroat bikers were watching them leave, their faces anything but friendly. *Oh shit!* She had to commend Brewer for not sprinting out of the bar like her legs desperately craved.

"Did you kill someone?"

"What? No. Please keep your mouth shut for once." His hand tightened and she fought the urge to spit venom-filled words at him. If they were hustling out of a biker bar, there had to be a good reason.

Almost there, she repeated until Brewer pushed the door open. The sun hit her seconds later, warming her fingers that she hadn't realized were ice cold. Instead of letting go, Brewer kept his hold, only releasing her when they reached his motorcycle.

"What was that all about?" She faced him, putting her back to the bar. "Did you piss them off or something?"

"Or something." Brewer fastened his helmet quickly, then went to work on hers. His fingers moved deftly under her chin, ensuring the helmet was snug before he hopped on the bike. "We really need to go."

"But—"

"Now," he growled. "I'll answer all your questions later." His blue eyes met hers. "Please just get on the bike."

The sincerity in his voice compelled her head to nod and body to slide in place behind him. Engine revving, they rolled out of the parking lot. Hugging her arms more tightly around him, she caught a glimpse of the town's MC members milling outside of the cantina, guns glimmering in the sunlight. *What the hell did he do?*

CHAPTER 11
BREWER

"What'd you say?"

The older biker blew a stream of smoke toward Brewer. "Is that Delphi Windsor?"

Clenching his jaw, Brewer sized up the man who was wearing a faded black cut with the Cutthroat emblem proudly displayed. The patch name said Sully, and Brewer racked his brain, trying to place him. He knew of most the Cutthroat MC patch members, but this one was older. He bet his dad would've known him.

Brewer rolled back his shoulders, standing a little taller now. "What's it to you?"

Sully cracked a half smile. "Old business, I suppose. Nothing that concerns you."

Before Brewer could question him, another biker nudged him.

"That your girl, or is she available?" The man was a few years older than Brewer, tattoos covering every inch of exposed skin. "I'd get her back to you in one piece."

"Fuck off. She's mine," Brewer growled. He curled his hands into fists, heat coursing up his skin.

"Pity. She looks like somebody Granite used to fuck." The man grabbed the front of his jeans, and the other patched members around him chuckled. "One hell of a lay, far as I can remember."

Another man stepped forward. It was Granite from the name on the patch. Brewer bit his cheek to keep from decking the guy. He deserved more than that after what Delphi had insinuated he'd done.

"Delphi's here?" Granite glanced behind Brewer. "I should probably go say hi. It's been a while since I saw her. We didn't get any breakup sex."

"She's taken, so go find somebody else," Brewer said, shoving Granite's chest. The man lived up to his name, but Brewer had a good fifty pounds of muscle on the other biker.

Granite laughed and shook his head. "She's not *that* good of a fuck. Hell, I'll finish up our business, then give the boys a bit of fun."

Brewer bristled but didn't give into the urge to

deck him. He glared at Granite, fingernails digging into the palms of his hands until he drew blood. It wasn't worth the risk. Not today at least.

He walked through the group of Cutthroats, hair on the back of his neck still upright. One wrong word and he'd be in deep shit. He could handle a couple Cutthroats, but definitely not a whole bar full of them.

Patting the small thumb drive in his front pocket, he nearly made it to the bar front before somebody called out his name. His club name.

"What the hell is a Macha bitch like Brewer doing here?"

Brewer turned around to see Skinner emerge from the dark area. "Just rolling through."

Five bikers flanked Skinner, the expressions on their faces clearly showing how eager they were to dish out a beating. "Thought we agreed Macha and the Cutthroats would stay away from each other."

Brewer ran a hand over his beard. He had to get out of there before something bad happened. Delphi couldn't fend off a Cutthroat horde.

"And that's exactly what I'm doing." He turned and hurried to the bar. Seeing Delphi seated there, he silently swore under his breath. If they were lucky, they'd make it out of there without getting pommeled.

BREWER GRIPPED THE HANDLEBARS TIGHTER, STILL ruminating on his conversations with the Cutthroats. The fact that she was asked about by name bothered him. Delphi wasn't the kind of woman anyone would forget so easily. She had a way about her. Even when she breathed fire, she was gorgeous. But he didn't like that more than one biker recognized her. The older biker, Sully, was more confusing, but maybe she'd shed some light on that later. He needed to talk to her, but not until they were safely back in Macha territory.

The road curved, and he clenched his jaw when Delphi hugged him at the turn.

The small flash drive in his pocket was filled with the intel his sister was promised. *Sure hope it's on there and we weren't played.*

A cold wind came from the west, buffeting the motorcycle slightly. He straightened out as he saw a sign for Snowshoe in the distance. The weather wasn't ready to relent to spring quite yet. It was a good thing they were headed back to the clubhouse anyhow. Delphi wasn't wearing enough clothes to keep her warm if the temperature dropped much further.

When they arrived in Snowshoe, he'd answer her

questions, but he had a few of his own as well. That was fine by him, but he'd be doing it at the clubhouse. His phone vibrated again. Without a doubt Dolly was blowing his phone up with text messages. If he had to guess, his sister's contact had reached out and dished on their hasty retreat. *Great.* Explaining the situation to Delphi was one thing, but his sister was a whole different story. *Especially if Dolly's looking to get out of club life.*

The moment his front tire hit Macha's clubhouse parking lot, he sensed a change in Delphi. He couldn't pinpoint what it was, but the air around him seemed denser somehow.

He drove into the garage and parked, but before he shut off the engine, Delphi was off the bike and in his face.

"You better fucking tell me what happened in Waverley, Brewer Stapleton." Her eyes shot blue daggers and her mouth was turned down in a fierce frown. If she wasn't so angry, he'd kiss her into submission.

"Somebody's old lady is pissed," one of the prospects sang in a joking manner.

Brewer whipped his gaze to him, and the man went silent. Even the machinery in the garage seemed to quiet. That never happened.

Delphi poked his chest, her voice rising. "They

had guns, Brewer. Guns. You know, the things that can kill you in an instant."

Brewer pulled off his helmet and rested it on the bike's seat. He stood with his arms crossed over his chest, letting her have at it. The growing crowd of Macha prospects dispersed the instant he glared at them. Nobody needed to hear Delphi go off the rails except him. The fear was evident in her tone but even more so in her eyes. It was a look he hated with every molecule of his being.

"I agreed to go on a harmless ride this afternoon, but instead I get ushered to the one place I loathe, and then you leave."

She flung her arms around, the garage emptying faster by the moment. Only Rubble and Kevlar stayed, but neither appeared to be listening, Kevlar hunched over the paperwork in the office while Rubble tinkered on a car. Brewer made a mental note to check in on them later. Rubble would want to see the flash drive.

"And to top it off, I end up running for my life because you went and said the wrong thing to somebody." Delphi stopped pacing; her eyes rimmed with red. She wasn't crying, but the tears were there just below the surface.

Brewer kept his temper in check. She wasn't

wrong, but she wasn't completely correct either. "Do you remember the Cutthroat you dated?"

"What?" She snapped her gaze away from the Chevy that Rubble was repainting. "Why are you asking that?"

"Because when I went back to get my information, one of the bikers sought me out. He saw you in the cantina and asked if you were available."

"So?"

Brewer did his damnedest to keep his anger simmering on low. This woman made him crave a shot of whiskey chased by five more. "He made it pretty clear he wanted to finish what he started last summer before passing you around the club."

Her face turned as white as a sheet, the blood draining instantly. "Oh, God."

Standing up, he slowly closed the distance between them and took both her hands in his. "I need you to be one-hundred-percent honest with me."

She searched his face, waiting for a question.

"Do you know a biker named Sully?"

She shook her head. "No, why?"

"Probably nothing, but I wanted to check." Brewer didn't fully know the connection with the old biker and Delphi, but for the time being, Sully wasn't the biker he was after.

"Is that all?"

"No."

Delphi caught her bottom lip between her teeth, and he had to remind himself of the urgency of the matter at hand.

"You know more about Shovelhead, don't you?"

If he thought she was pale before, Delphi turned practically transparent. "Wh-what?"

"Answer me."

Lowering her gaze to her boots, she let out a breath. Her bottom lip trembled, and his heart instantly seized. "Yes."

"And what is that?" He lifted her chin with his fingers. Pain overwhelmed her eyes and transferred straight to him.

"I didn't want to believe that my mom cheated on my dad." She sniffled. "But she did. She slept with a biker, and I was the product of their affair."

"What're you saying?"

"On his deathbed, my dad said that Shovelhead is my biological father." A forced laugh passed through her lips. "No wonder my parents made a big deal about me steering clear of bikers, huh? They didn't want me finding out who I really am."

Brewer felt as though she'd kicked him in the balls. Unearthing family skeletons was one thing, but this made the situation more complicated. "Shit."

"I wanted to help any way I could. Even offered to do a blood transfusion for my dad." She rubbed her lips together. "But the doctor told me I couldn't. My blood type wasn't a match. I screamed at them. I was so sure they gave me the wrong results. That's when he told me." She walked over to the bay door and looked out at the busy street. "I didn't want it to be true."

Brewer followed her and gently hugged her from behind.

"I had a perfect childhood. Sure, I was kind of chubby and was bullied because of it, but I was happy." She hugged his arms over her chest. "In retrospect, I always knew I was different. It's why I went in search for my biological dad. I did some research and found out he betrayed Macha. I still wanted to meet him. I wanted to meet the person who helped create me. He's family, and he's all I have left."

"Blood doesn't make you family, Delphi. Love does." He kissed the top of her head, his mind spinning over the connection only he knew about. "Shovelhead has done a lot of bad shit, but not knowing you is definitely the worst."

Her body shook against him, and he gripped her a little tighter. Receiving such a bombshell at the time both his parents died would've messed him up too.

"Why are you nice to me?" she asked, wiping her face and turning around. "I'm rude and horrible to you. Probably a lot like Shovelhead."

Brewer cradled her jaw, tipping up her face to meet his gaze. "I like you, Delphi. It's because of your brash rudeness too. Sweet girls aren't my vice. Sassy ones are."

"I'm not sassy, I'm—"

His lips covering hers silenced the rest of her retort. He didn't need to hear it to know it'd be just as plucky as her usual jabs. Delphi stiffened at the contact at first, but within seconds, she opened her mouth, accepting his kiss and taking it deeper than before. A soft moan slipped through her lips, igniting his lust. When she slid her arms around his neck and pulled him closer, Brewer swore he saw stars. She kissed with such passion and abandon. *I'm gonna have so much fun with this woman.*

"Ahem. Should we shut down the shop for the rest of the afternoon, or can you two suck face elsewhere?"

Delphi squeaked and jumped away from him. She traced her mouth with her fingers, her face flushed with the prettiest shade of pink.

Meeting Rubble's steely gaze, Brewer smirked. "Nah, brother. We'll let you get back to it."

Rubble grunted, the response normal for the

hulking man, then waved in the prospects Brewer scared away so he could take Delphi's tongue-lashing. *And a delicious one at that.* Her minty lip balm lingered on his lips even now.

Linking his arm around her waist, he led her toward the clubhouse.

"I need to go home," she suddenly said, tearing herself away.

"Why?"

"I, uh, should do some inventory."

Brewer tried to capture her gaze, but she wouldn't give it up. "Stay for dinner. It's Queenie's turn to cook, and I hear she's making meatloaf. It's amazing."

This got her attention. Food was her vice, just like it was for him. Still, she didn't give in. "Thanks, but I'll rain check for another day."

"All right, I'll drive you—"

"No, it's fine." She started walking toward the street, phone in her hand. He caught sight of a popular transportation app loading on her screen.

An SUV pulled into the lot, and Brewer sighed in relief. The driver's window rolled down, and Jupiter's cheery face greeted him. "Hey! What're you doing here, Delphi?"

Delphi spun around, face aflame. "Jupiter, hey. I was...." She looked to him for help.

"Delphi and I were just making out."

Jupiter's mouth dropped open and her eyes went wide. He looked at Delphi and saw a similar expression, but hers contained a hint of embarrassment and wrath.

"What the hell, Brewer?" Delphi said between her teeth.

He winked, then asked, "Mind dropping her at home? She wouldn't accept my help."

Jupiter nodded slowly. "I wonder why."

"Probably because she's too afraid she'll invite me upstairs for a follow-up to our kiss."

Stalking toward the SUV, Delphi shook her head vigorously and flipped him both middle fingers before climbing into the passenger seat.

"Looking forward to that sequel," he called as Jupiter turned the SUV away. He didn't see Delphi's reaction, but he'd bet good money she turned as red as a cherry. In only one day, she'd managed to wiggle further into his heart. For the first time in a long time, he didn't mind one bit.

CHAPTER 12
DELPHI

Delphi wished she could fake an illness so she didn't have to answer her friend. Instead, she opted for changing the subject. "I'm thinking about joining the springtime picnic in the park this year. Maybe the bakery could team up with me."

Jupiter flipped on her blinker and took a right turn. "Mm-hmm, I'm sure that's what you're thinking."

She laughed. "What? I am."

"Well, in that case, I think it's a great idea. Once the weather is more stable, I guarantee Snowshoe residents would love a reason to get out of the house and eat some delicious food." Jupiter offered her a smile. "Maybe Brewer can bring the booze."

Resigning herself to the fact that she wouldn't get

a word in without Brewer's name circulating until she faced the truth, Delphi rolled her neck, the muscles tight after her time on the back of a bike.

"He's a really good kisser." She met her friend's gaze. "There. Now can we focus on the picnic?"

"Nope. I want to hear every steamy detail. Did he grab your ass? Pick you up? Push you against a door and kiss you until your toes curled?"

Delphi cast a curious glance at Jupiter. "Asking from personal experience?"

"Honey, please. You don't want to hear all the dirty things Rubble does to me every night."

"Every night?"

"Or day. Or both." Jupiter smiled secretively. "My man is a sex addict if I ever saw one."

"And you're good with that?"

"Seeing how he gets me off every time, only has eyes for me, and makes me feel like a goddess—I freaking love it."

Delphi fell quiet. She'd heard tidbits from Jupiter over the months but never had any man to compare the stories to. Without a doubt, Brewer would put all her previous lovers to shame. *And we hardly even kissed.*

Her lips tingled, remembering his firm yet soft touch. He was handsome, and she'd always known he would make for one hell of a one-night stand, but when he kissed her, everything changed. Suddenly, Brewer wasn't an asshole biker trying to flame her temper. The way he had put his hands on her waist, pulling her close while his lips sent her into a frenzy cleared her mind of all the bullshit.

Their kiss replayed in her mind. It was the best first kiss—though she'd never admit it to him. *It'd only make him cockier.* Catching her bottom lip between her teeth, Delphi thought back to the large bulge pressed against her thigh while their tongues tangled. She shuddered at the thought of what he could do with that solid length.

"Hello, earth to Delphi."

Jupiter's voice broke into Delphi's fantasy. "Huh?"

"You're home."

Looking out the window, she spotted the bistro and her apartment on the floor above it. "Right. Thanks for the ride. I owe you one."

Jupiter put the SUV in gear and grinned. "You'll fall for a Macha man if you spend more time with Brewer."

She hopped out and closed the door. "I can't, Jupiter."

"Can't or won't?"

"Both." Delphi waved and started up the sidewalk to her door. Jupiter was right. If she and Brewer spent any time together, she'd lose control of her heart. *And that'll only end in disaster.*

She fished out her keys as she climbed the stairs. A large glass of red wine and a bubble bath were what her body craved. It'd be simple enough to steer clear of Brewer. She'd blow him off until he got the picture. Falling for a Macha man wasn't in her future.

<hr>

Ignoring Brewer's calls was easy. Delphi hated answering when anyone called, let alone the biker who kissed her earlier in the week. The text messages were also no trouble to dodge. The one thing she doubted she could get away with was not seeing him when he stopped by the bistro. But as luck would have it, one of the waitresses asked to move to the front, so Delphi was able to focus on cooking, her real passion.

By the time Sunday night came around, her calves were burning from the long week she'd put in as well as the recent jog around Snowshoe. She pushed up her thick headband, sweat dampening her matching athletic outfit.

She pressed her fingers against her neck to check her pulse as she walked slowly back to her apartment. The sun played hide-and-seek behind clouds, and a brisk spring chill cooled her body temperature. Her muscles ached from kneading bread all morning, then bussing tables when the busboy called in sick. All in all, she was ready for a day off. The familiar scent of Guinness drifted to her. *Brewer.* She'd done her damnedest to not think twice about him. It was easier said than done when her mind kept replaying the way his lips felt against hers. She shivered at the memory and turned off the music in her earbuds. After finishing work, then letting off steam with a jog, a long soak in the tub was next on her agenda.

"You're one hard girl to pin down."

His sexy voice stopped her from grasping the door handle. Her heart thudded against her ribcage, and she had to tell herself it was from the exercise and not the man behind her.

Turning slightly, Delphi took a moment to appreciate Brewer's appearance. His red hair stuck out beneath a dark wool cap, his blue eyes sparkling with mischief. The matching beard was neatly trimmed, and his lips were curled upward in a half smile. A pair of jeans with his Macha cut overtop a dark red hooded sweatshirt and black boots rounded out the biker vibe.

"Maybe I was avoiding you," she finally said, grabbing her phone out of her back pocket.

"Oh, I know that's what you were doing." He caught up with her.

"And yet you're still here." Instead of moving inside, she pressed her back to the door and met his gaze. "Remind me again: why are you standing on my stoop?"

"I missed you."

"Bullshit."

He smirked. "All right, well, I did miss your fiery mouth." His gaze dipped to her lips, and she unconsciously licked them. "But I did have another reason for showing up tonight."

Delphi cocked her head to the right, waiting for him to explain.

"I wanted to invite you to dinner."

"Tempting." She looked at her watch and her stomach took that as a cue to grumble. "What's on the menu?"

"I've been smoking some pork all day. Makes for delicious pulled barbecue sandwiches."

Her mouth watered. Delphi couldn't recall the last time she had smoked pulled pork. It sounded tastier by the moment. "I'm assuming the whole club will be there?"

He nodded. "Yep. Dinner at the club is family style. I'm in charge of the main course tonight, but there'll be several other options if you don't like meat."

"Oh, no, I like meat. I like it a lot."

A boyish grin covered his face, and she rolled her eyes, realizing where his mind had drifted. "Is your head ever out of the gutter?"

"Nope."

It didn't take her long to decide. She didn't have a plan for dinner, and the thought of microwaved Japanese noodles wasn't luring her like the idea of Brewer's meal.

"Fine, but I need to shower." She opened the door and wasn't even surprised when he followed her inside and up the staircase. *This man has zero boundaries.* Somehow it didn't bother her like it should. She felt comfortable around him. Safe even.

He glanced around the open-concept apartment. "You have a nice place."

"Thanks." She hung her jacket up and slipped off her shoes. "It came with the bistro, so I can't complain. A lot cheaper than renting a place separately."

Brewer sank into the couch, grabbing the remote and flipping on the television. Fiona immediately hopped up on his lap as if she'd known him her entire cat life.

"No, no. Make yourself at home," she said sarcastically, walking down the hallway. "I'll be out in a few minutes."

"Take your time," he called back, a boxing match droning through the screen in front of him.

Grabbing a fresh towel from the hallway closet, Delphi hurried into the bathroom and cranked on the shower. Steam filled the space, but that wasn't the reason she started sweating again. Brewer in her living room, mere feet away from her naked body, was the culprit.

Stop fantasizing about him, she told herself, stepping under the warm spray of water. If she made it through the night without kissing him again, she'd be surprised. Brewer was more dangerous by the hour, and her body knew it.

CHAPTER 13

BREWER

Brewer had an ulterior motive. Of course he wanted to spend more time with Delphi. Every inch of him wanted to do more than that, but he held back. Despite the apprehensive front, she was scared of both her past and future. He didn't blame her one bit.

Watching her in the passenger seat of his truck, Brewer wanted to tell her the truth. She was nervous enough if the way her thumbs were fidgeting was any indicator. Still, Reaper asked him to invite Delphi to dinner, and he finally succeeded. It had taken all week, thanks to her evading him at every attempt.

"Anything crucial I should know before I walk in there?" Delphi asked as they pulled into the club- house parking lot. "I know the basics about clubs, but they all have little nuances."

A ping of regret filtered through him. He put the truck in Park and shut off the engine. "Just have fun. Macha's one big, crazy, happy family." He smiled, coaxing a small answering smile from her. "Don't worry, sweet cheeks, I won't let anybody get too friendly with ya."

Delphi unbuckled and took a breath before opening the door. If he were a gentleman and they were on a date, he'd rush over and hold it open for her. *But this isn't a date.* He stepped outside, a hint of moisture in the air. *And I sure as hell am not a gentleman.*

Brewer noticed the parking lot was full tonight. Nobody missed a good pork sandwich—especially not his brothers. It made his stomach churn for new reasons. His brothers weren't anything she couldn't handle, but he also had underlying motives in bringing her tonight. If he wasn't careful, he'd lose her.

He walked in step with her, the scent of her perfume making it difficult to keep his hands off her voluptuous ass.

When they reached the front door, he suddenly craved a cigarette. Delphi seemed oblivious of his plight and grinned at him.

"Too late to turn back," she said, tugging on the door to the clubhouse.

Light streamed outside, cheery voices and laughter quickly following it. Brewer held his breath and stepped inside. Bringing a girl to dinner wasn't abnormal for any of the club members, but he rarely brought anyone who wasn't already part of Macha.

"There's Brewer," Hawk said, tipping back a bottle of beer. "I was about to take over your duties." He grinned when Delphi came into view. "But I can see why you took so long."

"Kevlar was babysitting the smoker for me," he replied, offering a beer to Delphi. She grabbed it, staying close beside him. The sweet scent from her perfume overtook him once more. In the truck there'd been a barrier, but now with her flush against him, the fruity mangos suddenly made him crave more than the fruit.

"You should probably go check on it," Hawk said, his dark eyes scanning Delphi.

Brewer had seen that perusal many a time before. His brother wasn't subtle in ogling women, and from the looks of it, Delphi caught wind of it.

"Take a picture, it'll last longer," she said, twisting the top off the beer and taking a drink.

Hawk chuckled and held up his hands in defeat. "All right, I get it. You're set on one Macha man." He took a step closer, and Brewer resisted the urge to deck him. "But if you get bored of this one or want to try two brothers, call me up. I'll make sure you don't forget a night with me."

Delphi's eyes flicked to him, then back to Hawk. "Are you always so forward with women one of your brothers brings to the clubhouse?"

Hawk smirked. "Yes, ma'am. Even stolen a few."

She snorted. "Not this one."

Brewer beamed with pride and grabbed Delphi's arm, leading them further into the clubhouse. They passed the dining area, where Isa was setting the table as Doc was trying to stop his very pregnant old lady from overexerting herself.

He paused in the doorway. "Don't make me call in the big guns, cousin."

Isa scowled at him, but it quickly morphed into a smile when she noticed Delphi. "When will you Macha men stop micromanaging?"

Doc crossed his arms over his chest. "Isa, you know full well none of Macha's men can micromanage their old ladies." He nodded at Delphi. "Nice to see you again."

Setting down the last plate, Isa walked—more of a waddle than a walk, from Brewer's perspective—and clasped Delphi's free hand. "So glad you're here for dinner. Brewer is the smoking aficionado."

Delphi smiled politely. "He more or less dragged me here, but I'm starving and couldn't resist."

"That's how they get you." Isa laughed, her eyes twinkling. "People always say diamonds are a girl's best friend, but they're wrong. It's food."

"Amen, sister," a new voice chimed in as Dolly walked into the room, her typical tank top with Macha stamped on it exposing her toned, tattooed arms. "I don't believe we've met yet." She held out her hand. "I'm Dolly, Brewer's little sister."

Delphi cast a curious glance at him before shaking hands. "Nice to meet you. Brewer didn't mention he had a sister."

Three sets of stunning eyes latched on to Brewer. Doc clapped him on the shoulder and slipped past him. "Good luck."

He swallowed, the beer bubbling in his throat. "Probably because my sister is so nosy, I half expected her to track you down and force you to listen to all our horrible childhood stories."

Dolly flipped him both middle fingers, then shrugged. "Actually, yeah, that does sound like me." She linked her arm through Delphi's. "Come on. I'll introduce you to the club. My brother has dinner to attend to."

Brewer wanted to argue, but she was right. He'd left Kevlar on pork duty almost two hours earlier. It was high time he got back to make sure the damn pig wasn't burned to a crisp. "If you're all right with it."

Delphi took another drink and rubbed her lips together. She was nervous, but not shy. He knew she could hold her own within Macha. It was part of what drew him to her. "I think I can handle a little one-on-one time with your sister and the club."

He met Dolly's gaze. They both heard the undercurrent to her words. While his sister didn't know the whole truth behind Delphi's parentage, she'd corner him later to uncover any information he was willing to part with. The rest of the club knew about Shovelhead and Delphi. It was why she was there.

"Have fun. I'll check on you in a few."

A hint of worry flashed across Delphi's beautiful face, but she quickly recovered before Dolly led her toward the rest of the clubhouse.

Brewer took a deep breath and hoped he'd done the right thing. He had orders from his president, but he also didn't want to fuck anything up with Delphi. She was much too special to lose.

CHAPTER 14
DELPHI

"So, how long have you and my brother been hooking up?"

Delphi choked on the last swig of her Guinness. "What?"

Dolly's blue eyes were rimmed to perfection with catlike black liner. The thick coats of mascara she'd applied only enhanced their stunning color. "Playing coy, huh? I get it. Not sure I want to hear the details anyhow."

They walked into a large living area. Club members were gathered around pool tables. Two women were making out on the couch while a group of men with Prospect on their vests watched. Rock music streamed through speakers on opposite walls. Despite the scene, it didn't seem raunchy or even wrong. It felt right. The décor was welcoming instead of harsh, and the vibe in the room was cheerful and sensual.

"It's a sight, isn't it?" Dolly pointed to a tall couple. The woman was wearing a jacket with FBI on the back. "That's Kevlar's old lady, Nikita. Beside her is Rubble, but you already know him."

Delphi smiled slightly at Rubble. The big man narrowed his eyes, but then offered her a curt nod.

"Cueball is over there, hustling a couple of my nymphs." Dolly chuckled. "The new girls don't know any better yet."

"The nymphs are club girls, right?"

Giving her a once-over, Dolly nodded. "Yep. They're my bread and butter."

"Who's that?" Delphi looked across the room.

A proud expression covered Dolly's face. "That's Queenie. She's basically a mother to all of us and old lady to Reaper. He's the club president. At least he will be for another few months."

Queenie raised a tumbler filled with what looked like whiskey and grinned. The man beside her glanced over. His kind blue eyes seemed to smile. They were old enough to be her parents, but seemed ready to have a good time.

"Is he stepping down?" She'd brushed up on Macha club life not long after discovering her connection to Shovelhead.

Dolly walked toward a room off the main one. "He's getting up there in years and wants to retire. The club will vote on a new president and vice president before summer."

"Who do you think will win?"

The next room was darker, with a fire roaring in the hearth. More bikers and women filled it, but the ambiance was cozier. Dolly sat on the couch and patted the spot next to her. "I've heard whisperings about Doc."

"Isa's old man?"

"The very one." Dolly grabbed two fresh beers from a nymph. "He's Reaper's nephew and a shoo-in. It makes sense. Reaper called him to Macha from his paramedic job in Iowa. I think it was to groom him for the presidency. Keep it in the family and all. But it's anyone's guess."

"And the vice president?"

"That one is up for grabs." She rested her arm on the back of the couch, facing Delphi. "Maybe even Brewer will toss his patch in the race."

"I didn't realize Brewer was interested in leadership." Delphi heard a deep chuckle across the room and immediately knew it was from the man she couldn't get out of her head. The tenor timbre sent shivers through her belly.

"Not sure if he is, but that's part of the reason

why I think he'd be great at it. My brother isn't a fan of being the center of attention." She jutted her chin toward a couple arguing by the pool table. "Others like Snoopy and his old lady only want to have everyone's eyes on them."

The couple stopped yelling in English and switched to Spanish. Delphi cringed but couldn't help but wonder what they were arguing about. "Think people will vote for him?"

Dolly's gaze focused on a woman playing pool. "Probably. Can't help stupid."

She couldn't agree more. Over the years, Delphi had anticipated how plenty of issues both personal and professional would play out while everyone else shook their head, unable to decipher the outcome.

"What about Rubble?"

"Nah, he likes being sergeant at arms." Dolly crossed one leg over the other. "So, you want to tell me what's going on with you and my big bro, or do I have to get you drunk first?"

"Nothing's going on."

"I heard you kissed."

Delphi snapped her eyes from the beer label to the other woman. "Who told you that?"

"Other than half the garage?" Dolly's eyes sparkled. "Brewer."

A new reason to drink came over her. She

tipped back the bottle until it was empty. If she was going to get through the evening, she'd need to stabilize her nerves a bit. "You two seem close."

"Yeah, I'd say we're close."

"That's really cool. I'm an only child." She placed the bottle on the coffee table. "But not for my parents' lack of trying."

"Hey, they got lucky once. Can't hate them for trying to give you a sibling."

Delphi hadn't thought of that in years. Not since she was a kid and complaining she had no one to play with. It suddenly made sense. "My dad couldn't have kids."

Dolly arched her brow. "Um, okay?"

"Shit, I didn't mean to say that out loud." She watched the logs burn. "I just realized. No wonder they tried so hard. They wanted someone who wasn't...." She left off there, unable to finish the thought.

"Wasn't what?"

"A mistake."

Dolly opened her mouth to respond, but Brewer chose that moment to step into the room. "Dinner's on. If you don't want Hawk eating it all, you better get in there," he said loud enough for everyone to hear.

Bikers and nymphs alike funneled down the hallways toward the dining area and kitchen.

"Come on. He wasn't joking about Hawk." Dolly stood up. "That man can put more food away than a dozen teenagers."

Delphi waited until Dolly disappeared into the throng of foodies before standing up herself. The weight of their conversation should've been light, but it turned heavy in the beat of her heart.

"Everything okay?" Brewer asked, coming up behind her. "Dolly didn't say anything to upset you, did she? My sister is very blunt. She didn't mean it. Probably."

Placing a hand on his forearm, she shook her head. "No, it wasn't her. She was great. Honestly."

"Then what's wrong?" He covered her hand with his. "I can see it in your eyes, Delphi. Talk to me."

"I'm just understanding more about my family, that's all."

"Being here did that?"

"Yeah. I don't know why." She offered him a look she hoped would make him stop staring at her like she was Pandora's box simply waiting to be opened. "I'm fine. Seriously. Unpacking family history is a bitch sometimes."

He wrapped his arms around her and hugged her

gently. "I may not understand completely, but I do get it, Delphi."

She snuggled deeper into his chest. The scent of firewood clung to his shirt. "What do you mean?"

"Well, Dolly and I are trying to find out what happened to our parents a few years back."

"When they died?"

"Yeah. We think somebody in Macha killed them."

Delphi dropped her hold and took a step back. "Who do you think it was?"

Brewer ran his fingers through his hair, chewing his bottom lip. Finally, he met her gaze and stole her breath. "Shovelhead."

CHAPTER 15

BREWER

The dining area never seemed fuller to Brewer than it did with Delphi sitting next to him. Most of the nymphs were there along with all his brothers, prospects, and the old ladies. Both the adjoining kitchen and dining table were packed to the brim.

He stared at the food heaped on his plate. He'd only been able to take a few bites since piling it on there. More than once, he'd had to tell one of the patches or prospects to leave Delphi alone. Nobody seemed to believe she was there with him.

Brewer gritted his teeth at the sound of Hawk flirting with Delphi. Sure, he was never attached to any one woman, but Delphi was literally sitting at his side. It rubbed him the wrong way, but he guessed his brothers were doing it on purpose.

He and Delphi hadn't had a chance to discuss his

bombshell yet. The club's need for dinner interrupted any response she could give. Since then, he kept trying to talk to her, but she wouldn't even look at him.

"So, Delphi, you work at that French bistro, right?" Kevlar asked, scooping cheesy mashed potatoes on his plate.

"Actually, I own it." Delphi smiled. "I've always loved food, especially French food, and when I came back from culinary school, I knew I had to open a restaurant in Snowshoe showcasing that kind of cuisine."

"Are you a chef too?" Hawk asked.

"Yes, but I did hire another chef, so I bounce around as needed."

"She makes the best cheese soufflé," Jupiter added from across the table. "It's my go-to comfort food."

Delphi blushed, the pink perfect against her light skin tone. "You're my number-one customer for those."

"More like the baby is," Rubble said, jumping into the conversation. "Jupiter hauls me out of bed on a Sunday morning for those soufflés." He offered Delphi a grin. "But I can't complain. Your food is incredible."

"Well, that settles it," Reaper said from the head

of the table. "We'll plan a club dinner there. Delphi, can we rent out the whole place?" He laughed at three youngsters running around the table. "We can be a bit of a rowdy bunch."

"Oh, of course." She looked at him, and for the first time, Brewer felt a zing of hope. "I'll let Brewer know when I have an opening. Unfortunately, we have reservations months in advance."

Reaper's face fell until she added, "But I can squeeze you in on a Monday."

Brewer frowned. "That's your one day off."

"It's fine." She shrugged and offered him a small smile. "Not like I do much on those days anyways."

Her wounded eyes nearly did him in. He'd fucked up by not telling her about Shovelhead when she told him about her possible parentage. Brewer wasn't about to give up on this woman. *If she gives me another shot.* Their relationship thus far was complicated, and her connection to Shovelhead only intensified that.

"We'll help out," Queenie said from beside Reaper.

"That's not—"

"She'll take the help," Brewer finished for her. "Won't you, sweet cheeks?"

The bite of creamed corn she was about to eat paused at her lips, and a hush drifted over the table.

Delphi met his gaze, but he couldn't guess her reaction. She was calm and collected. Not her normal Delphi self when it came to his teasing. It all came down to this. How she reacted would determine if he had a shot in hell with her or if he was better off sulking to the nymphs in the basement.

"You know I'd never turn down seeing you suds deep, honey buns."

Brewer's face heated until he knew it was as red as his hair. Laughter erupted in the large space. Snoopy choked on his bite of green beans, and Legs slapped his back. Rubble's shoulders shook when Kevlar offered a salute to Brewer.

"You got honey buns, Brewsky?" Hawk howled from his spot.

Delphi laced her left arm around Brewer's neck and kissed his flamed cheek. "The tastiest."

"Thank the goddess she's a freak too," Nikita chuckled, winking at Delphi. "We could use a few more."

"I'll second that." Doc said, raising a glass toward Delphi.

If he wanted to hide his face in his hands, Brewer thought better of it. He needed to keep an eye out since his brothers had gone from flirting to admiring Delphi. She had been officially accepted into the club, but as *his* and no one else's.

"How'd I do?" Delphi whispered a few minutes later once the attention drifted to Jupiter and the baby.

He squeezed her leg. "Perfect, just like I knew you would."

The club went back to eating, the presidency coming up in topic, but Delphi didn't seem to want to shift gears yet.

"You know I'm pissed at you, right?"

He met her gaze and frowned, the BBQ pork threatening to turn on him. "Yeah, I figured you might be."

Delphi sighed but kept a smile on her lips. "You can't drop that shit on me seconds before a family dinner."

"Sorry."

"God, you're infuriating." She stabbed a piece of meat with her fork. "It'll never work between us, Brewer. You know it too."

"No, I don't."

Instead of arguing further, she returned to her food and chatted with others for the remainder of the meal. Brewer, on the other hand, couldn't force another morsel past his lips. His burgeoning hope for a relationship with her was shattered.

"Reaper wants to talk to you after dinner," he said

when Queenie and the nymphs went to the kitchen to grab dessert.

"About what?" She didn't look concerned. Quite the opposite, really.

"You know what." He'd let Reaper tell her the rest. If Delphi truly wanted to know about her father, it may as well come from Macha's president himself.

CHAPTER 16

DELPHI

The pulled pork and creamed corn churned in Delphi's stomach. As much as she'd wanted to eat the blueberry cobbler for dessert, she couldn't manage it. Not after the forlorn look Brewer gave her. He'd lied to get her there, and she wasn't about to let him get off without a tongue-lashing. Setting foot in the club's inner sanctum only made her palms sweat more. The large wooden table carved with an image of their patron goddess, Macha, intimidated her. But not as much as the group of men did who were currently sitting around the table in twirly chairs. Those chairs were the only things not frightening her. Every part of this room demanded adoration and obedience.

She sank into one of the chairs, Brewer between her and the members of the club's cabinet.

She laced her fingers together in her lap, willing them to stop fidgeting. "So, what did you need to talk to me about?"

"It's come to our attention that you know Shovelhead."

"No, I know of him. I've never met him."

Reaper looked at her over his small pair of glasses. "You're his daughter."

Hearing it out loud made her cringe. "That's what my dad told me before he died. My hope is to track him down and find out if it's true or not."

Rubble slid a folder toward her. "This is what we've come up with. Thanks to what the FBI, Brewer, and Dolly have been able to discover, we think Shovelhead is hiding out somewhere outside of Waverley. He's been spotted at the Greenback Cutthroats' cantina several times last month and has a history there."

"I can understand why Macha is so set on capturing him, considering the way he betrayed them." She flipped through the pages of photos both in color and black-and-white. They were all of Shovelhead. Many of the shots were rough, but it was the same man throughout.

"Shovelhead's treachery is only part of the reason Macha needs to find him." Reaper looked past her to Brewer. "We have questions about a murder from a few years ago that has remained unsolved."

She turned to the redhead beside her. "Your parents' deaths."

Brewer's cheek twitched. His normally friendly eyes turned cold. "Yes."

"You honestly believe…." She couldn't finish the thought, but Brewer did it for her.

"Like I told you before, Dolly and I think Shovelhead killed our parents."

"No, it can't be true," Delphi said, shaking her head, but quickly realized she didn't have a legitimate reason to argue in his defense. Shovelhead wasn't someone she knew beyond his name. *And it's not even his legal name.*

"That's what we hope to find out," Rubble finished. His mismatched eyes kept her pinned to the chair. "We need you to help us."

"Wh-what?"

"Shovelhead will come out of hiding for his daughter," Reaper explained. "At least, we think he will chance it."

She pushed away from the table. "He doesn't even know I exist."

Rubble smirked. "Even more reason to address the issue personally instead of sending a lackey. Shovelhead's pride will be his downfall."

Glancing at Brewer, she noticed his discomfort. "How long have you known he might be my father? Since we met?"

He met her gaze. "No. Only since you mentioned it."

"That's correct," Reaper added.

Her hands shook for a new reason. Blaming Brewer wouldn't do either of them any good. She had two options, but only one would be fruitful. Finding Shovelhead on her own wasn't going well, and her ex now knew she was back in town. She had to trust Macha. She had no other choice if she wanted the truth. She looked at Brewer, but she knew she couldn't trust him. He lied to her. They hadn't known each other long, and he didn't owe her anything, but the lie hurt nonetheless.

She took a deep breath. "I'm in. How do we get in touch with him?"

The man sitting next to Rubble with the name Boulder on his patch piped up. "We have a contact in the Cutthroat dollhouse. She'll get the word out about Shovelhead's kid looking for him. You're a local, so he won't suspect anything. You keep running your restaurant. Macha will look out for you, and Shovelhead will do the rest."

Delphi nodded, but she hoped they'd repeat the plan ten more times because in that moment, she was barely listening. Her nerves were shot just from meeting the club—learning of her connection to Brewer sent her emotions into overdrive. "What if he comes to the bistro?"

"Brewer will be assigned to your protection detail until it's all over with," Reaper said.

"What?" both she and Brewer said at the same time.

"Prez, I don't think that's a good idea," Brewer said, pushing away from the table.

"Yeah, I agree."

Reaper's brows furrowed. "Why not? You two seemed chummy at dinner."

"Yeah, but not in the way I hoped," he explained, barely glancing over at Delphi. "Sweet cheeks here isn't a fan of my method of employment and has made it abundantly clear."

"You have a problem with Macha?" Boulder asked, his green eyes faded from years of club business.

"Uh, no. I mean, in a way, but nothing serious." She chewed her bottom lip. She'd lose out on everything if she let her past club issues bleed through. "I don't have an issue working with Macha on the Shovelhead thing."

"Just the Brewer thing?" Rubble said, a smirk playing his lips. "Got it." He met Brewer's eyes, and it seemed as if a silent conversation was exchanged between them. "Fine, we'll draw the security detail by lottery. It'll give the boys a chance to get out of the club for a bit anyways. All this presidency shit is driving them nuts."

Reaper looked from person to person before finally nodding once. "So be it. Delphi, Rubble and one of the boys will stop by tomorrow morning and get the details out of the way. Brewer can take you home tonight."

Brewer's previous statement had kept her hackles up. "No, that's okay. I'll take an Uber."

Rubble stood up and chuckled. "I don't think you heard right, Delphi," he said, his eyes narrowing in a new way. "Brewer is taking you home. You're under Macha protection. We don't fuck around with that."

She frowned. "I don't need your protection. I only need your contacts to meet my father."

Brewer also stood. "Sweet cheeks, the moment you cross paths with Shovelhead, you'll be begging for Macha's protection."

A shiver of realization ran down her spine. *If this club fears him, what kind of a man is Shovelhead?*

She finally nodded at Rubble, giving in to their protection. Finding out Shovelhead's history suddenly wasn't as high on her list of priorities as surviving. "Now what?"

"We wait," Rubble said, walking out the door.

Meeting Brewer's steely gaze, Delphi swallowed hard. "Wait?"

"It's all we can do." He pulled on his wool cap, his mass of red curls all but disappearing. "Hope you enjoy staying indoors and personal bodyguards." He chuckled. "But I have a feeling you won't."

Delphi followed him out of the room. His quick shift from sweet and teasing to annoyed and uptight frustrated her. He lied to her. She had a damn good reason to be pissed. Even though she truly enjoyed spending time with him, telling him outright how she felt wasn't fair to either of them. They couldn't be a couple. *Ever. It's better if we're enemies, not lovers.* Her heart disagreed, but she couldn't ignore the truth of the matter.

The drive back to her apartment was eerily quiet. Only the country music playing over the speakers cut into the silence. Brewer walked her all the way upstairs. Macha took their role seriously, and Delphi almost wished she'd taken back what she said about working with Brewer. He was the only biker she trusted to keep a watchful eye on her, as ironic as that was.

"Be sure to deadbolt the door after I leave," he instructed, checking the stability of the lock. "One of the boys will be posted outside tonight."

"I rarely lock the deadbolt. It's a safe neighborhood."

Brewer deadpanned and shook his head. "Woman, you're asking for trouble."

He started down the stairs, and she couldn't help herself. "Brewer, wait."

Pausing on the second step, he turned slightly. "What, Delphi?"

She rubbed her lips together, words suddenly difficult. "Um. You lied to me."

He frowned. "Yeah, well, so did you. Omission is still a lie."

Her mouth dried. She hated that he was right. "Yours hurt more."

"I don't know about that." He rubbed a hand over his face. "Thanks for putting on a good show at the clubhouse." He shoved his hands in his jeans pockets. "For once I didn't feel like an outcast with my married brothers."

The truth in his eyes struck her hard. She'd liked flirting with him. Hell, she loved it. She moved closer. "It wasn't all a show."

"Then which part was real?" He retraced his steps until he was in front of her. "Was the disdain real, or was the easy way you joked and acted like you cared the genuine part?" He shook his head. "Sadly, I think the real part was you hating bikers and everyone living under the club's rules. Including me." He laughed and pushed back his wool cap. "Especially me."

Before she could stop herself, Delphi grabbed the front of his cut, the leather tough yet smooth against her fingers. "It isn't as easy as that. I was raised to fear bikers. My family hated bikers, and if Shovelhead's my dad and he did the things your club says he did, I can understand why. I can't get over that in one night."

Brewer cradled her jaw. "I never asked you to, Delphi. I just want to know you." He placed a feathery kiss on her cheek. "Love you, even, if you let me. I like you. I really do. Spitfire and all. I think we could make it work if we tried."

Her pulse echoed in her ears. He was so gentle, it physically hurt. She hadn't expected this from a biker. There was a sensitivity about him that she craved more of. He wasn't like the other MC men she'd known. He was kind, even if he had an asshole attitude most days.

"But you have to let me in, Delphi. I like our cat-and-mouse games, but not when it comes to real feelings." His eyes sought out hers, the blue depths piercing straight to her soul. "I won't force you to do anything, least of all like me."

"I do like you, Brewer. You piss me off so damned

much sometimes, but I like spending time with you." She sighed, her actions from the night coming back to her in one big rush. "I'm afraid of what might happen if I like you too much."

He brushed a chaste kiss on her lips, then dropped his hold. "I'd like to find out, but that all depends on you, sweet cheeks. Let me know when and if you do too. Night, Delphi. Sweet dreams."

Delphi stood in her doorway until his shadow had long vanished from the bottom of the stairs. She wanted to go after him and somehow explain herself. But instead, she locked the door like he instructed and crawled into bed, Brewer never leaving her thoughts.

CHAPTER 17
BREWER

The attention of the entire club was fixed on the brunette next to Brewer. She flipped her long ponytail over her shoulder. "Affirmative, Sergeant. Sent." She waved the phone and lifted her eyes. "Need a read receipt, guys?"

Hawk snorted and Snoopy rolled his eyes. Each one of them was eager to get Shovelhead back in their grips. They'd lost men over the years due to Shovelhead's disloyalty. Brewer couldn't imagine the club would let him live. Not after what he'd done to Doc's old lady, Isa, as well as to his and Dolly's parents. Only Shovelhead knew the other sins he'd committed. The club was determined to get them out of the man.

Rubble cleared his throat, and the room hushed.

He'd be the instigator when the time came for blood-shed. There was no going back when it came to betrayal in Macha. "Keep us updated."

Giving him a mock salute, Dolly stood and sashayed toward the door. Brewer shook his head. His sister was anything but oblivious to the way men watched her. It was partly why her entrances and exits were overly dramatic. As the club's madam, she taught the nymphs anything they didn't already know about enticing men. Dolly was as close to a Macha patch as any other man.

"Now that business is complete, we'll discuss the protection detail." Rubble flipped through a stack of paperwork. "Looks like Tater is up for first shift."

The patches snickered at the man on the cusp of being inducted into Macha. He was tall and lanky, and nothing about him was even close to being shaped like a potato. Nevertheless, the name stuck because he had tripped over loose potatoes and lost his front tooth during his second week on kitchen duty.

"As always, check-ins on the hour." Rubble's mismatched eyes swept over the men. "No one steps away from their post until relieved. Got it?"

Brewer glanced across the table at Kevlar. They exchanged knowing looks. It was because of Rubble's own old lady, Jupiter, that he'd reiterated the rules of protection. The recent firefight with Jupiter's abusive ex changed them all, but especially Rubble. He was the same cantankerous MMA retiree and ex-military man turned club enforcer. Now, though, there was a softer side that they all witnessed.

A round of "Ayes" filled the room. Rubble nodded, then sat.

Reaper pulled on his small glasses. "The next topic is the upcoming election. I've spoken to a handful of you about the VP and Prez roles that're up for grabs, but I'm hoping for more nominees." His gaze landed on Brewer. "Some of you are more fit to run this club than you think."

Brewer shifted in his seat as Hawk nudged him with his elbow.

"Legacies are always welcome to run, boyos," Reaper finished with a grin. "And many of you are from Macha families. Let's make this difficult, yeah?"

Kevlar wiggled his brows at him, and Brewer not so subtly flipped him the bird.

"All right—enough talk. Queenie's been busting her arse all day with a roast and all the fixins." Reaper pounded the gavel. "May the goddess ride with you."

The men dispersed in intervals. The prospects eagerly made a dash for the kitchen, their bellies compelling them toward the tasty smells. A handful of patches lit up before leaving, while plenty more milled about the room.

"Brewer, why haven't you added your name?" Boulder asked, finishing his notes from the meeting.

"My dad was never in the cabinet." He shrugged. "And I'm not one to give orders."

Boulder chuckled and stood up. His movement was obviously slower than in years prior. Their treasurer and secretary was retiring too, which meant they would need another new cabinet member—or two, depending on if the men split the role between two members. "You sure about that? You practically run the bar on your own."

"That's different. It's the bar. Any fool could run it."

Hawk slung an arm around Brewer's shoulders. "I sure as hell could. Honestly, the tattoo parlor is easy, so I could totally run the bar too."

"You fuck more clients than ink them," Snoopy added, joining them. The few times the man was away from his old lady were the best. He was free to act like himself without Legs hanging around them, which was why Brewer liked the times she was working elsewhere. Legs was nice enough, but a little too high maintenance for his liking.

"And don't forget about the special discounts," Doc jibed, laughing.

"Is there a discount for blow jobs?" Dolly called from the doorway.

They all glanced toward her, unaware until that moment that she'd come back into the room.

Cueball joined them and nodded. "If Hawk could get paid to screw, he would." He snapped his fingers. "Hey, why don't you talk to Dolly about making man-nymphs a thing."

Dolly laced her arms around Hawk and Cueball. "Hell no. Could you just imagine trying to teach him how to give proper oral?"

Hawk shrugged out from Dolly's embrace. "Hey, what's wrong with my technique? You seemed to enjoy it once upon a time."

Brewer let out an exasperated grunt at the conversation. Talking sex was no big deal. However, it got minimally annoying when his sister offered bedroom tips.

Dolly's face scrunched. "Meh, you're decent at best. If you want, I can arrange some lessons. I know a nymph or two who could use a good lick."

"Oh, my fucking God, Dolly."

All eyes swung to the doorway where Nikita stood with her hands on her hips. Kevlar's breathing went shallow, and Brewer held in a laugh.

She closed the distance to them and grinned.

"You know I like to join in with sex advice. Stop giving it when I'm gone."

Dolly and Nikita shared a good laugh over this. The rest of the men in the room—not so much.

"Aw, lighten up, big brother." Dolly jabbed his stomach with her finger. "It's not like I asked about Delphi."

Hawk and Kevlar cooed like teenage girls. "How's that going, by the way?" Hawk asked.

"It's not. She's just a necessary chess piece to get to Shovelhead. Oh, and she hates my guts."

The men exchanged glances between themselves, then burst out laughing.

"Yeah, right," Doc said, walking to the door. "And Isa hates my cinnamon twists."

"Ew, Doc—nobody wants to hear about how Isa dips your dick into cinnamon," Kevlar teased.

"I don't know, I kinda do." Nikita shrugged when her old man gave her an appalled glance. "Gotta keep it spicy." She nodded toward Rubble. "Like Rubble and Jupiter."

Rubble stopped pushing in the chairs around the table. "Don't pull me into whatever mind orgy you got going with Kevlar. I've heard plenty from the two of you."

Brewer found himself agreeing. Nikita and Kevlar

were anything but discreet when it came to their rendezvous.

"And let's not forget Rubble and Jupiter," Brewer added when Rubble tried to escape. He wasn't about to let him leave that easily.

Rubble glared at him. "And how many times have I caught you getting head under a table at the bar?"

He laughed, unable to disagree. "Hey, I can't help if the ladies like a bartender."

"Kinda like that Delphi girl." Hawk pulled out a carton of cigarettes. "She has one fine pair of tits."

"And that ass…. I'd like to—" Snoopy started to whistle just as his old lady, Legs, walked in. It quickly morphed to a sputtering cough, sending his brothers into a collective fit of snickers.

"You guys jawing all night or you gonna eat?" Queenie called from the doorway.

Brewer joined the tail end of the parade of hungry men and women.

"Hang on there, Brewer."

Pausing at the threshold, he glanced over his shoulder. "What's up, Prez?"

Reaper moved sluggishly toward him, favoring his left knee. "Should I be concerned about your relationship with Delphi Windsor?"

"Absolutely not."

"Are you sure?"

Sighing, Brewer closed the door slightly. "Do I think it's an issue? Yes and no. She and I are fire and ice. We're connected in the worst possible way."

"I saw you two kiss the other day."

"So? Enemies kiss sometimes." He brushed his fingers through his beard. It really needed another trim, but it'd have to wait. It wasn't high on his list of priorities.

Reaper's light blue eyes twinkled. "You're right, they do. Just ask Queenie."

Brewer cocked his brow. "Queenie?"

"Aye. She and I didn't get off on the best foot."

"My parents told me you stole her from another guy."

Nodding, the club president glanced past Brewer. "And that's true. She was with somebody else when I met her." He chuckled. "I never said we got along. Quite the opposite, actually."

"Then what's the real story there? I've heard it five different ways."

Reaper smiled secretively. "Boyo, I'll tell you one day."

"When?"

"When you're in Macha's cabinet."

Rolling his eyes, Brewer shook his head. "Guess I'll never know the story, then. I'm not interested in playing politics, Prez. I just want to run the bar and enjoy club life."

"But you're not enjoying it." Reaper placed a fatherly hand on Brewer's shoulder. "You're cruising. Nobody wants that in life. I know your father would kick your arse for doing it."

Thinking back to his dad, Brewer couldn't argue with Reaper there. His parents never let a day go by without getting into some kind of trouble. They were as childishly in love as teenagers. That fact made it ten times harder for him to ever settle. He had to be himself with a woman the way his parents had been with each other. In Macha, he was just a tough biker who poured drinks at the bar and had to bounce drunk customers now and then.

Brewer let out a breath. "Delphi seems like a good girl. She's had a shit year."

"We can all relate to that."

"But she doesn't need more shit." Brewer's phone buzzed with a photo from Doc of a plate filled of food. "And Macha tends to draw a whole heap of drama whether we want it or not."

"True words." Reaper nodded approvingly. "You're halfway to a presidency already. If I could vote, you'd be at the very top of my list of choices."

The older biker left before Brewer could say anything else. If the club president wanted something to happen, it would. *Let's hope he changes his mind.* Being president was more responsibility than he wanted.

Brewer walked down the hallway, his stomach grumbling. A nymph brushed passed him, dark eyes seductive. He'd make do one way or another. Delphi didn't need a washed-up bartender. *Just like I don't need to taste her again.* He shook his head. *No.* He couldn't simply let that girl go, but he also wouldn't chase her into a corner. The times she let her guard down and jumped him had been few and far between. If Delphi wanted more, he'd give it to her until her legs shook. *But she has to make that move.*

CHAPTER 18
DELPHI

Whipping her head toward the voice, Delphi stopped stirring the tomato bisque. "Cooling on the racks." She nodded at the trays near the oven.

Tessa, the waitress, piled four into a basket and smiled. "Perfect. Thanks."

"I really need to talk to Yasmina and Jupiter about those." She hurried around the kitchen, taking up the slack for Edgar, who was on his fifth smoke break of the evening.

Five days had passed since she spoke with Macha about contacting Shovelhead. Since then, a parade of Macha bikers had come through her doors. She peeked out and saw the man dressed in all leather flip through a car magazine at one of the tables near the entrance.

After moving the ratatouille from the oven and onto warming racks, she double-checked the order scribbled on the notepad, then placed the food on plates. It was the night's special, and she was pleasantly surprised at how popular it was during the dinner rush.

"Hey, you have a visitor."

Delphi turned at the man's voice. It belonged to her Macha bodyguard. If the stocky man with Stones on his patch thought this visitor was approved, then so did she. "Okay, send them back."

Jupiter's head popped into the kitchen before the rest of her body. "Hey, stranger. Got room for one more?"

"Jupiter! Oh, it's great to see you." She motioned toward the small table in the kitchen. "It feels like it's been months."

Jupiter walked to the table and sighed when she sat. "Rubble's baby is going to be ginormous. I just know it." She patted her swollen stomach. "Thankfully, I haven't thrown up in a week, so there's my one ounce of good news."

Laughing, Delphi sat across from her. "Well, I'm glad to hear that. I've missed you."

"Where have you been? Playing tonsil hockey with a certain bartender?"

"He wishes." She brushed her hair out of her face. "I assume Rubble told you about the Shovelhead plan?"

"It came up. I have to say I'm shocked. I never knew Shovelhead, but I saw him once or twice. He's a scary guy and a conniving one from what Rubble's told me." Jupiter offered her a comforting smile. "I'm glad the club's involved. They'll protect you." She reached over and patted Delphi's hand. "How're you dealing with all this?"

"I've been okay. It's not like I know the guy. I'm still wrapping my head around the fact that my mom slept with someone else."

"Maybe she didn't."

"What, like immaculate conception?"

Jupiter laughed. "No, you goof. I meant, what if your mom and Shovelhead were together?"

"Ew."

"Be serious."

Delphi took a breath and thought it over. "It's possible, I guess. She was always kind of coy about when she and my dad got together."

Edgar returned from his break, the back door swinging noisily behind him. "You two look like you could use something to eat."

While Jupiter nodded enthusiastically, Delphi

slumped in her chair. Her mind whirled with the possibility that her parents weren't together when she was conceived. It'd make her feel better about the entire situation, but only for a moment. If Shovelhead refused to acknowledge siring her, the message that went out to him may come back unanswered.

Setting a small plate of pastries on the table, Edgar cooed about Jupiter's round belly. Delphi didn't hear them beyond muffled syllables. She stuffed a purple macaroon into her mouth, the sweet fluffiness calming her.

"My dad knew. He had to know." Her eyes bugged at the realization.

Edgar stepped back and left them to their conversation.

"Knew what?"

"That my mom was knocked up by a biker." She wracked her memories, trying to decipher something that would help her make sense of it all. "My parents were high school sweethearts."

Jupiter nibbled on a madeleine. "You think he married your mom because she was pregnant and because he loved her?"

She popped another macaroon in her cheek and nodded. "That's exactly what I think."

"Whoa."

"Yeah."

They were both silent for a minute. The sounds of the kitchen and bistro flooded Delphi's ears. It was oddly comforting to have something else overwhelm her thoughts. Suddenly, Delphi wished she had more time with her mom. Her death was so abrupt. They never even had the chance to talk about the truth of her conception.

"Do you think Shovelhead...?" Jupiter stopped, but Delphi knew exactly what she was going to ask. She was thinking the same.

"I don't know. I hope not."

"Damn, I came to raise your spirits, but I'm afraid my visit is having the opposite effect." Jupiter finished off another madeleine. "Do you want to hear about the spring picnic?"

Delphi managed a smile. "Yes, please. That will help keep my mind off things."

For the next twenty minutes, Jupiter gave Delphi the lowdown from the recent town hall meeting about the upcoming picnic. Snowshoe would host the event with Waverley joining in and bringing businesses along with its residents.

"If the bakery and bistro team up, we'll kick major ass." Jupiter tugged a small notebook out of her oversized purse and opened it. "Yasmina and I made a list of our most popular pastries, and I jotted down a few foods I thought would go well with them." She placed the book on the table and turned it toward Delphi. "If you think of any others or ones that'd go better, say the word. I'd rather combine forces than flop."

"I agree." Delphi quickly skimmed the pastries and entrees. "Is this buffet style or booths?"

"Buffet."

"Okay, then we can plan on a fondue station, and french onion soup is always a big hit." She snagged a pen and jotted notes. "Edgar and I will brainstorm some other options, and I'll text them to you."

Jupiter grinned. "Perfect."

"How's Isa by the way? Shouldn't she be having that kid any day now?"

Leaning over the table, Jupiter's eyes widened. "Right? It's like she's trying to set a new world record. She's so cute and little. I'm jealous."

Delphi laughed, glad to finally be back to normalcy. Just hanging out with Jupiter made her feel better about everything going on in her life.

"She's what, nine months?"

"This week."

"Damn, she's gonna pop any minute."

The two exchanged frantic expressions, then laughed.

"Doc will be a wreck." Jupiter smirked. "Can't wait to watch it all go down."

"Sadist," Delphi teased.

"Hardly. I'm more interested in seeing how Rubble reacts to everything. It'll give me a good idea how he'll be when this little one makes a grand debut."

Delphi watched her friend rub her stomach protectively. "Everything going well in the Rubble arena?"

A whimsical smile covered Jupiter's face, instantly making Delphi jealous. That was the expression she hoped to have herself someday. "Oh, yeah, you have no idea. He's such a sweetheart. Always doting and worrying about me."

"Rubble? The ex-MMA fighter and former military dude?"

"Don't forget foster kid."

"Wow, I never knew."

"There's a lot more to a Macha man than you realize," Jupiter said with a knowing wiggle of her brows. "Aren't you curious what Brewer's really like?"

She was. More than she'd admit, but still, she feigned disinterest. "Eh."

"Oh, whatever." Jupiter playfully shoved Delphi's elbows off the table. "You're a horrible liar."

"You say that like it's a bad thing." Delphi noticed Edgar's eyes bulging, and he looked ready to start muttering in Italian at them. "I should probably get back to work. The dinner rush must've gotten a second wind, and Edgar can't go it alone."

Jupiter stood. "Shit, sorry. I'm monopolizing you."

Delphi hugged her friend. "Never apologize for that. I enjoy spending time with you. And I'm more than happy to rest for a few minutes. I've been going nonstop the last five days."

"Hmm, I wonder why."

Delphi shook her finger at her friend. "None of that." She gently rubbed Jupiter's stomach. "I'll be by tomorrow to pick up those cherry pastries."

"Great. See you then."

Once Jupiter disappeared from her sight, Delphi let out a sigh. Asking about Brewer was more than tempting, but she'd refrained. *Somehow.*

"All right, Edgar. What do we have?"

She walked back into the throng of the dinner rush, ready to focus on something other than Macha and her sudden mess of a life.

By the time Delphi shut off the bistro lights, all she wanted was a breath of fresh air. Normally, she jogged in the morning, but tonight was different. She had a ball of pent-up energy she needed to get rid of fast. Hurrying to change, Delphi scratched Fiona's head before running down the stairs and out into the darkness. Her Macha bodyguard stayed in his truck but started the engine when she took a left toward the city square. Music filled her earbuds, her phone finally synced with a new playlist. The city lights flickered on the main drag, but she wasn't worried. Even if she couldn't outrun an attacker, the biker in the pickup would step in.

Cars passed slowly beside her on the sidewalk winding through the street. It felt good to be out and about again. The evening rush had been hell, and her unresolved issues with Brewer kept festering under the surface. The man drove her nuts, but her body craved for him to undress her and kiss her until she forgot why she was mad at him.

Delphi shook the thoughts away before she lost control. Looking in both directions, she crossed the street. The sweat sliding down her body felt good, but it also sent her mind spiraling to thoughts of how it'd feel if it was the result of spending naked time with Brewer. *Damn man won't get out of my mind even when I jog!* She paused at another stoplight, jogging in place.

"Hey, Delphi, is that you?" a muffled voice called. She barely heard it above the hum of the Enrique Iglesias melody.

Delphi pulled out one earbud and looked to her left. Her throat dried at the sight of the man hanging out of the blue Mustang. "Grant."

"I go by Granite these days, but yeah." His dark eyes skimmed her tight leggings. "You're looking good. Very good."

The light changed and she started running the opposite direction. It didn't take long for the rumble of the car to catch up with her.

"Aw, c'mon. I heard you were at the cantina. Sorry I missed you."

"I'm not."

"That mouth's gonna get you in trouble," he warned, the playfulness gone from his tone.

Deciding to switch it up, Delphi turned again to head down a one-way road. *Surely he won't follow.* To her dismay, he did. She glanced around, looking for her Macha bodyguard. The familiar truck was nowhere in sight. *Shit, shit, shit!*

"Where you off to so fast, Delphi? The boys and I would love for you to play a round of poker with us."

"No, thanks." She picked up her pace, but she was no match for a V6 engine.

"I can do this all night," Grant heckled. "Just get in the car." He pulled over and hopped out. He was bigger than he had been the last time she saw him. Meaner too, if she had to guess.

"Go away, Grant," she said, hoping he didn't hear the tremor in her voice.

Grant grabbed her wrist and yanked hard, causing her to trip and fall onto the pavement. "Just as clumsy as ever, aren't you?"

Adrenaline coursed through her body. She wanted to cry but wouldn't give him the satisfaction. "Fuck off, Grant. We're not together anymore, and we never will be again."

She tried to move out of his reach, but he followed her, grabbing her by the hair and pulling her to him.

"Aw, don't say that, baby." He nuzzled his nose into the back of her neck. The sickening sound of laughter from the car made her stomach pitch. "We could be good together again." He stroked her neck. "Let me show you I'm better than that Macha asshole I saw you with."

Rage fueled her next movements, and before she knew it, Grant was kneeling on the ground, cupping his balls.

"Stay away from me, or I'll send Macha to your door," she warned before sprinting down the road. Her pulse throbbed in her throat, the desire to wash his stench off her more overwhelming by the step. Suddenly, she didn't want just any Macha man to protect her. She wanted one in particular. *Brewer.*

CHAPTER 19
BREWER

Neon lights flickered in the windows, reminding Brewer to change the bulbs before the start of the next shift. The bar was jammed full of partiers celebrating St. Patrick's Day. He hurried to pour drinks and noticed the tip jar stuffed with cash. People were always more generous when they were buzzed. And in his line of work, tips were what made the world go 'round.

"Table four needs a new bottle of whiskey," one of the nymphs called.

Brewer stooped down and grabbed a bottle of Jameson from below the counter. "Don't forget to add it to their bill this time."

The nymph nodded, her long blonde ponytail swishing between her shoulder blades. That particular bartender tended to accept cash under the table instead of ringing customers into the system. He'd spoken to her about it several times, and she was receiving his last ounce of grace. It was time to get new blood in the bar.

A group of Macha bikers came in through the tattoo parlor and took their usual booth in the back. Brewer finished pouring the green-tinted beer for the man in front of him before grabbing a round of Guinness for his brothers and taking the bottles to the booth.

"Busy night," Boulder said, immediately twisting open and taking a large gulp of the beer.

"St. Paddy's Day always is." He finished passing out the beers as a nymph stopped by with two bowls of pretzels. Boulder caught the woman by the waist and pulled her to sit on his lap. The girl giggled, her low-cut shirt printed with a cartoon leprechaun giving off the ideal vibe for the holiday.

"Hawk said the parlor is packed too," Kevlar said, scanning the bar.

The Irish celebration wasn't complete without a plastic pot o' gold filled with plastic gold coins on the stage along with a DJ pumping out lively jams. The Irish jig competition would start after another few rounds, the prize being golden tickets for a night of bottomless tap beer.

"He's running a discount on Irish-themed tattoos." Brewer glanced toward the front. Two prospects were acting as bouncers tonight. Normally, they weren't necessary, but something about the green beer made the Snowshoe drinkers crazier.

"Where's your girl?" Kevlar asked with a knowing smile on his face.

The club had heard about the scheme to draw out Shovelhead that they'd come up with at church a week ago, but only a select few knew the truth about his and Delphi's relationship. *Or lack thereof.*

Brewer pasted on a grin. "At the bistro, I bet. Probably a busy night there too."

He turned on his heels and headed back to the bar before anyone else could give him shit. To his chagrin, Snoopy had been assigned to the first day of protection detail for Delphi. This kind of rotation among the club members was normal. *Except the part where my name hasn't come up.*

Over the next two hours, Brewer and his crew slung drinks over the bar and at the tables. The loud music, rowdy men, and flirtatious women should've distracted him. None of it did a damn thing to keep him from thinking about Delphi.

The illuminated clock above the back entrance displayed two in the morning. A group of women danced nearby, but even their seductive moves didn't tempt him. *I wonder what Delphi's doing.* He mind-lessly poured a Jack and Coke. It was all second nature to him after learning the ropes at the bar as a kid.

Kevlar and Hawk came up to the bar, finding open stools near the end.

"Kinda late for you two to be here," Brewer said, pouring them fresh beers.

Kevlar shrugged. "Kita's in Boston for work, so I have no reason to rush home to an empty bed. Plus, it's kinda depressing when she's not there."

"Fuck, you're so pussy whipped. It's adorably disgusting." Hawk took a shot of whiskey and pointed at their bartender. "And this guy's not far behind you."

"What're you talking about?" Brewer frowned. "You know I don't date."

"Because of me, right?" Dolly joined them, her normally clear eyes taking on a glassy sheen. "My job, not me personally. That'd be weird."

Pouring three glasses of water, Brewer handed them around. "Partly, yeah. You tell me way more about the nymphs than I care to know."

She took a sip, a good portion of the water spilling down the front of her white tank. Brewer rolled his eyes when both Kevlar and Hawk glanced over at her. While Kevlar had the manners to look away, Hawk continued to ogle her.

Brewer was used to it, but he still didn't appreciate it when it was his sister. His brothers staring at one of the nymphs was fine, but he made a point to make sure his younger sister was safe at all costs. He continued, "But it's mostly because no woman ever made me feel the *thing*, you know?"

Three blank stares met Brewer, and he chuckled. "I could say just about anything, and you three amigos would agree. Not like you'll remember in the morning anyways."

"Hey, isn't that Delphi?" Hawk said, nudging him.

At the very mention of her name, he felt the air escape his lungs. Turning in the direction Hawk was pointing, Brewer felt the bass from the song reverberate in his bones. It was enough to give him chills, the hair on his arms rising up on their own.

Standing inside the door was a vision with a shamrock headband sitting on top of her straightened hair. Even from his location, he knew she smelled as delicious as she looked. Her light-wash jeans hugged every curve of her legs, and his hands itched to reach out and grab her ass. An orange cardigan overlaid a white T-shirt dotted with four-leafed clovers. His gaze drifted to her feet. A pair of green ballet slipper shoes rounded out the outfit. She was dressed for the holiday to perfection.

"Holy shit," Dolly mumbled, then whistled low. She moved to stand, but Brewer laid a hand on her arm.

"You love Yasmina, remember?"

Hawk and Kevlar's eyes widened, and they exchanged a look. "Say what?" Hawk choked around a bite of pretzel.

Dolly shot him blue daggers, but Brewer only caught part of her seething glare. He was too busy walking toward the goddess who had recently stepped foot in his bar. Palms clammy, he cursed himself for feeling an ounce of nervousness. Never in his life had a woman affected him like this.

His boots were heavier with each step. Delphi hadn't noticed his approach yet, and he instantly second-guessed himself. She was out past midnight and in his bar. Surely that meant she wanted to see him.

The closer he got to her, the more his body demanded her undivided attention. The lights lowered yet again, leaving only the green lights from the stage to give the bar an Irish ambiance.

"Delphi," he whispered. If she heard, she didn't

let on. Her eyes were latched on to the DJ and the people dancing. For a long moment, Brewer simply watched her take in the nightlife. It was the first time he'd seen her hair straight. It fell in curtains, covering her supple breasts. He looked closer and noticed her peaked nipples beneath the white shirt. He stifled a groan, his dick jumping at the sight.

She moved her head slightly, catching him in the corner of her eye. Turning to face him, Delphi met his gaze. "Hey, Brewer."

Stomping down the possibility that she was merely drunk and looking for a good time, he leaned over. "What're you doing here so late?" He looked around but didn't see the prospect assigned to her protection. "And where's your bodyguard?"

Sighing, she shook her head. "He's around somewhere."

He immediately sensed something was wrong. "What happened?"

"Nothing."

"Delphi."

She glanced around, hesitating.

"Tell me."

"When I was on my jog the other night, the Cutthroat guy I used to date followed me." Her eyes slid down his chest, warming him to his toes. "I couldn't find my bodyguard, so I punched Grant in the balls and ran off."

Rage mixed with regret flooded his mind. "Are you all right? I'm gonna kill Leftie for losing you." He brushed his knuckles across her cheek, and she leaned into him.

"I'm fine, really." Her eyes dipped shyly to the floor. "But it made me think about the stupid fight we had. I was dumb, getting so mad at you."

He shook his head and motioned at a nymph to hop behind the bar. He could barely hear Delphi, and he wasn't okay with that. "C'mon."

Grabbing her hand, Brewer led her away from the door and to the back of the bar. Kevlar nodded approvingly and Hawk catcalled when they walked by. Dolly shoved them both, and Brewer made a note to thank his sister later.

The thud from the music lessened the farther away they got until they were standing at the saloon-style doors connecting the bar to the now closed tattoo parlor.

"Are you sure you're okay?"

She smirked. "Of course. Took a hot shower afterward and had a couple shots of whiskey." She ran a hand through her hair. "Had a couple more before coming here. The bistro was packed all night."

"You should go home and sleep it off. I'll make

sure one of the prospects keeps an eye out for that douche." Brewer bit his tongue. He didn't want to say it, but she was tired and had a scare recently. He needed to keep her safe above all else.

Delphi pushed through the doors and into the tattoo parlor. Brewer followed, ready to guide her to his truck parked out back. He'd take her home, then make sure someone was posted outside before he left.

She set her jaw. "I only want one of your biker guys following me—not a whole rotation."

"I don't think I'm the right person to talk to about demands." He pointed to their surroundings. "I run the bar, not the club."

"But you could." Delphi scanned the tattoo sketches pinned to the walls. "You could be the next president or vice president if you wanted."

"I don't." He sighed when she started walking around the parlor, stopping to look at each of the Polaroid photos taped above the artists' chairs. The display of artwork always impressed him. He couldn't draw for shit, and these men and women could use an ink gun to create masterpieces on skin. They deserved every dollar they charged and then some.

"Delphi, it's late. I'll take you back to your apartment."

She leaned on one of the tattoo artists' tables. "I don't want to go home yet." Glancing around the room, she hopped onto the table and lay on her back. "I want to be with you."

Taking her words as drunken gibberish, Brewer helped her up into a sitting position. "Come on, sweet cheeks. You need to sleep it off."

Shoving at his hold, Delphi scowled. "I've had a total of two shots, Brewer. I'm not drunk."

"Fine, you're buzzed. You need a clear head, and whiskey doesn't give anyone that."

She didn't budge. "I want to stay here for a while."

He scooped her off the table, and she didn't fight him like he expected. "We can do this the easy way or the hard way."

Delphi bopped his nose with her index finger. "I think I prefer the hard way. It gets your hands on me, and I like that."

He groaned, this time out loud. "Delphi, don't."

Ignoring him, she wiggled free of his arms and back onto the solid ground. "Don't tell me what to do, Brewer."

"Stop being a little brat and I won't."

Her eyes flashed with fury, and he steeled himself for a slap, punch, or harsh word. Instead, her lips against his caught him off guard. She wrapped her arms around his neck, urging him to kiss her back.

"Delphi, if we start this, I don't know if I can stop," he admitted softly, desire consuming his better sense.

She nipped his bottom lip. "Then don't."

CHAPTER 20
DELPHI

The past week had been shit. Macha sent a burly biker every day to keep watch over her, the bistro, and her apartment. To make things worse, not one of the seven men on duty was Brewer. The constant shadows annoyed her more than anything. They followed her to the local grocery store, trailed her when she went for a jog, took up a table in the bistro, and sat outside in the discreet pickup truck on the corner of the street. *But the one time I need a Macha biker, the man was nowhere in sight.* She shivered at the direction that happenstance could've gone in if she hadn't punched Grant.

Despite the aggravation that came with having Macha watching over her every move, she knew it was for the best. That was what she told herself every night before drifting into a fitful sleep in which she'd dream of Brewer and the wicked things she wanted him to do to her despite her better judgment.

Now as she stood with her arms locked around him, Delphi couldn't imagine a better way to end the week. The apprehension in his blue eyes encouraged her to rise up and lick his top lip.

Brewer growled, his back straightening. He was holding back. She saw it in his face. It would take very little to turn him into the sex beast his eyes promised to expose.

"Don't say shit like that. You're horny, and if I were a weaker man, I'd bend you over the table, spread your legs, and fuck you until the whole bar hears you cry my name."

Delphi's heart pulsed harder, her breath catching at the threat that sounded more like heaven than hell. "Then be weaker."

She trailed her hands down his chest, then, reaching just below his belt, she bit the inside of her cheek. The sizeable bulge beneath her fingers sent delirious chills through her. Lifting her eyes, she met his gaze and smiled.

"Fuck, woman, you've got that feisty smile that makes me want to do some very bad things to you." His hands lingered on her hips, fingers making small circles on her skin under the hem of her shirt.

Delphi traced his mouth with her tongue,

tempting him even more. He continued resisting her, and she had to commend him for his resilience. He wasn't the kind to take advantage of her. While honorable, it wasn't what she wanted. She'd take the respectful Brewer any other time. Right now, though, she needed—no, *craved*—the unrestrained, raw savage.

Delphi pulled both her shirt and sweater over her head and tossed them onto one of the chairs. Brewer's eyes didn't leave her, but he also didn't move to help. Determined to watch him break, Delphi kicked off her shoes and unzipped her jeans. She kept her eyes glued to him, slowly stripping until she stood in her matching green bra and panties.

Music from the bar continued to pound through the speakers, echoing over to the tattoo parlor like they were backstage at a concert. The twinkle lights lining the shop's walls cast a magical trance over them. The overhead ones would be too much for what she wanted to do next. A soft glow set the mood.

"Brewer, if you don't touch me, I'll do it myself."

His eyes went from blue to midnight. Taking a step closer to her, Brewer pulled her against him by the waist. Hovering his lips above her mouth, his hot breath clashed with hers. "Don't tempt me with a good time, girl. I'm liable to take you up on it."

Grinning, she raked her fingers through his hair, urging him to kiss her.

He grazed her lips briefly, then pulled back. "Next time you're doing exactly what you promised, because I really wanna watch." He tugged his shirt off, and she didn't even notice when it fluttered to the floor. The array of colorful tattoos on his chest stole her attention. "But tonight, I'm going to give you precisely what you want. What I want." He unzipped his jeans. "What *we* want."

Delphi's stomach dropped, a warm and fuzzy sensation pooling between her legs. The lust in his eyes sent her desire into overdrive. For a brief second, she second-guessed her bold move. Her gaze flickering to the door to the bar as her heart pounded.

"Nobody will come through that door," he promised, still too far away from her to touch. And she wanted to touch him, to kiss him, to let him do the same back.

He walked closer, sliding his hands around to cup her ass as he said, "How do you want it, sweet cheeks?" The manly groan that came from him when she inhaled sharply sent her grinding against his thigh.

"Just how you said it." She licked her lips. "I want you to fuck me from behind, pulling my hair and making me scream your name while I come."

Brewer's brows rose and he nodded approvingly. "Holy shit, you're a naughty girl, aren't you?"

Before she could answer, he twirled her around. His hands traveled up and down her body. He unclasped her bra and it fell to the floor. His hands took their place in an instant, cupping her breasts. Nipples aching at his touch, Delphi sighed and leaned back into his chest. He pinched her nipples, making them harder than before.

"I wanted you the first time I came in here," she said, the words breathy.

Brewer kissed the side of her neck, increasing his pressure on her nipples until she moaned. "Did you, now?"

"Yes."

"Did you want this?" He slipped his fingers into her panties. Delphi bucked at the welcome intrusion. "Did you want me touching your pussy and biting your neck?"

"God, yes."

He nipped her ear, and her giggle morphed into a moan when he slipped one finger into her wet pussy. "Fuck me, you're dripping."

Delphi locked her arms up around his neck, leaning back heavily against him. It'd been too many months since a man touched her like this. And this wasn't just any man. This was Brewer. The man who pissed her the hell off and turned her the hell on at the same time. "I can't help it. You do this to me."

He let go long enough to spin her around, setting her on the edge of the tattoo table. Tilting her face up, he scanned her eyes. "Every time?"

She nodded.

"Even when I make you mad?"

She bit her bottom lip. "Yes."

A cocky grin covered his face. "In that case, I need a taste for myself."

She didn't have a chance to react. He knelt and nudged her knees apart, pulling her panties down her thighs. She gripped the edge of the padded table, anticipation lining her stomach. He kissed one leg, then the other before he brushed his nose between her manicured curls and inhaled. That act alone sent a tremor of lust through her.

The coolness of his tongue stunned her into submission. As he pressed his mouth against her, she gripped his head, lacing her fingers in his curls. He drank her in, his strong hands holding her ass to keep her in place. Black dots exploded in her vision. Delphi slapped a hand over her mouth to mute her cries.

He pulled away and growled, "Don't you fucking dare."

The command in his voice urged her to let her

hand fall away. She kept his gaze as he rubbed circles on her clit with the fingers of his free hand. The tension he'd built quickly returned, prodding her closer to an orgasm.

"Let's hear it." He returned his tongue to her pussy, his fingers alternating between rubbing and thrusting.

Delphi clenched her legs around his head, the sensations building further. She didn't want to let go yet. She could hold out a little while longer.

As if hearing her thoughts, Brewer switched to his tongue on her clit and plunged two fingers into her soaking pussy. His name passed through her lips in a grateful prayer as she came. Her legs trembled, hips thrusting as the ecstasy dazed her. It was all she could do to not collapse. Brewer was there to keep her upright, never leaving his position, drinking in every ounce of her passion.

Her vision finally cleared of fireworks. Brewer stood up, his hands never leaving some part of her body. It was almost as if he was worried she'd fall if he let go.

He cradled her cheeks and pressed his mouth to hers. His tongue tangled with hers, the heady taste of her own desire thick on his lips.

"Yep, delicious—just like I thought," he

murmured, tucking her hair behind her ears. Nuzzling her ear, he licked it. "Do you want more?"

Her legs threatened to give out at his question that hinted at more sensuality. "Please."

Brewer kissed the spot right below her ear and took a step back. "What my girl wants, she gets."

Delphi's chest heaved despite her not doing a damn thing about what he intended to do next. But she wanted more of it. More of him.

Grabbing a condom from his back pocket, he pointed at the tattoo table. "Get up there."

A sizzle of danger sparked in his blue eyes, and she didn't dare decline. She moved to the table and started to climb on top. He placed his hands on her hips, stopping her from fully mounting it. He lifted her easily and set her ass on the edge of the table.

"You're more than a quick fuck, Delphi." He tilted up her chin. "We can do that another time. Tonight, I wanna see your face when I make you come again and again on my cock."

Shivers settled between her legs, her pussy ready for more. Any words she said would simply break his spell.

Brewer entered her in one swift move, and Delphi's lips parted as if on command. He kissed her slowly, his tongue exploring her mouth. Lifting her hips, she met his steady thrusts. Each time he drew back, she whimpered. Without him filling her to the brim, she felt empty, even lost. Delphi closed her eyes, wrapping her legs around his waist. This wasn't a fast fuck. It was intentional, and exactly what she never knew she needed.

His tempo increased, and she opened her eyes, not wanting to miss a moment. Beads of sweat lined Brewer's brow, and she realized then how much he was holding back.

"Give me everything, Brewer," she whispered, licking his neck.

He let out a guttural sound and grabbed her by the throat, forcing her mouth to his. The sheer intensity of his kiss sent her stomach into a nosedive. Her desire coated his dick, the slippery sound meeting her ears when he withdrew and then slammed back into her core. She came undone then and there. Her fingers clenched, nails digging into his shoulders.

Brewer didn't let her float down from the clouds. He thrust into her harder. The table beneath her scraped against the floor, the sound only outdone by her breathless moans coupled with the delicious groans from the man coaxing a third orgasm from her.

"Now I will." He kissed her hard, then spun her around. Delphi couldn't cry out at the loss before he slipped back into her dripping core and increased his speed. She grabbed at the table, but it did little to steady her against his thrusts.

Brewer lifted her up by her hips, cock jamming into her until Delphi swore she'd pass out from ecstasy. Her feet dangled above the floor, his strength keeping her upright while her forearms slid on the tabletop.

He kissed up her spine, goose bumps scattering along her skin. Heat bloomed between her legs again, and she let out a loud moan. She muttered his name over and over, the orgasm spreading faster and not letting go. Delphi's vision blurred. The sounds from the bar were mere muffles, her hearing all but murmured at the ferocity of the orgasm he induced.

"You had enough?" he asked, hips still going at full force.

She shook her head. "Never enough."

He chuckled. "If your makeup wasn't streaking your face, I just may believe you."

Touching her cheeks, she realized her mascara had indeed made its way down her face. She also felt wetness there. Whether it was sweat or tears, she suddenly didn't care. Brewer had successfully fucked every concern right out of her.

"But as it is, I came five minutes ago, and I'm about to come again," he said, putting her feet back on the floor and pulling her upright. As he kissed the side of her neck, Delphi turned and met his lips. She arched into his thrusts and felt his cock swell, emptying inside her. Tangling her arms around his neck, she leaned against him as he finished.

Her hands shook but she didn't let go. This was as close as they could get, but somehow, she wanted to be closer.

His mouth grazed her shoulder. "You all right?"

"More than."

Chuckling, he carefully picked her up and placed her back on the tattoo table. Crouching beside it, he pushed her hair away from her breasts, merely taking her in. "You're stunning, Delphi. I mean it."

She leaned up on her elbow and smiled. "You're not bad yourself."

"I hope not." He trailed his fingers over her breasts and her nipples peaked. "As much as I'd like to take you again right here, we should probably go. The bar closes soon, and I don't want anybody seeing you like this." He leaned over and kissed her. "You're much too precious for any of my brothers to witness."

A pang of worry churned in her stomach, and she looked past him to the door. "Shit, you're right." Sitting up, she laughed at the turn of events she'd encouraged. She swung her legs over the side of the table and watched Brewer pick up the strewn clothes.

"Don't take this the wrong way…."

Delphi's body seized at the impending words.

He yanked his shirt over his shoulders. "But I'd really like to sleep with you tonight."

A wave of relief washed over her. Quickly dressing, she watched him finish doing the same. His red hair was mussed in a sexy and irresistible way. If she let herself have more than a mere fling with Brewer, she was certain she'd fall head over heels for him.

"What do you say?" He brought her shoes over and slipped them onto her feet one at a time. "Want to be the little spoon all night? I can't promise my dick won't poke you, but if all we do is sleep, I'm okay with that."

Standing up, she took his hand. "Believe me, I'll want a lot more than sleep tonight."

CHAPTER 21
BREWER

 Horribly terrific.

Brewer glanced over at her sleeping form. Curtains of dark brown hair spilled over the white pillowcase. Even in the dim lighting, her pale skin looked radiant. The makeup on her face was now long gone, her natural beauty keeping his eyes glued to every exposed inch.

Delphi's arm jerked in her sleep, and he held in a chuckle. She truly was adorable, both awake and asleep. He shifted in his seated position, sleep evading him. He was a shit sleeper. Had been one his entire adult life. The time glowed on his cell phone. Even though it was nearly dawn, he knew he could survive off a few short hours.

He gently traced Delphi's eyebrows. They were

relaxed. She was somewhere in REM sleep, dreams overtaking her, no doubt. After locking up the bar, he'd followed her home, half expecting her to change her mind. She hadn't. Instead, she'd all but mauled him on the stairway, not that he was complaining. *Hell, we didn't even make it to her apartment.*

The coupling on the stairs wasn't about to be outdone by the one on the couch, kitchen counter, shower, and then the finale in her bed. A small part of him worried she'd regret inviting him to stay. He'd fully intended to do precisely what he suggested. Cuddle with her all night. Nothing more, nothing less.

He smirked. That went straight out the window, and he didn't give a damn. A glow from outside her window caught his eye. The sunrise would be beautiful—he just knew it. Most days, he was awake to see the sun wake on the horizon.

Swinging his feet to the floor, he winced at the squeaky bedsprings. The cool hardwood beneath his toes should've chilled him, but he ran hot most times. With Delphi next to him, it was impossible to be cold. She turned on every facet of his warmth. *Gotta heat up those damn freezing feet of hers somehow.*

The kitchen was right across from her bedroom. He carefully closed the door and padded to the sliding door that led to a small balcony. Spring hung in the air, birds chirping nearby despite the frost on the ground.

Closing his eyes, he inhaled the earthy aroma filling the air. Hands down, it was his favorite season. Starting fresh all around and looking forward to the summer heat. But mostly because after months of cold, he could get back on his motorcycle and ride until he exhausted himself.

"Early riser, huh?"

Her sleep-riddled voice made him smile. Turning, he took in the morning glory of Delphi Windsor. Her hair was piled high on her head in the messiest of buns with strands falling around her face. The baggy pair of green plaid pants she was wearing hung on her hips, and she'd paired it with a black tank top, her nipples peaked in the cool breeze. Topping the entire outfit was a fuzzy blue wrap that looked like a blanket cut to size.

She stepped out onto the balcony and rested her forearms on the metal railing. "My dad always liked watching the sunrise. My mom was more of a sunset kind of girl." She smiled, their memories no doubt haunting her. "It made sneaking in at dawn kind of difficult."

"Did you do that often?"

She shrugged. "Here and there. Mostly during the

last few years I lived at home. You know how the teenage hormones make you crazy."

"No shit. My mom got so pissed when she found out I was with a nymph for my first time." He laughed, the image of his mom's furious face coming to mind.

"Your first time was with a club girl?"

He bit the inside of his cheek. "Um, yeah. My dad actually encouraged me to start with a nymph."

"Guys are so weird."

"Can't argue with you there." Brewer noticed her shiver and pulled her back against his chest, enveloping her from behind. The familiar scent of sex lingered on her skin, instantly stirring his cock.

"Are you a coffee drinker?"

He nuzzled the back of her hair. "I'm Irish but more American, lass—of course I love a good coffee."

Without looking, he knew she was rolling those perfect blue eyes at his attempted Irish accent.

"Good, because I don't think I could invite you over again if you didn't like it." She made a move toward the kitchen, but he held her in place.

"Let's watch the sunrise first." He kissed the side of her neck. "Then I'll make you breakfast."

She hummed her agreement and settled back in his embrace. They didn't have to wait long for the sun to poke through, its yellow rays casting a stunning glow over the city below. The scent of freshly baked bread wafted toward them, and his stomach rumbled.

"Smells like Yasmina's baking," she said before he could. "Are you hungry?"

"I won't lie, I'm starving." He slipped his hands beneath the soft tank top. "But all I want is you."

Delphi let out a breathy moan and turned around, her lips pressed to his in the next second. Her tongue darted into his mouth, exploring him thoroughly. Brewer's resolve dissolved when she rubbed up against his hard dick.

"What a coincidence." She nipped his bottom lip, eyes glazed with lust. "Because I want to taste you."

Brewer inhaled to speak, but Delphi was on her knees before he could utter one word. She tossed him her blanket and freed his cock in the same motion. Using the blanket to shield her act, he watched her lick the head of his dick. She was anything but timid, teasing him with her tongue before sliding him deep in her mouth.

"Damn, Delphi." He wanted to grab her head, thread his fingers through her hair, but he couldn't. If he moved, he'd expose them both to the world. As much of a turn-on as it might be, there was no way he'd do that without her permission.

Delphi cupped his balls in her right hand,

massaging them in time with the fluid way her mouth bobbed along his dick. She increased the pressure with her tongue, and he clenched his jaw tighter. The cool air hit his bare chest, giving him a moment of reprieve. He couldn't burst this easily. He was a Macha man, after all. He'd grown up in a club and with club nymphs. He should be a pro at holding off, but he wasn't. Not with Delphi. She made his cock yearn for more of her flesh.

Thrusting into her mouth, he hit the back of her throat, making her gag. Brewer looked down, expecting her to pull away. Instead, Delphi met his eyes and smiled before repeating the act herself. That was almost enough to make him come on her tongue.

"That hot mouth of yours is gonna get fucked daily if you're not careful," he warned, bracing his hand on the back of her head.

"I wouldn't mind that one bit," she said around his cock. His length disappeared into her mouth once more, and he groaned.

"As much as I want you to swallow every bit of me...." He tugged her up off her knees and kissed her roughly. "I want to fuck you more."

Delphi turned around, and he eagerly pulled down her pants, cock growing harder at the sight of no panties beneath. She looked back at him and spread her legs. "Then fuck me hard, Brewer."

He didn't need to be told twice and quickly pulled on a condom. In one swift move, her pussy enveloped his cock that was so recently sheathed in her mouth. The warm wetness made him close his eyes. She was so fucking perfect.

Delphi grabbed the railing, her hips meeting every thrust he gave her. The way her ass bounced against him inspired Brewer to grapple for her breasts. Despite the light tank covering them, he felt her stiff nipples. Whether it was the chill in the air or their activity, he wasn't sure of the real culprit.

Her moans drifted back to him, the sounds only turning him on more. Knowing the hour and that people would be heading to work right then, Brewer reached over and clasped a hand loosely over her lips. Giving the neighborhood a show wasn't something they'd discussed beforehand, and he wasn't about to share this with strangers.

"Nobody gets to hear that this morning except me," he said against her neck, thrusting deeper.

Her body shuddered and he felt her pussy grip his cock like a vise. Sweat slid off his forehead. Keeping himself from coming until she had at least two more orgasms was his only goal.

When she stopped shaking, he repositioned them so he could play with her clit while hitting her from behind. In response to the additional attention,

Delphi licked his fingers that he still held over her mouth. It was worth the agony of self-restraint when he felt her shudder beneath his ministrations. He could hold out for one more. *Maybe.*

When she started sucking two of his fingers at the same time, Brewer swore under his breath. "You're killing me, Delphi."

She looked back and smirked. "Good," she mumbled between his fingers.

"Fuck it." Shaking his head, he turned and picked her up, pushing her back against the sliding glass door. She wrapped her legs around him, welcoming his jagged thrusts.

Catching her lips under his, Brewer swallowed her cry. Hearing her moan his name was the most erotic thing she'd done thus far. Just as he started to lose control, another orgasm crashed into her, encouraging him to let go. He growled into the nape of her neck, filling the condom to the brim.

Her chest heaved against him, her breath falling across his exposed skin. It warred with the cold breeze, the perfect combination of temperatures.

Meeting her gaze, he searched her blue eyes. They were still laced with desire but there was something else hidden in their beautiful depths. He gently kissed her, never once dropping her gaze. "Did I earn my breakfast?"

She giggled and nodded. "Yeah, I think you did." She brushed her hands over his beard and tugged slightly. "You make breakfast, I'll give you dessert."

The familiar longing filled her eyes once more, and he could've come again at the sight. "Deal."

Swatting her ass playfully, Brewer felt his heart lighten. He wanted to fuck this woman until the day he died.

CHAPTER 22
DELPHI

A knock on the apartment door popped the sex bubble they'd been living in since returning to her place. Brewer patted her knee and got off the couch while she stayed cozied underneath a Sherpa blanket with Fiona purring underneath it. A Macha biker stood in the doorway. Rubble, by the looks of the tall, bald man.

Delphi slouched deeper into the cushion. If she wanted to hear what they said, she'd need dog ears. They spoke in low tones, Brewer's body blocking any chance of reading Rubble's lips.

Muting the television, she craned her neck toward them but frowned when no sounds reached her. Thankfully, it was the slowest day of the week, and she'd be able to catch up on paperwork and orders before the bistro opened.

I need to take a shower first. She stretched her legs. Her entire body was sore after time spent with Brewer. *Maybe a long soak would be better.*

Brewer turned to her, his lips in a thin line.

Her stomach dropped. "What's wrong?"

"I gotta go talk to Reaper." He crouched down beside the couch. "You still want me to watch over you?"

"Of course."

He offered her a small smile. "Good. I already updated Rubble, but I have to talk with Prez to make sure we're on the same page. I'm guessing they'll want a guy outside until Shovelhead shows up."

"Okay, sure. That makes sense." She looked around him to Rubble. "Will he stay until you come back?"

"Rubble's coming with me." He smoothed a hand over his beard. "But don't worry, I personally put the fear of my wrath in the prospect stationed on the corner if he fucks up."

Delphi nodded, unsure what else to do. Brewer was a mere cog in Macha's machine. He didn't run the club, so getting approval was a necessity.

"But I'll be back." He kissed her forehead. "Oh, and for the love of the goddess, lock the deadbolt. Anybody can bust down a door if they try hard enough."

"Yeah, yeah."

Standing up, she walked around the couch and into the kitchen. The first cup of coffee wasn't hitting her yet. She poured a second cup and yawned. "I'll be fine for an hour or so."

"Lock it." Moving to the front door, he turned the lock for good measure before closing it behind them.

Sighing, Delphi sipped the coffee and made her way to the bathroom. She turned on the water, testing it with her fingers. Once it was properly warm, she set the coffee cup on the counter and went in search of an outfit for the day.

In need of tunes, she found a playlist on her phone and synced it to the Bluetooth speaker in the bathroom. Soon Keith Urban was crooning beautifully, thanks to the bathroom's acoustics. Stripping as she walked to the closet, she tossed her clothes into the laundry hamper. Neatly folded piles of leggings beckoned to her. Spring in Snowshoe was unpredictable.

Picking out a violet pair and a long-sleeved shirt, she danced her way to the bathroom. The bathtub was halfway full, so she grabbed a magazine. Despite having the information readily available online, there was something irresistible about gossip in print form.

She poured a healthy serving of bath salts into the water and glanced at her reflection. Her cheeks were flushed with a rosy hue. She smiled at the reason. *Brewer*.

Tracing her fingers down her neck, she noticed the small marks. She shivered, recalling his teeth grazing her there more than once. Nibbling was a turn-on she didn't know she had until he came along.

The elastic band that she'd used to hold all her hair on top of her head was sorely inadequate. She chuckled and pulled it free, her locks falling to her shoulders. He was worth all the trouble and some.

The scent of the lavender bath salts filled the air, and she turned off the water. Testing the temperature with her toe, Delphi tossed aside the last bit of clothing she was wearing, then slowly submerged into the water. Sighing in relief, she closed her eyes and let the warmth wash over her strained muscles.

She'd just gotten comfortable when her phone buzzed. Glancing at it on the floor, she frowned at the number. She picked it up and opened the message.

Grant: I heard you want to meet your father.

Delphi's pulse skyrocketed. After her run-in with him, she'd hoped it was a singular event. How she answered would affect not only her life, but Macha as well.

Delphi: What do you know?

She brought her knees up and rested her chin on them, waiting for a response. She hadn't been this nervous about texting since high school.

Grant: I'll be in touch.

Not bothering to reply, Delphi immediately took a screenshot of the conversation and sent it to Brewer. *He'll know what to do next.* She, on the other hand, didn't. Suddenly, the hot water was doing the opposite of what she intended it to.

After washing, she'd get back to work. It was the only thing that'd keep her sane until Brewer returned. Delphi swore under her breath, both loving and hating that truth.

CHAPTER 23

BREWER

Reviewing the text message from Delphi, Brewer suddenly needed a cigarette. Bumming one from Hawk, he lit it up and inhaled. He didn't like the idea of her running into her ex, let alone the fact that he'd texted her about her father.

"I thought you were cutting back," Kevlar said, walking toward the clubhouse from the garage.

Brewer took another drag. "I was." He laughed. "Then I met Delphi, and that all went to shit."

He handed the pack to his brother, who immediately lit one up. "Yeah, I get it. I promised Kita I'd stop, but it's harder than you think." He blew out a steady stream of smoke. "I slip up every now and then. Only human nature."

"How's Nikita, by the way?" Brewer glanced over

at Kevlar. He hadn't spent much time with the ex-Army soldier outside club functions.

"Kicking ass and taking names." Kevlar grinned around the cigarette. "Wouldn't trade Kita for the world."

"She seems pretty cool."

"She is." Kevlar flicked ash onto the dark pavement. "Never met a better woman than my Kita."

Brewer watched the smoke curl in the air above them. "I'm concerned about the Shovelhead plan."

Kevlar didn't seem to mind the extreme shift in conversation. "I'd be worried if you weren't." He looked toward the garage. "You tell Rubble your concerns yet?"

"No. I think it's just me." He brushed a hand over his beard. "I'm too close to it."

"Ah, overly protective." Kevlar tossed the rest of the cigarette on the ground and crushed it with his boot. "I get it. Almost every man in Macha gets it."

Turning to face him, Brewer frowned. "How do I stop being that way?"

"You don't," Kevlar chuckled. "Not when feelings are involved. Just ask me or Doc—hell, even Rubble. We got too close and risked it all. Thankfully, the club had our backs." He clasped a hand on Brewer's shoulder. "Like we have yours and that pretty chef's. We'll make it out alive. Macha will make sure of it."

Snorting, Brewer wanted to disagree but couldn't. Kevlar was right. "At least I can learn from all you dumbasses and not make the same mistakes."

Kevlar punched him in the stomach good-naturedly. "What the hell? I try to calm you down, and you're giving me shit."

Brewer grinned. "It's kind of what I do."

Not seeing Rubble approach, Brewer suddenly found himself in a tight headlock. "What was that you were saying, Brewsky? How awesome Kev and I are?"

He tapped on the big man's forearm. "Yeah, that must've been it." Rubble dropped his hold, and Brewer stumbled away. "Asshole."

Rubble shrugged. "Never said I wasn't one." He nodded at Brewer. "Your girl heard from Dolly's contact yet?"

"Yeah." Brewer fixed his hooded sweatshirt under his leather cut. "It doesn't feel right."

"Never does, brother." Rubble's mismatched eyes turned serious. "But we'll be ready. One of the nymphs offered to drop by the cantina in case Shovelhead stops by. She'll keep us updated. I'm surprised Dolly didn't tell you already."

"Dolly's mind is on other things lately," he said under his breath. "I'm glad to hear we have a contingency plan in place."

"We'll get the bastard." Rubble exchanged a glance with Kevlar. "Nikita's keeping the FBI on his trail, so he'll pop his ugly head out one of these days."

"As long as we get there before the FBI, we're golden," Kevlar added. "Kita can only do so much, which is why it's important we catch him first. The Feds want Shovelhead for multiple cases."

This kept Brewer homed in on the conversation. "Other than the ones we know about?"

Kevlar nodded. "Yep. The Twelve Brothers, Diablos, and Greenback Cutthroats seem to be the tip of the MC iceberg for this guy."

"Too bad he never stepped into the ring with me." Rubble cracked his knuckles, a menacing gleam in his eyes.

"He's too old to go a single round with you," Kevlar reminded him. "The club will have their vengeance." He swiveled to Brewer. "And so will you."

"But what about Delphi?" Brewer suddenly needed another hit of nicotine. He fished his lighter out of his back pocket and lit a fresh cigarette. "If Shovelhead is actually her dad like she thinks, we can't just off him."

Rubble kicked at the slush on the sidewalk. "This

is a club matter, Brewer. If Delphi wants to meet her dad, she'd better do it before Macha gets ahold of him."

He'd been in club life long enough to know the veracity of Rubble's words. What Shovelhead did was beyond forgivable. *And that's only part of his sins.*

Resting the cigarette between his lips, he nodded. Discovering more about Shovelhead wouldn't happen without catching the man. Having Nikita on Macha's team helped. They'd get their answers or at least try before handing the traitor over to the FBI.

"You gonna be able to handle this?" Kevlar asked. "I know it was difficult for Kita."

"Her situation was a bit different," Rubble reminded him. "She knew her dad."

"Okay, yes, but she also had to deal with the shit she found out later." Kevlar offered him an encouraging smile. "How do you think Delphi will handle things?"

"Not sure. My guess is, it'll depend on the circumstances of her conception."

Rubble's left brow cocked. "You mean...."

"It's one of the scenarios Delphi's tossed around since finding out."

Kevlar coughed. "Shit."

"Either way, I think Delphi just wants answers.

We all do. If Shovelhead will readily give them up, things will go much smoother for everyone."

Both men hummed their agreement. Macha wasn't about to let Shovelhead ride away into the sunset. The man had done it more than once before.

Brewer pulled his sunglasses out of his pocket and put them on. It was a perfect day for a ride around town. *Maybe I can convince Delphi to come too.*

"Yo, Kevlar, your phone's been ringing off the hook in here," one of the prospects called from the garage.

Kevlar patted his pockets. "Shit, I really need to remember that thing. See you boys later."

Rubble moved toward the motorcycles in the parking lot with Brewer walking alongside him. "You got somebody watching your girl?"

"She's not—" Brewer stopped there. Delphi *was* his. Maybe not officially or technically, but he'd seen the way she came undone under his touch and felt her body tighten with passion. Delphi was his goddess. "Yeah, one of the prospects. I'll relieve him at three this afternoon."

"Good. I'm itching for the open road, and you look like you could use a few miles too."

They reached the bikes and strapped on their helmets before starting the engines. The motorcycles purred, glad to be rid of the safe and cozy garage they stayed in during hibernation. It was more than time to start the riding season.

He'd get Delphi on the back soon enough. For now, he followed Rubble to the street. Macha had to come first. He just hoped when the time came, he could uphold that oath.

CHAPTER 24
DELPHI

DDELPHI EYED THE TEXT MESSAGE AND WIPED HER FLOURY hands on her pink apron.

Delphi: The bistro kitchen. Why?

Her mind spun to the possibility that something was wrong.

Brewer: Can you slip away for a bit?

She glanced at Edgar currently playing solitaire on his phone. The dinner rush was two hours away. If she wanted, she could sneak out. *Especially if Brewer is involved.* Her skin heated at the memories the redheaded biker enticed.

Delphi: Since you asked so nicely.

Brewer: Great. Grab a jacket and meet me out front.

A giddy sensation filled her gut. Without even asking, she already knew he was on his motorcycle.

"Edgar, I'll be back for dinner."

Edgar looked up and nodded. "No problem. I can handle tonight if you need me to."

She hung up the apron. "I'll keep that in mind and text you."

The older man waved her out of the kitchen, and she eagerly hurried up the stairs to her apartment. After quickly fixing her hair and washing the flour from her cheek, Delphi changed into an outfit befitting a biker chick. She nodded at her reflection. Or at least, this was what she imagined a biker chick looked like.

Hustling down the steps, she opened the door and hid a smile. Brewer sat astride his motorcycle, sunglasses hiding his eyes. The typical jeans and hoodie under his cut were almost to be expected by now. A teasing grin on his kissable lips stood out beneath his neatly trimmed beard.

"Where are we going?" she asked when she closed the distance to him.

Brewer handed her a helmet. "For a ride."

She buckled the helmet and easily mounted the motorcycle. "That's what I usually do when you're around."

He reached back and tickled her side, starting the engine with his free hand. "Keep it up, sweet cheeks. See where that gets you."

Delphi's laughter was drowned out by the bike. She loosely laced her arms around Brewer's waist and kissed the back of his neck. No matter where they were headed, she was certain they'd have an intensely fun time.

THE WINDING ROADS SURROUNDING SNOWSHOE KEPT Delphi's arms glued to Brewer's waist. She couldn't complain. In fact, she rather liked feeling his muscles jerk slightly whenever she slid her hands up his torso.

They reached the club's mountain retreat much too quickly for her liking. Walking toward the large log cabin, Delphi pushed up her sunglasses.

"Have you ever seen it?" Brewer asked coming up beside her.

"No, but I've driven by several times over the years." She tossed a thumb behind them. "The locked gate isn't exactly inviting."

He smirked and took her hand in his. "For good reason. This is the club's getaway spot."

As they walked up the front steps, Delphi had to hand it to the designer. It looked exactly like a ritzy log cabin, not a bunker. The more she looked, the more she noticed the reinforced walls, cameras, and all-around security involved in the multiple buildings hidden among tall trees.

"How often does the club come up here?"

He opened the large door and walked in first, punching in a code on the alarm monitor before answering. "It's not just for bad times. It's for good ones too."

Brewer flipped on the lights and the entryway came to life. A large modern chandelier hung from above, illuminating the space perfectly. "Last summer we had a complete lockdown."

"Why?"

"Some drama with a club in Ireland."

Delphi vaguely recalled reading about a shooting the previous summer. "What happened?"

He walked further into the open concept space, heading toward the large kitchen. "You've met Isa, right?"

Recalling the pretty woman with an Irish accent, she nodded.

"Isa was targeted in an MC war in Ireland. Her

dad sent her to us for protection, but the other club followed."

"Oh." Her mind whirled with questions.

"And before you ask, her dad was the reason she got involved." He grabbed a bottle of whiskey and two glasses. "But it ended happily. She and Doc hit it off." He smirked. "Eventually."

"What do you mean?"

Brewer poured the whiskey and motioned to the barstools pushed up against the kitchen bar. "I'll let my cousin tell that tale. She takes pride in her story-telling capabilities."

Delphi took a seat and sipped the whiskey. The brown liquid burned but settled her nerves almost instantly. "She mentioned you were related. Did you know when she arrived?"

"Nope." He leaned over the counter. "But when I started hitting on her, it came out. Pissed Doc off too until he found out."

"Hey, isn't she due, like, any day now?"

"Oh, yeah, but knowing Isa, her kid is just as stubborn by not refusing to be born on time." He finished his whiskey in one long gulp and held out his hand. "I'll give you the grand tour if you'd like."

Mirroring his act, she swallowed the liquor and placed her hand in his. For the next twenty minutes, Brewer walked them through each room in Macha's mountain stronghold. It was state-of-the-art, and not one part was cheaply made. From the pool to the escape tunnels, she was amazed by the intuitiveness of the club's planning. They didn't leave anything to chance. Somehow it made her feel better about the meeting with Shovelhead. No matter how she looked at it, Macha could protect her.

"The nymphs have the basement level, but it's nothing to brag about." He nodded to the stairs to the basement. "There's also the booze cellar that I predominately maintain and a couple other rooms."

Curiosity getting the better of her, Delphi watched Brewer walk away still talking about the history of the house before she carefully walked down the dark stairs. She found a light at the bottom and flipped it on. There were two doors on the landing space opposite each other. One she was sure led to the cellar. The other was what she wanted to see.

Trying the door on the right, she felt along the wall for a light switch. Finding one, she braced herself for the worst. To her surprise, it was filled with bottles of assorted liquors and kegs of beer.

"You sure you want to see the nymph lair?"

Delphi yelped, hand going to her mouth. "Dammit, Brewer, you scared me." She lightly smacked his chest.

"Sorry." He offered her a sheepish grin.

"And yes, I do. All the bikers talk about nymphs, and I've met a few." She lifted her chin. "I want to see what's so alluring."

Brewer parted his lips, then seemed to think better of it. He moved to the other door and opened it, turning on the lights. "Dolly likes to rearrange a lot down here, so I have no clue what's waiting."

Entering the space felt wrong on some level, but Delphi didn't let that stop her. She took it all in. The walls were painted a light gray. Several pool tables were set up, and there was a bar at the far end. Large speakers sat in every corner, a DJ booth was stationed near a door on the opposite wall. If she had to guess, it led to a patio area. Couches were set up sporadically throughout the space, and a few tables for cards also filled the room. The south wall held four televisions, no doubt for watching sporting events and to give the club members variety.

In all, it appeared like a haven for any red-blooded man. But it was the curtained off area that drew her attention the most.

"And behind curtain number one," she mumbled heading toward it.

The closer she got, the more her hands shook. Instead of an actual curtain, she realized it was a maze of curtained rooms separated only by fabric.

She walked along the row of cubicles, each one sporting a bed and chair. She didn't have to think too hard about what occurred there.

"For the club members who want more privacy," Brewer explained, suddenly appearing beside her.

"I figured."

The north wall caught her eye, and she moved toward it. "Holy shit. Are those toys?"

Brewer cleared his throat. "Um, yeah."

She noticed several racks of wigs with colors every shade of the rainbow. Nodding, she met Brewer's gaze. "Macha knows how to do sex."

"You could say that, yeah, but it's mostly Dolly." He scratched his nose. "Before her, Macha's nymphs were different. When my sister took over, she created a whole new look. Sex became better for the guys. My dad would probably have a heart attack if he saw this. She's really come into her own since my parents passed."

Delphi slowly made her way around the large room. It was a combination of a sex shop and strip club. Her mind spun at the things that happened in their very location. A surge of desire sprang through her, and she bit her bottom lip. *Being here shouldn't turn me on so much.* But it did. And all she wanted to do was use one of the makeshift rooms to her advantage.

"Say something, Delphi. Your silence is killing me."

"Do the nymphs clean up down here?"

He shifted his weight. "Yeah, the girls do, then Dolly after them."

Nodding, she reviewed the toys on the wall. Each one tempted her, but she wasn't sure how Brewer would react.

"What's your favorite position?"

Brewer's brows lifted, nearly disappearing into his hairline. "What?"

Delphi carefully pushed Brewer into one of the rooms and onto the bed. "You heard me."

"Uh, um." He chuckled, his face a shade red. "I like them all."

She shook her head. "Not good enough." She leaned over and kissed the side of his neck. "Which position gets your cock hard and makes you want to fuck?"

Brewer's eyes turned a shade darker. "What are you doing, Delphi?"

Grabbing his chin, she kissed him hard. "I should think it's fairly obvious, Macha man."

He let out a strangled cry, tongue desperately tangling with hers. She pulled back and licked his lips. "What do you want?"

"You."

She smirked and rotated her hips. Brewer caught her earlobe between his teeth, kneading her breasts through her shirt. There were too many clothes between them. She slipped her hands under his cut, her fingers crawling along his muscular torso.

"Delphi?"

"Yeah?" She straddled his lap, instantly feeling his body's reaction beneath her.

"How attached to that shirt are you?"

She glanced down at the button-up shirt. "Not very."

"Good." He reached up and tugged on the front of the shirt, sending buttons flying in every direction.

Delphi gasped at the rush of cold air to her chest. Catching his lips with hers, she moaned when Brewer's fingers slipped under her bra and grazed her breasts. He made quick work of the rest of her shirt, tossing it to the floor along with her rose-colored bra.

The thick bulge in his jeans pressed against her, and she rocked her hips, teasing his length. His low growl made her repeat the act. Brewer grabbed the back of her neck and fused their mouths together.

The brutal force sent a ripple of lust to the pit of her stomach. She laced her hands into his hair and pulled. He gripped her jeans, squeezing her ass. Arching her back, Delphi pushed her breasts forward, begging to be touched. But he didn't give in. Instead, he pulled his lips away and frantically grasped at her pants. He didn't stop at the jeans but took her matching panties as well.

He slid his fingers between her folds, and Delphi twitched automatically. His cool fingers plunged into her slippery core, a hiss leaving his lips. "I think being down here turned you on."

Delphi swayed her hips in tempo with his thrusts. "Maybe a little."

Brewer pulled his fingers out and traced her lips with them. "More like a lot, sweet cheeks."

Darting out her tongue, she tasted her own passion. Swirling her tongue around his fingers, she purred, and he groaned.

"Damn, Delphi, you know how to make me rock hard."

She grinned, her hands busy with his belt. She desperately wanted to feel his cock's warmth in her palm. The jeans fell to the floor with a thud. Meeting his eyes, she lowered to her knees.

"Oh, no you don't." Brewer hauled her back to her feet, and she pouted. "Don't give me that either." He caught her nipples between his fingers and pinched. "You asked what I wanted."

"And what do you want?"

His lust-rimmed eyes searched her face. "I want you to ride me until you come on my cock."

Delphi's pussy clenched, a new flood of desire drenching her. "I think I can do that."

Brewer kicked off the rest of his clothes before he sprawled out on the bed. "Hop up, girl, and show me what you got."

Taking her time, Delphi walked over to the bed. She ran her fingers up his leg, taking in the freckles and goose bumps on his flesh. When she made it to his groin, she licked her lips. Her hand grazed his jutting length, making it bounce. Leaning over, she ran her tongue along the underside of his cock. He squirmed on the bed, and she moved lower, capturing his balls in her mouth one at a time. Having power over him was intoxicating. His groans only spurred her on.

"Enough, Delphi," he commanded, voice shaky. "Fuck me." His eyes latched on her. "Now."

The tone of his voice made her pulse quicken. Giving his cock one last lick, she sheathed him with a condom and straddled him on the bed. Her breasts dangled precariously over his mouth, and he reached up, catching one with his mouth.

He guided her closer, and in one swift move, Brewer's hardness overwhelmed her core. Delphi froze on impact, her body adjusting to his girth. When she was ready, she rolled her hips, taking him deeper.

Brewer sat up halfway and captured her lips, stealing her attention from the fireworks already threatening to detonate. His tongue teased her mouth, igniting a passion she long thought diminished. She pressed him down, hands splayed on his tattooed chest. If she wasn't desperate for completion, she'd take her time examining the elaborate art.

Rocking against him faster, her toes curled. The position perfectly rubbed her clit and G-spot at the same time. She arched and Brewer grabbed her hips, equally determined to get her there.

A familiar hum crept into her mind, fuzzing it immediately. She let out a cry, Brewer's name the only word she could manage, while cresting the mountaintop. Her orgasm washed over him, pussy clenching him tight.

Brewer caught her nipple in his mouth and sucked hard, enticing her ecstasy to deepen. He sat up, kissing up her neck as he let her ride out the orgasm. He caught her bottom lip between his teeth and tugged.

Delphi gasped, the sound airy and seductive to her own ears. Desire pooled at their connection, drenching Brewer's stomach.

"Two in a row, huh?" He kissed her collarbone and held her closer, pumping into her. "Let's make it three."

Delphi gripped his shoulders, steadying herself the best she could. She failed miserably. Brewer was in control, lifting and slamming her down on his cock. Her pussy quivered at each thrust, coating him repeatedly.

Brewer kissed her chin, his hands momentarily busy with her breasts. "I'm not gonna last much longer."

She clenched her thighs and caught his jaw between her hands. Searching his face, she marveled at the sheen of sweat on his brow, blue eyes wild with need.

"Come deep in my pussy, Brewer," she urged him, on the cusp of yet another orgasm.

His face tightened and she felt him swell inside her. The friction between their bodies sent her into the heavenly abyss once more. She came hard, crying out. Brewer joined her on the wave of release, arms keeping her close while they drifted together.

Delphi closed her eyes and rested her forehead against Brewer's. Her thoughts were still foggy, and she couldn't help but let a satisfied smile cover her face.

"What're you smiling for?" he teased, pushing back the hair plastered to her face. She hadn't even noticed.

Kissing his forehead, she shrugged. "Endorphins, that's all."

Brewer laughed and tickled her sides. Delphi giggled, trying to tickle him back. It felt good to laugh with and tease a man.

"You ready to head back to Snowshoe?"

She sighed. "Or we could stay here the rest of the night."

"Don't you have a restaurant to run?"

She scrunched her nose. "Yeah, I guess. But it'd be a lot more fun here."

He kissed her softly. "I have no doubt about that."

Brewer rolled her onto the bed with him, snuggling her against his chest. "All right, we'll rest here for a few minutes, then drive to town."

Cuddling closer, Delphi shut her eyes and focused on the beat of his heart. Suddenly, she didn't want to go anywhere without him. That thought sent chills up her spine.

"You cold?" He rubbed her arm, feeling the goose bumps.

"Not really. Just thinking."

"Don't do that. You're liable to regret something."

She leaned up on her elbow and met his gaze. "I'll never regret spending time with you, Brewer."

He wrapped her hair around his hand and tugged lightly. "I hope not, because I sure as hell don't."

Their lips met briefly, Delphi sighing at the simple yet erotic act. Being comfortable around a man wasn't normal for her. *But Brewer isn't just any man.* She kissed him again, already feeling him stiffen, ready for a second round. Brewer was the man who could easily break her heart.

Brewer pulled her beneath him, kissing the side of her neck and stoking the fire between them. For the time being, Delphi promised herself she wouldn't give in to her deepest fears. Brewer would never do anything to hurt her. She had to believe that. She couldn't go back to a life without him.

CHAPTER 25
BREWER

The sun stayed low on the horizon, hiding behind the mountains during their drive back to Snowshoe. Having Delphi pressed against his back shouldn't have been a turn-on, but it was. He was semihard the entire way to her bistro. More than once, he almost pulled over and fucked her up against a tree. He'd resisted. *Somehow.*

Now, an hour later, he sat at a small table. Soft music streamed through the speakers. The ambiance in the restaurant made him smile behind his cup of coffee. Couples in love were situated sporadically throughout the small space. He immediately wondered if the staff seated them there on purpose. One couldn't look far without seeing romance.

"Need a refill?" Delphi asked, holding up a fancy coffeepot.

He held out his cup. "Won't turn it down."

She smirked, and he noticed a splash of pink on her cheeks. She barely had time to change before the dinner rush started. Knowing that her skin still held the residue of their lovemaking sent his dick right back to the cabin in the mountain.

"How's everything going?" He glanced around but didn't see anything out of the ordinary. "Any issues I should handle?"

Delphi rolled her blue eyes. "I don't need a bouncer, Brewer."

"Nobody thinks they do… until they do." His gaze drifted to the front lobby. It was filled with people waiting to be seated. No one seemed out of place, but he wouldn't overlook anyone.

"Want anything to eat? I have a few madeleines in the kitchen. The tray tipped, so they aren't the prettiest, but they still taste good."

"You know I can't pass on those." He winked. "Or on you."

The pink on her cheeks deepened. She walked away and disappeared through the swinging kitchen doors. He'd never get sick of the way her hips swayed, mesmerizing him with every step.

"You're Dolly's brother, right?"

Brewer whipped his eyes to the left and noticed a

short woman with strawberry blonde hair. "Yeah, that's me."

The woman sat. "He wants to meet Delphi."

"Shovelhead?"

She nodded and lowered her voice. "He's been at the Rusty Cantina a lot this week. I managed to get his phone number. He'll want it to happen somewhere public."

"Would the city picnic work?"

"It should."

She looked over her shoulder, her features ragged like her clothes. It didn't take much to deduce she was one of the Cutthroat dolls. The Greenback Cutthroats didn't treat their women very well. It was one of the reasons he hated them so much. But the few times Macha tried to help, they never succeeded.

"Do you need help?" He had to ask. He wouldn't be able to live with himself if he didn't at least try.

He felt Delphi's presence before he saw her. She stood with a plate full of madeleines, the concern on her face making his stomach clench.

She stood and laughed. "Honey, I don't need anything but sleep." She eyed Delphi and helped herself to the pastries.

He let her go without another word. Anything he said would fall on stubborn ears. The Cutthroats mistreated their club girls but somehow maintained their allegiance. He'd never understand it.

"Who was that?"

Brewer met Delphi's skeptical eyes. "Dolly's contact."

"Really? What'd she say?" She planted herself in the same spot across from him, her brow raised.

"Shovelhead wants to meet you."

Delphi caught her bottom lip between her teeth. "I guess that's good, then."

He caught sight of the club girl before she completely disappeared into the darkness. "I suggested the city picnic. Plenty of public space, but Rubble will ensure Macha is around every corner, waiting for him to show up."

"Can't say I love it, but it makes the most sense." She stood up and grabbed the empty plate. "I'll be back with more."

"Don't worry about it." He caught her wrist and rubbed it gently. "I'm not very hungry at the moment."

Delphi didn't ask why, but her slight nod told him she understood. "After I lock up, do you want to go to the clubhouse?"

If Brewer thought she couldn't surprise him, he was sorely mistaken. "Are you serious?"

"Yeah. I feel safe with you, and you feel safe at the clubhouse."

She had him there. Macha's clubhouse wasn't as secure as their mountain cabin, but it had plenty of protective measures in place.

"All right, sure." He grinned and tried not to get too excited. Just because Delphi suggested it didn't mean she was all right with the club. It was the one sticking point that kept him from falling for her. He'd never give up Macha. Not even for her.

"Great. I'll pack a bag." She started walking away, then turned to say, "You know, so I can see your room for the first time. I bet it's horribly messy."

He shrugged. "Guess you won't know until you get there."

She laughed, the sound salving the worry in his heart. He had to protect her. If he didn't, it might kill him. Delphi had a murky family history and he wanted to fix it for her. He wasn't sure how, but meeting her biological father was a start. *Somehow, some way, I will, Delphi. I'll make it better for you.*

"THERE'S THE MAN OF THE HOUR." HAWK SLUNG AN arm over Brewer's shoulders.

"Oh, yeah? For what?" Brewer watched Delphi

walk toward the bathrooms. He didn't like letting her out of his sight, but she was safe here.

"The election, of course." Hawk handed him a bottle of beer. "We all think you'd make a damn good VP or Prez."

The beer in Brewer's mouth fizzed out at the words. "Nah, not my thing, boys."

He looked around the room but only saw men nodding in agreement with Hawk's statement. "I'm not so sure, but I'll keep it in mind," he said to placate them. He didn't intend to be president, but they wouldn't stop unless he gave them the answer they wanted.

Snoopy and Cueball shook their heads. The men of Macha didn't mince feelings or hide their opinions. It was part of the reason Brewer loved the club so much.

"I think you'd be a bomb prez," Cueball said.

"Yeah, me too." Snoopy grabbed a nymph by the waist and pulled her to him. "Plus, you run the bar and your sis runs the girls. We'd have one hell of a club with that combo. Just imagine the parties. I'm sure we could even make some cash on the side. Everybody loves our nymphs."

Brewer clenched the bottle a little tighter. "That isn't how this club works, and you know it." He finished off the beer in one long swig.

Snoopy shrugged. "Doesn't mean we can't tweak the code a bit. Clubs evolve with new leadership."

Brewer's jaw hurt from gritting it. Men like Snoopy were part of the problem with MCs. They took advantage of women instead of treating them like human beings. He wasn't about to let Macha turn down that rocky path.

Straightening his shoulders, he nodded at Kevlar and Rubble who recently joined the group. "No matter who's VP or Prez, one thing's never gonna change, and that's how we treat the women under our care. My sister will always agree with me too. Macha isn't in that business and never will be."

Snoopy rolled his eyes and walked away with the nymph in tow. Brewer moved to follow him, but Rubble placed a hand on his shoulder.

"He's not worth the fight." He nodded in the direction Delphi had recently disappeared in. "Not tonight at least. You might scare her off if you do." He smirked and waved at his old lady, Jupiter. "Your girl is a bit more standoffish with club matters, like Jupiter. Best leave those details out of the equation until she's more comfortable with us."

Brewer nodded, acknowledging the veracity of the sergeant's words. Other women were used to fist fights and bar brawls. Even if Delphi grew up in

Snowshoe, her mother kept her away from club life for a reason.

"Hey, Brewer, is Delphi here?" Jupiter asked, reaching them. Her little belly was cute on the lanky woman. Brewer was grateful the two were friends. It helped his cause a little more.

"Yeah, she's around somewhere." He grabbed another bottle of beer and did his damnedest to calm his temper. Delphi deserved a nice night at the clubhouse, and he intended to give it to her. Dealing with Snoopy and the rowdier club members could wait. One thing was certain: if his brothers voted him into office, he'd make damn sure Macha didn't change for the worse.

CHAPTER 26
DELPHI

"Want another round?"

Delphi shook the empty beer bottle in her hand and shrugged. "Sure, why not. I'm not driving home."

Brewer gave her an odd glance but headed toward the kitchen while she perused the rest of the clubhouse. It was the same as any day. There were nymphs being drooled over by both patched members and prospects alike, booze flowed from an unlimited tap, and curls of cigarette smoke lingered in the air.

Closing her eyes, Delphi listened to the sounds of Macha's clubhouse. Swearing was abundant as were the innuendos and jokes. Despite the dark places clubs could venture, she liked spending time with them.

She opened her eyes, and reality struck her hard. Hawk sat across the room, a redheaded nymph openly sucking his dick. It wasn't atypical in club life, she knew, but it also wasn't something she was immune to, and she never would be.

"It's probably hard to believe, but this is a tame night for the lads," Isa said, taking a seat next to her. She rubbed her stomach, face wrinkling in pain. "I've seen them much worse, believe me. You'll get used to it."

"No, I don't think I will." Delphi set down the empty bottle of beer. "I grew up terrified of motor-cycle clubs."

"What changed your mind?"

"Who said it changed?"

Isa rolled her eyes and flipped her long hair over her shoulder. "Seeing how you're currently screwing a biker and enjoying it, from what I gather, I'd assume you."

Thinking back over her time with Brewer, Delphi couldn't entirely disagree. Her perception of club life *had* changed, but not because she was sleeping with Brewer. "Macha is different."

"Thank the goddess for that." Isa sipped on her bottle of strawberry-flavored water. "I didn't grow up around clubs either." She nodded to the woman at Kevlar's side. "Only Nikita did."

Delphi noticed Dolly making her rounds in the clubhouse, typical tank top and high ponytail in place. She was the epitome of a club girl and wore that identity like a badass.

Isa shifted on her seat. "Och, this baby is getting too big."

"May I?"

Isa nodded, and Delphi placed both hands on the large bump. The baby kicked hard, sending a smile to her face. "Whoa, it's amazing."

"More like painful, after a bit," she said wearily. "But aye, very incredible."

Brewer finally returned, beers in hand. He fondly rubbed Isa's belly. "This guy is gonna be one hell of a biker."

"Is *she*?" Doc said, joining the conversation. He kissed the top of Isa's head. "I could get used to having a little princess running around the clubhouse."

"You sure about that?" Isa teased. "I'm quite the handful."

"It's why I have two hands, princess."

Watching the depth of love exchanged between the two, Delphi choked back tears. That was what she wanted. *Can I really find that here? In a motorcycle club?*

She coughed and wiped her eyes. When she

looked up, she saw Brewer notice the sheen of tears. Instead of saying anything, he pulled her to his side and tucked her comfortably against him. Delphi took a sip of beer and did her best to smother a contented smile. Even without hearing her thoughts, it was as if Brewer knew what she needed just then. *Maybe I can find love in peculiar places.*

"Oh my God."

All eyes shot to the very pregnant Isa doubled over in pain.

Doc hunkered down in front of her, worry scribbled over his face. "What's happening? Are you okay?"

Isa grabbed Doc's shoulder so hard her hand went white. "I think your baby doesn't want to wait to meet you."

"What?"

"The baby is coming."

Doc's eyes bugged out, and he quickly stood and started barking orders. "Kevlar, go get the truck. You can drive us to the hospital. Hawk, I need you to check in on the prospect I patched up this afternoon. Cueball, can you—"

"Love, there's no time," Isa managed in between contractions.

"What? Why? How do you know?"

Isa offered him a guilty face. "My water may have broken a few hours ago."

Reaper chuckled, the commotion catching his attention. "Of course it did. Isa's a stubborn lass. Why do you think her babe would be any different?"

Doc scowled at him. "Uncle, not now."

A knowing smirk covered the president's face, but he didn't say anything else.

Queenie joined them, and her features lit up at the scene. "Good God, Doc, we gotta get her in the infirmary."

Kevlar burst through the side door. "Truck's ready."

"I don't think there's time." Doc gingerly helped Isa to her feet with Rubble's help.

"Want me to call for an ambulance?" Snoopy offered.

Delphi watched the club members suddenly put aside their plans for the evening to help one of their own. She moved out of the way and watched the flurry of hands.

"Delphi, come with us," Jupiter said.

She looked over with wide eyes but didn't resist. Following Jupiter down the hallway, Delphi looked back and noticed Brewer helping his brothers with Isa.

Delphi lost track of how they got to the small

infirmary. Jupiter seemed to know what she was doing, flipping on lights, and opening cabinets for supplies.

"Grab those blankets, will ya?"

Quickly getting to work, Delphi took an armful of blankets from the closet and placed them on the counter.

"Ach, put me down. I can walk, you fools," Isa said from the hallway.

Delphi looked over and couldn't help but chuckle. Isa waddled into the room, one hand on the small of her back, the other on her stomach. Doc followed, cursing under his breath about his old lady's stubbornness. Rubble came through the door next, followed by Brewer, Hawk, Reaper, Kevlar, and Nikita.

Suddenly the decent-sized room was as small as a shoebox. Everyone was talking at once, the noise level above average, even for the club. Isa climbed onto the hospital bed, making herself comfortable despite the audience.

A loud whistle pierced the air, silencing everyone. Queenie moved through the throng, her expression one of motherly concern.

"There are far too many bodies here, and there's about to be one more, so if you don't have medical training, get out."

The bikers shuffled toward the door, voicing their respect and encouragement to Doc and Isa.

"There'll be plenty of time for you to see the baby later," Queenie added with a proud smile. "It's been too long since we had a newborn."

Making for the door, Delphi paused at the threshold when someone called her name.

"Delphi, please stay. We could use your hands."

She turned and shook her head. "I'm the last person you want near anything medical related."

Isa let out a cry and immediately pulled Delphi from her spot. She wasn't sure why, but all of a sudden, she had to do something to help the sweet woman. She snatched a washcloth from the counter and flipped on the faucet, running it under cold water.

"Yasmina has some experience with midwifery," Dolly chimed in from the door with the woman at her side.

Doc's worried eyes looked over. "You do?"

Yasmina offered a small nod. "My aunt is a midwife in my country. Sometimes, I would go with her."

"Well, between you and me, we have decent skills." Doc pointed to Brewer. "Call the hospital and have them send an ambulance. Since she insisted on having our baby here, she's going straight to the hospital afterward."

"On it." Brewer squeezed Delphi's hand before walking out of the room.

Doc turned to Isa and shook his head. "Damn woman, you're gonna give me a heart attack."

Isa laughed, then doubled over in pain. "Worth it."

Doc rolled his eyes and his gaze landed on her. "You doing all right, Delphi? You look pretty pale."

Delphi swallowed the bile in her throat, her hands clammy. She placed the washcloth on Isa's forehead and stepped backward. "I should go."

Yasmina set up camp at Isa's feet, and Delphi's stomach lurched.

"Shit, she's gonna pass out," she heard Doc yell.

Strong arms caught her before she completely collapsed to the hard floor. Her mind spun, the lights brighter than moments earlier. She tried to keep her eyes open, but her eyelids were too heavy.

"Note to self, don't let Delphi anywhere near a delivery room," she heard Brewer's teasing voice.

Her lips failed an automatic snarky reply, but they didn't miss the feathery kiss he brushed on them. Black overtook her sight, Brewer's the last face she saw.

"Just over an hour."

"I guess that isn't terrible." She shrugged. "A nice evening nap."

Noticing the way she crossed her arms over her chest, Brewer knew she was still upset with herself. That wouldn't do for a minute.

"Let's go play some pool."

"I'm horrible at pool."

He held out his hand. "All the more reason. Gotta step up your game if you're gonna hang with Macha."

Delphi looked at his hand, then sighed. "All right, fine, but no betting. I'm not about to lose my shirt or something."

Brewer helped her off the bed. "Don't worry, sweet cheeks, you'd lose your pants first." He playfully swatted her ass. "But now that I think of it, I don't want my brothers seeing that, so you better wear lots of layers if you ever play any strip game with us."

She lifted both her middle fingers. "Eat me."

"Oh, I plan to." He wiggled his brows and she giggled, her face going red. "I'll eat your pussy until you scream."

"Are you ever serious?"

Circling her waist with his arm, he drew her close. The scent of her perfume overwhelmed his nostrils. She smelled like fresh cookies and roses. Surely there had to be something wrong with her, because all he saw was perfection.

"Now, why would I want to be serious?" He nuzzled his nose against hers. "If I'm serious, I don't get to see your temper flare, or your eyes roll, or your cheeks go red."

The joking expression left her face, and her eyes dipped to his mouth. "You do it on purpose."

"Yeah, I do." He leaned over, softly kissing the side of her neck. Her pulse thrummed against his lips and her breathing hitched. "And that's why I'm not serious very often, Delphi. I like to see the fire burn in your eyes."

Her hands rested on his hips, fingers sneaking beneath his belt and pulling him slightly closer. "You take great pride in that, don't you?"

"Sure, I do, but there's something I take more pride in."

"And what's that?"

He brushed her hair out of her face. "Making you come over and over until you're too exhausted to do anything but smile in satisfaction."

Delphi licked her lips, eyes searching his. "I like when you do that."

"I know." He smirked when she rolled her eyes.

"We should probably go see if Isa had the baby."

Brewer nipped her bottom lip. "I don't want to yet. Believe me, Doc will pound on all these doors when he has a baby to brag about."

She grinned. "As a good daddy should."

"Wanna know what I'd rather do?" He cupped her ass and pressed the bulge in his jeans against her.

She lifted her brow. "Go dancing?"

"A kind of dance, yeah."

"Or we could go play pool like you suggested."

He let out a disappointed sigh. "Yeah, we could. The guys would love to give you a run for your money."

Turning the door handle, Brewer was caught off guard when Delphi reached up and kissed him hard. Too stunned to do anything but kiss her back, he stood there, letting her take the lead. She grabbed his hand and placed it over her pussy. The heat there consumed him.

Her fingers weaved into his hair, her kiss more frantic with each flick of her tongue against his. Brewer slid his hand down her pants and groaned at the lack of panties beneath them. He found her core hot and wet. Slipping two fingers in and out of her, Brewer moaned. No matter how many times he felt this, he'd never take it for granted.

"Maybe we have a few minutes," she said, shutting the door. It slammed, but not as hard as when he picked her up and pressed her against it.

Devouring her neck, Brewer didn't want a slow and leisurely session with her. From the way she was sucking on his bottom lip, neither did she.

She deftly undid his belt and lifted his dick out of his boxer briefs. His heart pounded at how much she wanted him. Brewer hissed in a groan, her hand encompassing his hardness and sliding him up and down in her soft palm.

"Damn, Delphi." He pulled down her leggings and quickly sheathed his cock with a condom. "You're making this way too easy for me."

"Can't play hard to get all the time." She grinned and guided him toward her entrance.

Not one to argue with her needs Brewer plunged into her pussy in one smooth move. She gasped, adjusting to him, but he didn't stop moving his hips. He pressed two fingers to her clit. She arched her back, her body shaking. Using her own wetness as lube, he kept up the pressure, rubbing her the way she liked. He paused and saw the white slickness coating his cock.

"Hot damn, Delphi, did you come already?"

The cutest smirk covered her face. "Maybe."

"I'll take that as a yes."

Delphi wrapped her legs tighter around him,

making it harder for him to pound her as hard as he wanted. He squeezed her ass, licking the side of her neck. When he nibbled at her throat, she mewed, and her nails dug into his shoulders.

Brewer picked up his pace, the sensation of her pussy clenching him making it increasingly difficult to not empty into her then and there.

He thrust into her once more before the inevitable sound reached their ears.

"Holy shit, I'm a dad! It's a girl!" Doc yelled, running down the hallways. As expected, he beat on the doors with his fists, and he whooped with joy.

Brewer paused his thrusts. "Dammit, Doc. Fucking cockblock."

Chuckling, Delphi kissed his nose. "To be continued."

"Whoa, whoa, you got off, but I didn't. Give me another minute and I'm there."

A wickedly adorable gleam filled her eyes. "Nah." She wiggled free and pulled up her leggings.

Brewer's mouth dropped open at her next-level sass.

She rose up and kissed him so thoroughly, he almost tossed her to the bed and said *fuck it* to Doc and his baby.

"We'll finish this later." She cupped his still-hard cock. "If you're lucky."

"Delphi, do you know what I'd do to you?" He gripped the back of her head, tilting her face up. The fiery look in her eyes couldn't be extinguished even if he tried. It sent his stomach spiraling down a path he'd never been on before.

Delphi arched her brow. "What would you do, Brewer? Would you fuck me until I moan your name? Maybe tie me to your bed and spank me until my ass is as red as a cherry. Or how about eat my pussy until I come on your beard?"

Every word she uttered enticed him to do exactly that. He'd keep them up all night, checking off her list until there was nothing left. But he knew better. She was teasing him to get a reaction. He deserved it, he knew, but it also made him three times harder for her.

"I'll tell you what." Her eyes took on a mischievous glint. "If you let me suck your dick right now, you can do whatever you want to me later tonight."

His cock bounced approvingly, but Brewer wasn't in agreement. He wanted to fuck her right this instant, not in a few hours.

"No deal, sweet cheeks." He regretfully tucked his dick back into his jeans and zipped them. "I don't like one-sided gratification unless you're the one getting it."

"But—"

He cut off the rest of her argument with a kiss. She melted under his touch, clinging to the front of his cut. When he pulled back, he watched her eyes slowly open. They were filled with desire, and he desperately wanted to give in to her. "Now, if you made a different deal, I might agree."

"Like what?"

"Hmm, like I get to lick your pussy until you come right now, then later, I get to fuck you until you're hoarse from screaming."

Delphi shivered, and he knew without a doubt it wasn't from a chill in the room. "There you go, teasing me again." She shook her head. "How about a compromise?"

"Such as?"

"We both get to tease each other." He opened his mouth to interrupt, but she placed her index finger on his lips. "Except neither of us gets to come. Not until later."

Brewer didn't have to think long. He wouldn't keep his end of the bargain. She'd be coming on his tongue within a minute. "Deal, now lose the pants."

CHAPTER 28

DELPHI

Delphi felt like she'd just stepped into a sauna. The heat emanating from Brewer was nothing compared to the way her body flushed every time he looked at her. The way his hands searched out her body was unlike any other, and she welcomed them whenever possible.

Dolly and Yasmina walked past the couch, the two cooing about the recently delivered newborn. Delphi didn't get the chance to drop her leggings like Brewer demanded. They'd been interrupted yet again, but that time by the club president. They couldn't exactly turn down Reaper's plea to join the happy new family. So, they'd put their sensual escapades aside. An hour had passed since Reaper called the entire club from their beds. The time on the wall flashed the start of a new hour, one much later than her usual bedtime.

Brewer was talking with his brothers, Kevlar and Hawk, but every now and then his gaze gravitated back to her. In an odd way, she didn't feel worthy of such adoring glances. Judging from the way he never went very far away from her lately, she wouldn't have to wait long until they were alone once more.

"Make a path," a paramedic called, wheeling Isa and her baby on a gurney down the hallway. Doc followed, his brow furrowed while he parroted the man in uniform.

Delphi swallowed a giggle at the sight of the manly biker. It was endearing in the best way. Macha's men didn't merely see women as possessions. Women were goddesses just like their patron. It was a steep difference compared to any other motorcycle club portrayed on television or in real life.

"She's glowing," Jupiter said, walking to Delphi.

"You're next, you know." Delphi reached out and rubbed Jupiter's growing belly.

Jupiter worried her lips together. "After seeing childbirth firsthand, I'm seriously reconsidering."

Rubble snaked one of his heavily tattooed arms around his old lady's waist. "Too late for that, baby girl."

Looking up at him, Jupiter smiled. "The things I do for you."

Rubble tilted up her chin and kissed her gently. "The things I do for you."

Delphi should've been uncomfortable. It was a private moment, after all. Instead, she was envious of them. Rubble was as badass a biker as she'd ever seen, but he was beyond tender with Jupiter.

Looking around the room, she couldn't help but notice the bikers with old ladies were all the same beneath their rough-and-tumble façades. Doc worshipped the ground Isa stood on. Kevlar bent over backward to support Nikita's FBI occupation. And then there was Rubble and Jupiter. Two unlikely souls that were perfect for each other.

She sighed, suddenly craving a stiff drink. The expectant couple's history was one she couldn't find fault in. Even though she only heard whisperings about the other couples, Jupiter had told her all about the love that blossomed despite their pasts. *Maybe Brewer and I can have that too.*

Delphi turned her head away and focused on the rest of the clubhouse. *But Brewer and I have a different kind of history.* The man circulating in her thoughts met her gaze, and she didn't dare look away. *A murderous one.*

"We're going to the hospital. Want to come, Delphi?"

Breaking Brewer's gaze, she looked at his sister. "Maybe tomorrow. It's kind of late." She yawned, not realizing how tired she truly was after a busy day at the restaurant. "Thanks, though."

Dolly slung an arm around Yasmina and nodded. "Catch you later."

Brewer walked over and tugged on her wrist. "You look tired."

"Don't you know it's rude to say that to a lady," she said around a yawn.

He held out both hands. "Mm-hmm, now, let's get you to bed."

She took them and stood. To her surprise, he didn't drop his hold as he led her down the hallway. A few of his brothers called after them, encouraging them with suggested sexual activities. He simply laughed and shook his head.

"They're my brothers, what can I say?" he said, opening the bedroom door and dropping her hands. Walking over to the bed, he pulled back the quilt. "Hop in, sweet cheeks."

For a second, she almost refused merely because she wanted to do more than sleep. But the better half of her brain, the tired part, swayed her against it.

She slipped off her shoes and crawled between

the cool sheets. The light overhead flicked off before she had a chance to fluff the pillow. The mattress sank under Brewer's weight, his warmth spreading to her in a flash.

Pulling her against his chest, he nuzzled his nose against the back of her head. "Sweet dreams."

Delphi hummed the same, sleep already crowding her mind. She snuggled closer, hugging his arm against her chest. The steady repetition of his breathing lulled her to a dreamless state, Brewer the last thing she thought of before succumbing to darkness yet again.

"Delphi, wake up."

"Didn't we talk about my coffee requirement?" Delphi slowly pried her eyes open and groaned. "It's too early."

Brewer hovered above her, a cheeky smile on his face. She couldn't help that she wasn't a morning person.

"Nah, it's almost ten in the morning. You got about six hours of sleep." He kissed her cheek, his beard tickling her. "That's enough."

"You're the devil," she mumbled, face-planting into the pillow. The heat from his body combined with the comfortable bed made it almost impossible for her to move.

"That's normally not what you say about me." He trailed his lips along her arm. "You're usually calling out my name in the holiest of ways."

The familiar desire spread from her toes to her lips the longer he kissed her. "Doesn't sound like me."

He tickled the spot behind her knee, getting an immediate reaction. Her eyes flashed open, a laugh bubbling from her belly. Delphi's entire body jerked, the coverings flying off. Brewer pinned her beneath him, coaxing her lips to match his fervor. Having too much of Brewer was impossible.

Delphi wrapped her right leg around his leg and used his body weight against him, flipping them over. She detached their mouths and lingered above him. His red hair was disheveled, his beard in the same state.

"Hmm, what should I do with you, Brewer Stapleton?"

He gently tugged her hair. "I'm pretty good at naked Twister."

She shook her head. "I'm the least flexible person in the world."

"Strip poker?"

"I think you're already halfway there, mister."

She wiggled against his boxer briefs and smirked at the immediate response. He was already at half-mast, but her movement added another inch to him.

"You know, I think you're wearing way too many clothes for bed." Brewer tugged on her shirt. She'd completely forgotten to take even her bra off before falling asleep. In one swift move, she unlatched her bra and pulled it out from under her shirt.

"Tada!"

"I really wish I had that skill." He teased her hips with his fingers.

"Sorry, you have to be a girl to master it." She kissed one side of his neck, then the other, licking and nibbling as she went down each side. "Can't give you more ammo to get us naked." She kissed down his chest, tongue darting out to taste his coppery-colored nipples.

Brewer squirmed but didn't try to undress her more. The lower she slid down his body, the more his breath hitched. "You're lucky you don't know what it's like sleeping with your fine ass up against my dick."

She paused at his dark green boxer briefs and looked up. "Why? Was it difficult to keep your hands off me?"

"You have no idea."

Delphi pulled down his boxers and freed his cock.

"Almost woke you up several times with my hard-on."

She flicked her tongue against the tip of his length, adoring the control she had over him. Brewer's blue eyes turned cobalt, lust filling his gaze. "I wouldn't have minded."

He managed a strangled chuckle. "You say that now, but I'm pretty sure you would've shoved me off the bed after the third time."

Leisurely licking the underside of his dick, Delphi made sure to keep eye contact with him. It turned her on almost as much as when he played with her clit. Knowing he'd come apart by her touch sent a shot of longing between her legs.

"I don't know, I like sex," she paused and swallowed his cock, then popped it out to finish. "And I really like sex with you, so I'm willing to give up sleep for a few rounds."

Brewer managed a smile before Delphi slid him back into her mouth. She sucked him to the back of her throat and gagged on the length. Between his girth and solid inches, there wasn't anything Brewer lacked south of the border. She kept bobbing up and down on him, mercilessly teasing him. When she fondled his balls between her fingers, his hips shot up in reaction.

"You know that's not fair, right?" He reached for

her hair, and she chose that moment to increase her suction, and a groan escaped him. He clenched his fingers on the bed but found nothing to grab.

"Now you know how I feel," she said around his cock. Returning to the job at hand, Delphi started bobbing faster. Her eyes watered the more she bottomed him out in her mouth, but she wouldn't stop. The anxious thrusts of his hips only encouraged her. Taking a moment to focus on his balls, she sucked one into her mouth while she pumped his dick with her hand. Only once she'd repeated the act with the other ball did she lick them, then return his cock to her lips.

"Delphi, please, I need to be inside you." Brewer said, brow furrowed. His torso muscles bunched deliciously, the tattoos showing off all the hours he'd spent under the needle.

Letting him pop free from her mouth once more, she quickly shed her leggings and tossed them out of the way. Not giving him the chance to argue, she sheathed him with a condom, then plunged his cock into her wet pussy. Biting the inside of her cheek, Delphi tried not to come then and there. The way he filled her to the brim was enough to send her crying toward the clouds.

After adjusting, she rolled forward, taking him

deeper. He immediately clung to her hips, urging her to repeat the act.

"As much as I like watching your tits tempt me, I need to fucking pound that pussy." He rolled them over and brought both her legs over his shoulders before thrusting in deep.

Delphi silenced a scream with the back of her hand. This position wasn't new, but the way Brewer consumed her made it feel like the first time. He grabbed her thighs, pumping her against him as his hips mirrored the movement. It was all too much for her. The orgasms washed over her in pummeling waves, one after another until she lost count.

She didn't know how long she shuddered her releases. Her eyes were too blurry to know what was happening. Brewer rolled her over, her ass on full display to him on her hands and knees.

Brewer cupped her breasts under her shirt, pinching her nipples. The already sensitive buds shot desire to her pussy, teasing another orgasm from her. Knees wobbling, Delphi rose to accept his thrusts, his balls slapping the back of her ass.

"I could do this every damn day." His voice tightened, each syllable more breathless than the last.

She whimpered her approval, her mind too jumbled to manage a coherent sentence. It happened whenever they had sex. He obliterated her with ecstasy.

Grabbing a handful of her hair, he coaxed her neck up, making any sounds impossible for her to utter. He paused and kissed up her spine.

"I don't want to fuck anyone else, Delphi. Only you." He dropped his hold and his dick slid free.

Delphi let out a cry, missing him already. She didn't have to wait long before he flipped her over. With one ankle settled on his shoulder and one under his body, Delphi was trapped in the best way.

Brewer leaned down and caught her lips, his tongue invading her mouth. She desperately kissed him back, needing to feel him in every orifice she had to offer.

As if reading her thoughts, he dipped a finger into her pussy, stealing her juices. Keeping her gaze, he parted her ass cheeks and teased the forbidden pleasure hole there.

Delphi gasped, focus suddenly on a place her body had never been breached. It didn't feel wrong like she expected. In fact, the naughty sensations he caused were more than taboo.

"One of these days, I'm taking your ass." He squeezed her cheek with his free hand, the other still playing with her virgin hole. "But today, I'm gonna make your pussy flood with your come."

Delphi's sex clenched automatically, the low promise more than enough to get her closer to the edge. Brewer kissed her roughly, pounding his dick into her pussy. While his left hand rimmed her tight ring, his right hand played with her clit. He pinched the bundle of nerves, and she shattered around his cock.

"That's my girl." His thrusts turned wild and erratic until he finally growled his completion.

Collapsing on her, Brewer kissed the base of her neck. Delphi closed her eyes, her body humming from the pleasure he invoked. She ran her fingers up and down his spine, goose bumps scattering along his freckles. She had no doubt Brewer would do exactly as he promised. Kissing his head, she listened as their heartbeats thrummed and their breathing synchronized. She couldn't fight what she was feeling any longer. He was it. He was who she wanted.

CHAPTER 29

BREWER

"Brewer, you got a second?"

Pausing outside the door following church, Brewer looked back and waited for Rubble to catch up.

"Yeah, what's up?"

Rubble pulled off his wool cap, his tattoo-covered bald head coming into view. "Your girl all set for the Snowshoe picnic?"

As they walked through the clubhouse, he thought back to earlier that morning. He'd left Delphi with a prospect at the bistro for a few short hours. They'd briefly discussed the picnic, their attentions not keen on talking versus making other sounds.

"Uh, yeah, I think so. She and Jupiter got together the other day to go over the menu."

They turned a corner, the pool tables coming into view. "It's nice that Macha and a local business are going in together. It'll really help the community outlook."

"I thought the same thing." Brewer passed on the offer for a Guinness from the nymph in front of them. It wasn't too early for a drink, but his mind needed to be laser focused on Delphi's protection until after Shovelhead was taken care of however Macha chose to do exactly that.

"She and Jupiter really get along." Rubble led him into the kitchen where Brewer sat at one of the barstools and Rubble opened the fridge door. "It's good for Jupiter. After all the bullshit she's been through over the last few years, I'm glad she found a friend here."

"Me too."

Rubble handed him a bottled water and Brewer cranked the top until it opened.

"You worried about her?"

Brewer sipped the water. "I can't stop worrying about her."

Smirking, Rubble lifted his bottle toward Brewer before drinking. "Get used to that. It never stops."

"Great."

"But once we know what's going on with Shovel-head, it'll ease a bit." Rubble leaned against the counter. "You honestly think she's up for a meet and greet of that intensity?"

"She's wanted the truth since her parents died last year. Delphi may not be ready to face the reality of it all, but she doesn't want to be left in the dark about anything. Especially when it comes to her parents." Brewer scratched at the label on the bottle with his thumb. "Kind of like me."

"You need to know if Shovelhead killed your parents."

"Yep, I do." He met his brother's unique eyes. "Dolly does too. Hell, the whole club needs to know if one of our own—our VP, for Christ's sake—called for a hit on my parents."

Rubble clapped a hand to Brewer's shoulder and squeezed. "We'll get the son of a bitch. If he did it, you can count on Macha's vengeance."

"See, that's where it gets tricky."

"With Delphi."

"Exactly."

Sighing, Rubble took a seat beside him. "She knows the risks, right?"

"I explained them, yes."

"Not much we can do otherwise, brother."

Brewer nodded, accepting Rubble's words as gospel. They dug at him, nonetheless. "Would my parents want that? Revenge against their murderer?"

Rubble stopped drinking and capped the water. "Not sure. I knew them, of course. Your dad was my brother, but I never connected with him like you and I have. Same with your mom. She was great, but other than knowing her as an old lady, that's the extent of my knowledge."

Finishing off the water, Brewer steepled his hands over his nose.

Rubble swiveled his chair to face him. "But you know them better than most of us. You and Dolly. And you two will be the ones we turn to when the truth comes out. If you want Macha to stand down, you'll both have to say the word. We all have skin in this fight, but yours is in it the most."

"And if Dolly wants one thing and I want another?"

"We vote on it like anything else."

"I was afraid you'd say something like that."

Dolly walked down the hall just then and stopped in the kitchen. "Hey, boys, what's new?"

"Your ears must've been burning," Rubble joked. "We were just talking about you."

"Oh? All good things, I hope." She leaned her forearms on the counter, her hair down for the first time in a while. It fell in dark sheets around her shoulders, the lengths hiding the Macha stamp on the front of her black sweatshirt. She looked more like their mom with each passing day. It sent Brewer's stomach into a nosedive. No matter how many years went by, he'd never stop missing them.

"We were discussing Shovelhead and your parents."

Her makeup-free face clouded. "Never a fun topic. Anything new on that front?"

"Just the meeting at the picnic." Rubble stood up and tossed his bottle into the recycling bin. "I'll keep you both updated if anything changes."

Once Rubble was halfway down the hall, Dolly took his spot next to Brewer. "I'm way too excited to bring the bastard down. He's gonna pay for what he did to Mom and Dad."

Brewer wanted to agree but couldn't. "What if he didn't do it?"

"He did."

"Dolls, what if he didn't?"

Dolly's bright blue eyes searched his, her brow furrowed as if she was trying to decipher a code written on his face. "This is about Delphi, isn't it?"

"No." He glanced at his black boots.

"Liar. You always look away when you lie." She sighed. "It's okay if it's about her, but it won't change my mind about anything. If Shovelhead shot our parents, he's going on a very long trip to hell."

It was exactly as he expected. A month prior, he

was right there alongside her on the retaliation train. But now it was different. Something had changed him. *More like someone.*

"Delphi's a big girl. She can handle the truth." Dolly gave him a side hug. "And we'll all live happily ever after."

"Speaking of—how're things going with Yasmina?"

A sly smile crossed her lips. "Now that, big brother, is none of your business."

"It is if you're leaving Macha to be with her."

Dolly's eyes flashed a warning. "Keep your voice down." She stood and poked her head out in the hallway, then returned to the edge of the counter. "I never said I was *leaving* leaving."

"What the hell does that mean?"

"Yasmina works at Macha's bakery and she freaking loves it. I couldn't pull her away from there. Not after all the hell she's been through."

"Little sister, there are other towns that need a kick-ass bakery." He stood up and offered her a sympathetic hug. "If you want to start over, you can. Macha would never turn their back on you, and if things didn't work out, you'd be more than welcome to return."

Dolly rested her chin on her fist. "You sound more like a cabinet member than a brother right now."

"What? That's not… never mind."

"Careful, Brewer, your brothers may vote you in yet." She playfully punched his stomach, then started walking down the hallway toward the nymph lair in the basement. "You'd make a damn good VP or president too, you know."

He didn't have a chance to refute her statement. The door to the basement shut behind her, ending the conversation. Brewer shoved the thought aside. He didn't want to be anything in the club except a member. *It might be nice.*

Walking out the side door, he pushed all notions of the upcoming cabinet vote to the side. If his brothers wanted him there, they'd say so. He wasn't about to campaign for a spot at the head of Macha's table. *Whatever happens, happens.*

His phone buzzed with a new text message from Delphi.

Delphi: Received a new message from Grant.

Brewer: Be right over. Hang tight.

He found his recently waxed motorcycle in the parking lot and thanked the goddess for the fine spring day. Many more of those were to come, and he couldn't wait to spend them with Delphi.

CHAPTER 30
DELPHI

Grant: You can't handle the truth. But you're about to find out anyways.

THE MESSAGE KEPT RUNNING THROUGH HER MIND WHILE Delphi prepped vegetables for the dinner rush. Brewer had driven over right after she received the message. He read it, then forwarded it to the club's sergeant at arms, Rubble, before leaving once more.

I can *handle the truth. I think.* She stopped dicing celery and stared at the cutting board. *Can't I?* Delphi wasn't even sure what Grant meant.

The multi-city picnic was in three days. There was plenty of time to back out, but she wouldn't. *I can't. Not when I'm so close to finding out what happened.*

She started chopping again, this time green onions. Jupiter would stop by after work to pick her up so they could visit Isa and the baby at the hospital. Doc being Doc, he had somehow finagled the hospital to let her stay longer than usual.

In a small way, Delphi was looking forward to seeing the baby and Isa. Another part of her wanted nothing to do with the place where her parents died. *Nothing good ever happens in a hospital.* It'd been her mantra for years and had held true up until now.

"Hey, are you ready to go?"

Looking up, Delphi met Jupiter's gaze. "It's time already?" She glanced to the clock and made a face. "Damn, how long have I been dicing?"

Jupiter walked around the kitchen island and chuckled. "Long enough to have everything ready for the picnic prep."

"Give me five minutes and let's go." She quickly washed her hands in the sink. "Did you get a present?"

"Yep, and don't worry, I signed your name too."

Delphi lifted her brows. "Why?"

"Because you haven't exactly had a lot of time to do anything but Brewer."

She wanted to object, plead innocence even, but she couldn't. Heat rushed to her cheeks, and she walked to the stairs. "That's neither here nor there."

"Oh, are those the places you haven't had sex yet?" Jupiter teased.

Rolling her eyes, Delphi hurried up the stairs, changed, then rushed back down. Ten minutes later, they were on the road, and ten minutes after that, they stood in Isa's hospital room.

"Oh my God, Isa, she's adorable," Jupiter cooed, rocking the baby wrapped in pink blankets.

"She is, but she's also a pain in the arse." Isa laughed at the matching expressions on Jupiter and Delphi's faces. "What? She's like her father. Wants my tits every few hours."

Jupiter carefully handed the newborn to Delphi. "Sounds like Doc, yeah."

Delphi looked down at the sleeping baby. For a brief second, she couldn't breathe. All she could do was stare at the perfect little nose and the eyelashes longer than what should be permitted on an infant. "What's her name?"

"Cliodhna."

"How's that spelled?"

"The Irish way." Isa's eyes sparkled. "Took Doc forever to spell it correctly, but once he got it down, neither of us could think of a better one.

"So Clee-na?" Jupiter said, trying out the Gaelic name.

"Aye. Cliodhna is the goddess of love and beauty. In some myths, she's also Queen of the Banshees."

"The way she wails, she sure is so far," Doc said, walking into the room.

Isa nodded, a content smile on her face. It was obvious to anyone who saw them how in love they were with each other and their daughter.

"It's a beautiful name," Jupiter said, grinning at little Cliodhna.

"Yes, it really is." Delphi froze at the baby's stirring and gratefully passed her off to Doc.

"Not used to holding babes, are you?"

Glancing at Isa, she shook her head. "Never had much of a chance, growing up as a single child. I never babysat either. Most of my friends moved away, so if they had kids, I never met them."

"Don't worry. If you hang out with the club long enough, you'll have plenty of babies to hold," Doc said, sitting on the edge of Isa's bed. "I mean, you're friends with Jupiter, so that's another one right there."

"And if Rubble has any say, they'll have more than one," Isa said with a cheerful smile.

Jupiter rested both hands on her protruding stomach and sat in one of the chairs by the bed. "This one is a miracle. I'm not holding my breath for a sibling, but I'm all for having plenty of sex, just in case."

Delphi was well aware of the story behind

Jupiter's reasoning, and she couldn't fault her one bit. Neither Jupiter nor Rubble thought they could have biological children, so when Jupiter found out she was expecting, they'd taken every precaution to ensure a healthy pregnancy.

"Plus, if you and Brewer ever have children...." Isa let the rest of her sentence hang there for them all to speculate on.

For the second time that afternoon, Delphi's skin flamed with warmth, and not in her preferred way.

"We're nowhere near talking about that. We barely know each other."

Doc gave Cliodhna a pacifier when she started to fuss. "Pretty sure that's the beginning of all our stories, Delphi."

Isa nodded and Jupiter mirrored the act before saying, "The only exception is Nikita. She and Kevlar had a history, so they rekindled their affection."

Shifting on her feet, Delphi averted her eyes from the two women who were her closest friends, even after such a short time. They weren't wrong, but she wasn't ready to admit it.

"How's the picnic planning going?" Doc asked, steering the conversation another direction. Delphi could've kissed him for reading between the lines of her silence.

"Delphi and Yasmina have all the prep work

done. Rubble said he and Kevlar would set up the tents in case it rains. Plus, if it's sunny, it'll draw more people to the shade." Jupiter grinned. "Oh, and I made a few calls to the women's shelter. They'll be participating too. Some of the women have quilts, blankets, and other items to sell. All proceeds from their goods will go to the shelter to help the women get back on their feet."

Doc nodded, a proud smile on his face. "You've done a great job there, Jupiter. Rubble never shuts up about it."

Isa waved for their baby at the next whimper. "As he should. Jupiter works harder than five Macha men combined."

"You're one to talk," Jupiter added. "You and Queenie kick ass at the boutique every day, and you design the clothes."

Isa shrugged, latching Cliodhna to her breast. The infant sucked greedily, her tiny hands outstretched toward her mother. "Ach, child, just like your father."

The women shared a good laugh at Doc's expense. He didn't seem to mind. In fact, he pressed a kiss to his daughter's head, ignoring their teasing altogether.

The sentiment made Delphi's heart lurch. This same sweet gentleness was what she'd seen in

Brewer whenever he touched her. It wasn't a learned ability, but an innate one. *All Macha men seem to have it.* She cringed. *All but one, but I guess Shovelhead isn't Macha anymore.*

Delphi's phone rang, stealing her away from the room. "Hey, Brewer, what's up?"

"Where the hell are you?"

She scrunched her face. "Shit, sorry, I forgot to tell you Jupiter and I were visiting Isa and the baby. My prospect is around here somewhere."

Brewer sighed, but his voice held a sharp tone. "You can't up and leave like that, Delphi. Not when you're under Macha's protection."

She shifted her weight. "I can't put my life on hold, Brewer."

"You don't know Shovelhead. If he senses anything is fishy, he'll come after you, daughter or not."

Delphi's temper flared, and she tried to tamp it down. She failed miserably. "Stop treating me like a helpless child. He's my dad, Brewer. He wouldn't hurt me."

"Sure, just like he wouldn't gun down members of his own club."

Delphi felt three gazes on her, so she quietly walked down the hallway. "What's got you so on edge?"

"How long have you been gone?"

She glanced at the digital clock on the wall. "I don't know. An hour maybe. Brewer, what's going on?"

"Is Doc there?"

"Yeah, why?"

"Okay, good." She heard his motorcycle start in the background. "Stay put, I'll be there shortly."

"Brewer, tell me what happened." She gripped the phone tighter, worry filling her stomach.

"It's your restaurant. Someone busted out all the windows. The place is a mess. Glass everywhere."

She gritted her teeth. "Probably some dumb kids. It's no big deal."

"It is. There was a note that said, 'Stay away from Macha.'"

Her eyes widened, and she suddenly felt out of breath. "Shit."

"Shovelhead knows you're hanging with Macha, Delphi, and that's bad news. If he knows, it also means he's watching you. Or at least, one of his guys is."

Delphi found a bench outside Isa's room and managed to sit before she collapsed, her leg muscles suddenly gelatinous. "Oh my God."

"Stay in Isa's room and tell Doc I'll fill him in

when I get there. And for the love of the goddess, don't try to fix this. Macha has it handled."

"Evidently not, if Macha let someone destroy my restaurant." She hung up before he could come up with a response. It didn't feel good snipping at him, but neither did dealing with an insurance agent she'd no doubt have to call about the windows.

Bending over, she rested her forehead in her hands and closed her eyes tight. Finding out the truth wasn't supposed to be this messy. *But it is. And I have a feeling it's going to get worse.*

CHAPTER 31
BREWER

HE COULDN'T SEE STRAIGHT. ALL HE SAW WAS RED. AT every stoplight and intersection, crimson blurred his vision. It was one thing to come after Macha, but to fuck up Delphi's bistro was different. It was personal, and he didn't like it one bit.

By now, the whole club knew about the warning. Nikita reached out to her FBI contacts and promised to get security footage from nearby businesses. In the meantime, Rubble sent over a dozen Macha members and prospects to clean up and board the windows until replacements could be found. It all aggravated Brewer more by the minute.

He clenched the handlebars tight and pulled into the hospital lot. Parking, he discarded his helmet and sprinted toward the door. He wasn't about to let someone hurt any of Macha's family who were inside.

Finding Isa's room, he sighed a breath of relief when he noticed Doc outside, his face grim.

"Brewer, glad to see you." He hugged him with one arm. "Rubble filled me in on the situation."

"Thanks for keeping an eye on her." Brewer glanced around the room, relaxing slightly when he saw the woman who made his pulse quicken. "I'll take Delphi back to the clubhouse."

"She won't like it," Jupiter said, poking her nose out the door.

"She won't like it at all," Delphi added, joining her friend.

"Tough nuts." Brewer folded his arms over his chest. "You're coming back with me and staying by my side until we have this figured out."

Delphi shook her head defiantly. "Hell no. I have a restaurant to run. If that means we relocate until windows are in, then fine. We can set up tables on the lawn and serve outside. The weather's been cooperating lately." She grinned, clearly proud of herself for thinking up the scheme. "A romantic, starlit dinner will be a big hit. It'll help make some extra cash too."

Brewer ran his fingers through his hair, yanking on it slightly to keep from barking orders. That wasn't who he was. He barely got involved in fights, let alone protection detail, but for some reason this was different. This was Delphi, and her life meant something more to him. "If I have to toss you over my shoulder, I will."

She crossed her arms over her breasts and narrowed her gaze. "You wouldn't dare."

"Don't bet on it, sweet cheeks." He took a step closer, eyes never deviating from her stubborn ones. "I'd enjoy it, and I know my brothers would too."

For a brief second, Brewer was worried she'd resist him. Instead, Delphi exchanged a glance with Jupiter, who shrugged, before she sighed in defeat.

"Fine, but I was serious about not closing." She shook her finger at him, and he pushed down the urge to kiss it. "My restaurant can't afford to lose customers."

"Why don't you make food for the club instead?" a new voice chimed in from behind him.

Turning, Brewer never thought he'd be glad to see Boulder, the club treasurer.

"I came to see the baby," Boulder said, holding up a pink gift bag. "But I'm serious. It'll give Queenie and the girls some rest and with the picnic this weekend. We could all use some of that."

Knowing Boulder wouldn't suggest it if the club couldn't afford it, Brewer nodded. "I think it's a great idea. Delphi, you still get cash in the door while your windows get fixed, and Macha gets food. Win-win situation."

"I agree. Delphi's food is the best," Isa called from the hospital room.

Brewer looked around Jupiter and Delphi to see Isa nodding with a smile on her face, the newborn glued to her chest. "If Isa approves, you know it's kosher."

"That does seem like a no-brainer," Delphi finally relented. "All right. I hope the club likes French food because that's all I have to offer."

Boulder patted his big belly and walked toward the room. "We like all food, don't worry about that."

Everyone laughed, even Brewer. A weight lifted from his shoulders, but then pressed back down when Delphi walked his way. Her expression was frustrated, no doubt from the way he spoke to her.

"Delphi—"

"Save it, Macha man." She brushed past him, her focus on the exit. "I need to clean up the restaurant. My staff is probably working overtime."

"Already taken care of," Doc said, waving his phone. "Rubble just sent a message saying they have it covered."

Delphi turned around but didn't look altogether pleased by being thwarted. "Okay, but I need to pick up some clothes."

"We can do that."

"You have it all figured out, don't you?" She rolled her eyes, and Brewer swore then and there he'd bend her over and smack her ass for more than one rebellious act that afternoon.

"When it comes to your safety, yes, I do." He waved goodbye to the rest of his family, then followed her out the doors. Delphi was a strong, independent entrepreneur, but he'd make sure she understood the severity of the situation. Protecting her would either drive him insane or bring them closer.

CHAPTER 32
DELPHI

The small restaurant was a mess. Glass covered the tables and floors. *But it could be worse. Thankfully, no one was hurt.* She took a cleansing breath and reminded herself of that twice more before hopping on the back of Brewer's bike.

Macha sent enough men over to clean up, and after she sent the staff home, Delphi felt comfortable enough to leave. Four prospects would stay at the shop overnight to see if anything else happened. She doubted anything would, as did Brewer.

Brewer didn't say a word to her. Not on the ride to the clubhouse. Not when they arrived and walked through the halls. And not even when he opened his bedroom door and tossed her backpack on his bed.

Joining her bag, Delphi watched him pace the

room. The sun was almost gone, the last streams of its light coming through his window.

"Until Shovelhead is caught, you can't go off on your own."

She crossed her legs over each other and pulled out a book. He could save the speech, but he wouldn't. Cracking open the romance novel Jupiter had recommended, she tried to focus on the words.

"Delphi, I'm serious."

"Okay, I won't go anywhere without a body-guard." She glanced up and saw the frown beneath his red beard. "Happy now?"

"Not even remotely."

Returning her gaze to the book, she reread the same page. It didn't do her any good. Not when Brewer's eyes were glued to her. She wouldn't give him the satisfaction of putting the book down yet.

"Club life can be very difficult."

"I've gathered as much." She turned a page.

"Particularly for women."

This got her attention. "Why? Doesn't Macha revere them?"

"Yes, but other clubs don't, hence the prob-lem." He crouched next to the bed, his face a combination of concern and frustration. "MCs we don't get along with take what's ours too often, thinking it'll get us to back down. It never works.

In fact, it creates more reason for Macha to get involved."

"But I'm not yours, Brewer. I'm not anyone's. I'm the bastard child of a traitorous biker."

Grabbing the book, Brewer tossed it to the other side of the bed. He gripped her chin in his hand. "Don't you dare say that. You're mine, Delphi. I don't care what anyone else says. I don't even care who your biological father is." His gaze softened. "I love you, Delphi, and that means you're my person. Mine and nobody else's. I'll do anything to keep you safe."

Tears sprang to her eyes, his words hitting a chord deep in her soul. "You… you love me?"

"You think I'd say it if I didn't mean it?"

She searched his blue eyes, the truth emanating from their gorgeous depths. "No. I don't think you'd say anything you didn't mean."

Brewer moved to the edge of the bed and cupped her face. "I'd only lie to keep you safe, sweet cheeks, and I wouldn't like doing it either."

She didn't realize tears had fallen until he tenderly wiped them away with his thumbs. "I love you too, Brewer. I think I have for a while but was too afraid to admit it."

A broad smile covered his bearded face. "About damn time you admitted it."

He kissed her before she could offer a sassy

remark. His tongue met hers and she moaned, slipping her arms around his shoulders and drawing him further onto the bed.

"Wait." She pulled her lips free and sat back. "What about the club and their vendetta against Shovelhead?"

He slid into the spot next to her and pulled her against his chest. "Shovelhead has a lot to account for when it comes to Macha. But if you want him saved, I'll do everything in my power to make it happen."

"Even if he killed your parents?"

His features tightened, the decision clearly splitting him in half. "Yeah, Delphi, even then." He kissed her brow. "They're gone. Nothing I do is going to bring them back. But you...." He tilted her chin up, his eyes shimmering with love. "You're right here in my arms and in my bed. I can't lose you. If it comes down to it, I choose you over revenge every time."

Delphi swallowed down the emotions that so desperately wanted to escape. She wasn't sure how to react. He'd spent the last year tracking down Shovelhead, the man who had potentially killed his parents, and then he'd give up all retribution for her. It didn't sit well in her gut.

Brewer's tongue drifted over the side of her throat, his attempts to quell her thoughts almost succeeding.

"But, Brewer, what about Dolly? She's even more set on—"

He placed his hand over her mouth and shook his head. "Delphi, we just exchanged the most important three words in existence, and you want to talk about my sister?"

She bit her bottom lip. "No, I guess not."

Rolling her beneath him, Brewer kissed her until she felt light-headed. "Good, because all I want to do right now is make love to you. Can I do that?"

"How could I resist such an offer?" she teased, kissing the base of his throat.

Brewer wiggled his eyebrows and immediately got to work on her shirt. Delphi pushed pause on their shared Shovelhead problem. They'd deal with it later. For this night, all they wanted was to celebrate their love. Delphi had no doubt they'd be doing simply that all night long.

THE FIRST NIGHT SHE'D STEPPED INTO BOOZE & Tattoos, Delphi liked it. Then again, she'd also been with her best friend, Jupiter, ready to sing her heart out. Tonight, she sat in one of the corner booths and scanned the bar. The photo above the booth had a small plaque beneath it that said RK and Alannah. It didn't take her long to figure out that the couple smiling back at her were Brewer and Dolly's parents. If the bright red hair wasn't a dead giveaway, Alannah's blue eyes hit it home. A part of Delphi felt guilty for sitting there. She was most probably the daughter of the man who slaughtered those loving faces. *I really hope Shovelhead didn't kill them.*

Swallowing the shot of whiskey, she focused her gaze on Brewer behind the bar. Dwelling on his parents would get her nowhere good. She loved their son. *Surely that rights a wrong.*

"You doing okay?" a nymph asked, breaking into Delphi's musings.

"Uh, yeah, thanks." She watched the thin woman walk away and couldn't help but stare at her shapely ass and solid C-cup breasts. She wasn't drop-dead gorgeous, but some of the other nymphs were. *What a place to grow up.* She shook her head and noticed Brewer making margaritas for the two women sitting at the bar. *And what an environment to be in day in and day out.* He was consistently surrounded by beautiful women. Instead of being jealous, Delphi felt a sense of pride. He chose her. Even though they hadn't discussed what that meant outside the bedroom, she trusted him.

The song overhead ended, and a popular country anthem came on next. A group of men in overalls whooped with joy and she smirked. Snowshoe was many things, but the town's collective love of country music would never change.

After taking a sip of the Guinness, Delphi sat back and closed her eyes. The sounds of the bar and tattoo parlor mingled together. From teasing voices to the noisy tattoo guns, she found she rather liked the harmonies.

"You look way too comfortable here," Brewer's teasing voice said.

Opening her eyes, she grinned cheekily. "Isn't that how I should feel?"

He slid into the booth across from her. "Yeah, I'm glad. A little surprised, but definitely glad to hear it."

Delphi stretched lazily. Coming here after the bistro closed wore on her, but she wanted to see Brewer as often as possible. Not being near him felt wrong.

"You want to go back to my place tonight?" she offered. "I need to feed the cat. She'll yell at me tomorrow if I don't."

"Works for me." Brewer scratched his chin, but his eyes weren't on her anymore. Following his gaze, she swallowed hard at the sight of a group of men who walked into the bar. From their cuts, it was obvious they were Greenback Cutthroats. A sense of dread filled her stomach.

"Maybe I should go home now."

Reaching across the table, he grabbed her hand and squeezed it once. "If you want to go, I'll take you now. But if you only want to get away from that crowd, don't let them scare you off." His blue eyes searched her. "Nobody fucks with my girl. And nobody fucks around in Macha's bar. If those boys want anything other than booze, I'll kick them out. I don't care what patch they're wearing."

Squeezing his hand back, she offered him a tiny smile. "You're really a big teddy bear, aren't you?"

He growled in a low tone and wiggled his eyebrows up and down. "If that's what you want, then hell yes, sweet cheeks." He stood and leaned down. "Don't you forget what I said. You're mine. Nobody will mess with you in my bar or my club." He kissed her hard, and she had to catch her breath when he pulled back. "Got it?"

Delphi nodded mutely. She wasn't sure she could put a sentence together if she tried. The love Brewer made her feel after one kiss was ten times the amount any other man had shown her. Sighing, she watched him walk back to the bar. His presence dominated the space. This was his domain. This was clearly evident in the ways the nymphs and bikers treated him with respect. Even if he wasn't wearing his Macha cut, his role in the club was clear.

Pulling out her phone, Delphi reviewed her social media accounts. Nothing on them held her attention. Not when her eyes constantly gravitated to Brewer. She could get used to coming here on a daily or weekly basis. His lithe movements and easy smile were addictive. Watching him was more than enough entertainment. She pressed her legs together. She couldn't wait until she was all alone with him in her bed.

CHAPTER 33

BREWER

The day of the city picnic, the sky was filled with big, fluffy clouds. The tint of gray worried Brewer at first, but Snowshoe was more than prepared for the chance of rain. Everywhere he looked, tents had popped up with vendors inside them, ready to share and sell their goods.

"Need me to grab anything else?" he asked, his arms full of folding chairs.

Yasmina and Delphi looked his way while Jupiter kept unfolding the chairs. After he and Rubble finished hauling the necessities to the tent, the setup was nearly complete.

Delphi shook her head, unpackaging the plastic silverware and paper plates. "I think we're good."

"The mayor said he'll make announcements in an hour," Brewer filled in. He'd gotten up early for the

Snowshoe city meeting and was damned glad he hadn't missed it. The local authorities had also been there, and Brewer was among the tight-knit group that discussed Macha's upcoming plan to corner Shovelhead.

"Great. We'll be ready by then." Yasmina grinned and walked around the table that held the cash register. The two shops would share any of the profits from the day, and the main courses were offered on a donation basis for the women's shelter.

He finished placing the last chair at the long table and watched the trio of women scurry around, trying to prepare for the incoming onslaught of hungry citizens from Snowshoe and Waverley.

Gripping the back of one of the chairs, Brewer's pulse quickened the longer he took in Delphi's fluid movements. Her hair was partially pinned out of her face, the rest spiraling down the light brown cardigan she was wearing over her maroon shirt. Knee-high boots covered leggings with a spring-inspired design, her ass tempting him to reach out and smack it.

All in all, every inch of his girl was scrumptious. His dick pulsed and he adjusted his jeans. *Not now.* There swas enough time to sneak her away, but he wouldn't suggest it. Not when her nerves were already bundled and frantic due to meeting Shovelhead sometime during the picnic. The exact time it would happen was unknown, keeping her and all of Macha on high alert.

Delphi had woken early that morning, sleep having evaded her but not from his doing. The day meant a lot to both of them, but it might almost mean more to her. Brewer watched her now as she brushed powdered sugar over a plate of beignets from the bakery, a sprinkling landing on her shirt. She seemed off today. He couldn't blame her for being uncertain about what the day would bring.

"Brewer, can you give me a hand with the last table?" Rubble asked, breaking into his observations.

"Yeah, you bet." He moved toward the line of vehicles parked on the street. The town square was quickly filling with people from both cities.

"She ready for this?" Rubble flipped down the tailgate and hopped into the truck bed.

Brewer grabbed the end and pulled the table closer to the edge. "As ready as she can be. I think she's pretty nervous."

Jumping down, Rubble nodded. "Don't blame her." He grabbed the other side of the lightweight table. There was no need for both men to hold it, either one more than capable, but it allowed them to step away for a brief moment. "Our guys are scattered throughout the square. Got two guys on scopes at opposite ends if the need arises too."

"I wish all this wasn't necessary." They stopped before they reached the tent.

"It's Shovelhead, Brewer. Of course it's necessary."

"I know, I know." He shook his head. "And who knows who else he has on his payroll? Just sucks that Delphi has to see all this."

Rubble pushed up his cap and scratched his forehead. "My guys are well camouflaged. Unless Shovelhead does something dickish, she'll never see them."

"Let's hope not." He patted the table. "Better get this to them before one of the girls comes looking for us."

Grunting, Rubble picked it up by himself. "Knowing those three, it'll be my old lady. She'd haul it herself if I let her."

"Got to love gutsy women," Brewer said with a smirk.

Rubble nodded appreciatively. "Especially in the bedroom."

Brewer chuckled and walked past him. Macha's bikers did their fair share of bragging, but when it came to old ladies, the men were far more selective in telling stories, but Rubble and Jupiter's bedroom antics wasn't something he wanted to dwell on right then.

Coming up behind Delphi, he wrapped his arms around her waist. "How're you holding up?"

She smiled, pausing her hands above the tray of madeleines. "Pretty well, all things considered." She kissed his cheek, then returned to her work. "What're you going to be doing during all this?"

A crowd had started closing in on the focal point in the center of the lawn. Snowshoe's mayor stood with Waverley's on the elevated stage, testing the microphone.

Brewer checked the time. "Hanging around the tent."

"Is that why you're in regular clothes?" She gestured toward his plain sweatshirt. Not wearing his cut overtop felt weird, but it was necessary.

"Yeah. We're all trying to blend in." He looked across the square. "Except at Macha's tent. It's easier this way."

Delphi rearranged the desserts on the tables. "Makes sense. Shovelhead is probably already wary of showing up at a town event where Macha will be participating."

Brewer caught her between his arms before she could return behind the table. Meeting her gaze, he swore to himself at the timidness he saw in her beautiful eyes. "It's going to be all right, sweet cheeks." He squeezed her ass for good measure, and a smile crossed her face in response. "After today, it'll be a cake walk."

She rolled her eyes. "Yeah, right."

He kissed her soundly, hoping his confidence transferred to her. She needed every ounce he could spare. "You got this."

"I know." She playfully tugged on his beard. "Thanks, Brewer. No matter what happens today, I'm glad I walked into your bar."

"Me too." He hugged her tight. "More than you know."

Delphi let go before he did. Brewer made himself scarce at the tent, but not before assuring her he wouldn't be far. Shovelhead knew who he was, so keeping out of sight was the best course of action.

He exchanged a glance with Rubble from across the lawn. The picnic was set to last three hours. It was time to see if Shovelhead meant to keep his promise to his daughter or not.

CHAPTER 34
DELPHI

The first hour and a half of the picnic flew by before Delphi had the chance to take a break. Yasmina operated the register while Jupiter and she manned the buffet assembly. Two of her waitstaff assisted with cleanup while people milled from tent to tent, trying all the delicious cuisine.

"Can someone grab more buttered rolls?" Yasmina asked, giving away the last one.

"Got it," Delphi offered. She could use a breather, and her stomach needed one of the freshly baked rolls she could eat on the way back.

Grabbing four empty trays, Delphi walked to the truck to replenish them. She rustled through the totes, finding the rolls Yasmina requested before she stepped away.

"Delphi Windsor?"

She paused and turned toward the gruff voice. A man in his early sixties stood next to the truck. His silver hair was longer than average, faded tattoos standing out against sun-weathered skin. She didn't have to ask to know who he was, but she found herself doing it anyways.

"Who's asking?"

The man stepped closer, his boots clinking on the pavement. "Shovelhead. I heard you wanted to meet me."

He didn't offer an outstretched hand or friendly embrace, not that she expected it from a man she'd known nothing of until last summer.

Dropping the rolls, Delphi nodded and shut the door. "Yeah, I did."

Shovelhead pulled the handkerchief off his head, exposing a receding hairline. "Well, I'm here."

She crossed her arms over her chest. "I don't know what I was expecting, but it definitely wasn't this." She shook her head at her idiocy. It was clear this man didn't give a shit.

"Why do you think I'm your dad?" he asked, glancing around at the passing vehicles.

He wasn't comfortable there. *Good.* She didn't want him anywhere near comfortable. The desire to send Brewer a message gnawed at her, but she resisted. If she tipped off Macha, she'd get no answers.

"Why don't we talk?" She motioned to a nearby bench.

Nodding, Shovelhead led them to a shaded area. They both sat down, leaving a good three feet of space between them.

"My mother was Marjory Windsor." She watched his face for any recognition, but his features didn't change. "She died last summer. She and my dad." Delphi tucked her hands beneath her thighs, memories flooding to the surface. "My dad admitted he wasn't my biological father. He mentioned a biker named Shovelhead, so unless there's another one, I think you're it."

The biker unzipped his leather jacket, his face turning a light shade of red. His beady, dark eyes seemed to be latched on the tree in the distance while he digested her words. "Are you sure?"

She nodded. "There's only one definitive way to know."

Shovelhead turned to face her. "I can't be your dad, Delphi. I'm not fit, for starters."

"I'm not asking you to be one. I wanted to meet you, that's all. I have zero expectations." She shrugged. It was the truth. The only part she left out was Macha's involvement in her life.

"How'd you find me?"

"I stopped by the Rusty Cantina. One of the girls said you frequented the restaurant and offered to help."

He seemed to accept the answer she and Brewer concocted that morning. It wasn't false. *Technically.*

"It's possible I'm your dad." Shovelhead sighed. "There were quite a few ladies back then." He chuckled. "But I do remember an MJ. She looked a lot like you. Well, I guess it's the other way around, isn't it?"

Delphi wasn't sure if his admittance should comfort or perturb her. If her mother was simply another notch on his endless bedpost, why would he know her name?

"If you remember her, maybe you two were together."

He shook his head. "I've never done relationships. Too much drama."

"Surely she meant more than just one night," she pressed. There was more to the story, and she'd be damned if she didn't get it out of him.

A cloud shaded the sun's usually bright rays, casting them in a dark shadow. Shovelhead rubbed his wrinkled hands up and down his thighs.

"You sure you want to hear this, girl?"

"Absolutely."

He picked at a scab on the back of his knuckles,

eyes averted. "Your mom was a club hopper back then."

Delphi's eyes bugged and she choked on her saliva. "Excuse me?"

Shovelhead shrugged and leaned back against the bench. "You heard me right. MJ was well known around the clubs."

"Which clubs?" Her stomach felt queasy. She couldn't accept his words. Surely he was lying.

"The Greenback Cutthroats for the most part, but I'd seen her at Macha too, on occasion."

Leaning over, she breathed in through her nose and exhaled out her mouth. "No, no, that's not possible. My mom was a kindergarten teacher."

"Yeah, she was, but only afterward. During college, MJ…. Well, she was popular with the MCs."

The food in Delphi's stomach crept up her throat. Suddenly, the truth didn't seem so important. "I think I'm going to be sick."

Shovelhead offered her a weak smile. "Sorry, kid. Either way, I might be your daddy, but there are plenty of other possibilities." He looked her over and she tried not to squirm under the intense scrutiny. "I don't see any resemblances between us. You kind of remind me of a guy from back then, but no clue if your mom slept with him too."

Delphi covered her mouth, bile rising faster than

she could control. Before she could stop it, she leaned behind the bench and emptied the remnants of her breakfast.

A large hand patted her back, but she felt anything but reassured. *No wonder Mom wanted to keep me away from the clubs. One of the bikers was my dad, and she didn't know which one.* Avoiding clubs meant she could keep avoiding the truth and also keep Delphi from anyone else she was potentially related to. Considering her mother remained adamant about that, then her father must still be around Snowshoe somewhere.

Sitting up, she wiped her mouth. A flash of metal caught her eye, and she noticed Brewer closing in on them. Rubble flanked his left, with more Macha bikers heading their direction. A new surge of bitterness crawled up her throat, but she pushed it down. There'd be time to discuss this with Brewer later.

"Your mom was a good lady. Really sweet and quite the looker."

"Yeah, I guess."

He chuckled. "I mean it. MJ was special. It's probably why your dad was so insistent on getting her out of club life."

His words temporarily calmed her. Even if the man she grew up calling Dad wasn't biologically hers, he was still ten times the man who'd impregnated her mother.

"I'm not a good man, Delphi." His eyes momentarily met hers. "I'm the worst kind, in fact. You'd do yourself good staying as far away from me as possible."

"What do you mean?" She straightened, needing to hear more even if it'd make her sick again. "What'd you do?"

The sun peeked out from behind the clouds, and Shovelhead closed his eyes. When he opened them again, she noticed a sense of urgency in his words. If he'd seen the approaching MC members, he didn't let on.

"I've betrayed my closest friends, deceived my brothers and sisters and committed the worst sins, all for money."

"Then it's true."

"What is?"

"That you killed two Macha bikers."

He smiled sadly. "I've done worse than that, if you'd believe it. I deserve every and any punishment that's heading my way."

Delphi felt Brewer's presence before he rested a hand on her shoulder.

"Then I guess I don't feel bad about what's going

to happen next," she said, standing up. "I'm sorry it had to be this way, Shovelhead."

Taking her hands in his, Shovelhead squeezed them twice. "But you should know, if I'm not him, your real daddy's out there. If I were you, I'd stop looking for him. No good can come of it. If your momma didn't tell you, there was a reason."

Rubble and Hawk each grabbed one of Shovelhead's arms while Snoopy took his side piece.

"I'd say it's good to see you again, boys, but it's not." Shovelhead stood up but didn't take his gaze from Delphi. "If I'm not back at my clubhouse by midnight, they'll send someone for me. And if they think you're my daughter, you'll be the first person they take."

Rubble and Hawk manhandled him in the opposite direction. "Mark my words," he called before the group of bikers escorted him from the town center.

Delphi watched him go, unable to look away until he was completely out of sight. Brewer stayed by her side. He hadn't touched her anywhere but her shoulder, and she found she desperately needed him to.

Standing up, she turned to face him, tears flowing down her cheeks. "Did you know about my mom?"

"No." He shook his head. "If I did, I would've said something."

"I don't know if I can believe him."

She moved closer and rested her forehead on his chest. Brewer wrapped his arms around her, bringing her against him fully.

"If you want to find out, we can, Delphi." He tilted up her chin, his blue eyes lined with concern. "But if you don't, that's okay too."

She thought it over for the tenth time since Shovelhead's bombshell. "I can't. I need to know who my biological dad is even if I won't like the answer."

He brushed a chaste kiss on her forehead. "Then I'll help in any way I can, and so will Macha."

"Thank you." She wrapped her arms around him and buried her face in his sweatshirt that smelled of motorcycle oil and cedar. "Is the picnic over?"

Brewer's right hand smoothed her hair. "It is for you."

She stepped back. "But what about Jupiter and Yasmina? They need my help."

Turning her to face the tent, he chuckled. "I think between the nymphs and prospects who stepped in, they more than have it covered." He grabbed her hand. "C'mon, sweet cheeks. We're off to wherever you want. Home? The clubhouse? Your choice."

Delphi wiped the tears from her cheeks. She desired an answer to the question that had burned in her mind over the last year. Brewer offered her a boyish grin. But she also wanted to escape from the havoc the recent meeting had caused. Only Brewer could offer such an escape.

"Let's go to the clubhouse." She pressed her hand against his lips to keep him from replying. "But only so we're there in case I change my mind about wanting to talk to Shovelhead after we're done in your room."

Brewer lifted his brows. "And what do you think is going to happen in my room, young lady?"

She rose up and kissed him. "Whatever we want."

He cradled her face, deepening the kiss. "Needing a distraction?"

"Something like that."

"Well, I'll do everything in my power to make sure you get it." He picked her up off the ground, and she giggled when he swatted her ass. "But afterward, I want to hear every damn word he said to you."

"Deal."

Delphi laughed louder when he practically skipped toward his motorcycle. She may not have the truth, but she had something better. *Someone* better. A man who loved her.

CHAPTER 35
BREWER

Watching the rhythmic rise and fall of Delphi's chest made Brewer's tighten in response. He reached over and pushed the few strands of hair out her face, holding his breath when she stirred.

When they reached the clubhouse, she'd poured her heart out. It killed him to hear Shovelhead's words regurgitated like that. He couldn't be mad at her for needing the truth. *Or at least the truth as Shovelhead sees it.*

Brewer carefully climbed out of the bed and turned to see Delphi move slightly. The sheet fell away, exposing the curve of her breast. The desire to softly kiss it until she woke overwhelmed him. He shook his head. She needed to rest, and he needed to find out what his brothers had done with Shovelhead.

Slipping on his clothes, he silently promised to make it up to her. He wasn't sure how, but he'd find a way. He pulled on his cut, the scent of leather invading his nostrils. It was one he'd grown up craving. Being part of Macha was all he'd ever dreamt of.

Delphi let out a small snore and his stomach dropped. He walked over to the bed, pulse pounding in his eardrums. But now all he wanted was Delphi. He gently ran his thumb along her soft skin. All he craved was Delphi. She was his new dream. Macha may be the club's goddess, but Delphi was his.

The basement of Macha's lodge had never looked so damning. What most visitors didn't know was that the secret door hidden at the very back of the liquor storage led to another more menacing room. The lighting was dingy at best, but none of Macha's patches seemed to mind. Their focus was on the man strapped to the metal chair in the center of the fortified room. Macha didn't fuck around with traitors. They had a specific location to deal with them.

Brewer cautiously glanced around at his brothers. Not one looked happy to be there. Hell, he'd rather be cozied up with Delphi than have the stench of stale sweat linger in his nostrils. This part wasn't what he liked about club life. *But we have no other choice. He's a traitor.*

Reaper took a step forward, a large leather-clad book in his hands. His tiny glasses looked out of place on his nose, almost as if he should be holed up in a library instead of staring at a man they all used to love.

"Shovelhead, you're accused of sabotaging Macha and her members. How do you plead?"

Shovelhead spit blood mixed with saliva on the floor in response to Reaper's question. He managed a slight grin, his lower lip cracking from having been repeatedly punched. "You're not the law. Hand me over to them, and I'll take my chances."

A rumble of discourse spread through the tight-knit group of men, but none moved. They stayed in their spots despite the murder written on their faces. Brewer had only seen one other judgment day before now. No one betrayed Macha.

Reaper met Brewer's eyes and nodded once. Tugging on Dolly's arm, Brewer stepped toward Shovelhead. They weren't the only two who had beef with the man in question, but they'd lost the most.

Dolly reared back and punched Shovelhead in the gut before anyone could react. He doubled over, and she yanked on his hair until he met her gaze. "Did you kill my parents?"

"And what if I did?" he snarled.

Dolly's blue eyes flashed with fury. She tightened her grip until Shovelhead winced with pain. "Speak the truth, motherfucker. You aren't getting out of this room intact until you do."

Brewer had to hand it to his little sister. She was venom and acid when she got going. It was a wonder she'd never demanded the club change its rules so she could patch. She'd be one hell of a member.

"Look, I did some bad shit, but I did it on my own. Nobody else from this club was involved." Shovelhead's eyes swiveled to the president. "I worked with other clubs and set up Macha to take the blame for the trafficking shit with the Cutthroats and Diablos. I took some cash off the top whenever I got the chance. I'm not the devil here. I'm just a product of my environment."

Not able to hold back his rage any longer, Brewer's fist connected with Shovelhead's nose. Blood sprayed the air, droplets landing on Brewer's vest. "Did you kill our parents?" He gripped the front of Shovelhead's bloodstained shirt. "I won't ask you again."

A glimmer of fear crossed the other man's dark eyes. "Yes. Yes, I killed your ma and pa. They kept sticking their noses in where they didn't belong. They would've exposed my allegiance to the Greenback Cutthroats and Diablos. If I hadn't, someone else would've. Better to end it quick than make them suffer. Diablos wanted a slow death. I was kind to put them out like I did."

The room went silent, then erupted into a flurry of curses and calls for vengeance. Brewer dropped his hold on Shovelhead and watched as Dolly screamed and pommeled her fists into the man. After all this time, the truth was out in the open. The weight of their deaths lessened on his shoulders. Where he expected a need for retaliation, his brain could only process grief. Tears dripped down his cheeks and into his beard. He didn't try to hide them. He'd waited so long to hear it from the murderer's lips that now all he wanted to do was leave. Leave the pain behind him and never look back.

"Everybody, shut it!" Rubble growled, prying Dolly off Shovelhead's bloody body.

Dolly opened her mouth to argue, but one glare from Rubble made her stop. "We aren't done with him yet," she stated instead.

Rubble shook his head. "No, you're not, but neither am I. There are still some questions Macha needs answers to. Shovelhead will pay for his betrayal." His mismatched eyes swept over the room. "But we won't become murderers in the process."

The bikers started talking all at once again. Snoopy called for the ultimate punishment while Hawk wanted to see Shovelhead eat the burned patch. Three months ago, Brewer would've joined them. But now, he wasn't sure what to feel. He didn't know how it was possible. One thing was certain: he had to find the answer to Delphi's paternity.

Finding Doc at the other end of the room, Brewer lowered his voice. "Think you can get a DNA swab from this guy?"

Doc pulled out a small vial with a swab brush in it. "Already ahead of you, brother." He handed it over. "Nikita offered the FBI's help with this. Get Delphi's and Shovelhead's DNA over to her, and she'll have the lab run it."

Brewer tucked the tube into his breast pocket. "Thanks, Doc."

"You'd do the same for me." Doc's brows furrowed when Boulder and Cueball started wailing on Shovelhead again. "For as upstanding an MC as we are, I don't think I'll ever get used to this part."

"Not something we usually have to do." Brewer eyed the man who had patched the previous year. "I hope to the goddess neither of us has to see it again."

Doc nodded, then sighed. "Better go check his

vitals. Don't wanna drop a dead man on the sheriff's door."

Brewer watched Doc cut through the crowd toward Shovelhead. The malice seemed to pause for the moment, and suddenly all Brewer craved was a stiff shot of whiskey.

Rubble whistled, and the room went quiet once more. "Doc says the traitor needs a bit of rest. Grab a drink and be back in an hour."

Grumblings echoed, but none of the men dared to talk back with Rubble's steely gaze simply waiting for someone to get out of line. The brute may be a kindred spirit with his old lady, but every man in Macha feared the ex-MMA fighter for good reason.

Brewer waited until the room emptied. He remained, along with Dolly, Doc, and Reaper. Each pair of eyes were fastened to Shovelhead. Dolly's makeup was smeared from rubbing her eyes and crying. He didn't blame her one bit. They'd both found out the reason their parents died. It wasn't an easy thing to swallow.

He looped his arm around Dolly's shoulders and pulled her into his chest. Her body shook with silent sobs, and he squeezed her tighter. Dolly'd been one foot out the door since their parents' death, but now he wasn't sure how much longer she'd stay Macha's madam. Not with her own love life taking a turn for the better.

He met Reaper's eyes and immediately recognized the wear and tear on the older man. Years at the helm of Macha showed in his eyes. He'd step down in a month, and it wasn't a secret whom Reaper wanted as his successor. Doc was a shoo-in, but it'd be a close call for both president and VP.

"I can't do it," Brewer said softly. "Surely you understand."

Reaper smiled sadly. "Boyo, it's not up to me anymore. The club votes in two weeks. You have until then to convince them you're not up for a cabinet gig."

Doc cleared his throat, finished with his examination. "If it makes you feel any better, Brewer, Isa absolutely hates the idea of me in charge too."

Brewer rested his chin on the top of Dolly's head. "Not really. You were born to lead. I sling drinks, and I'm good at it."

"But you've also managed to capture Macha's traitor," Reaper pointed out.

"Only because of Delphi." His sister smacked him in the gut and pulled away. "And Dolly."

Dolly wiped at her eyes and nodded. "Fuck yeah."

"Women are what make Macha great. Not the men. They should be in leadership roles."

Tucking his small glasses into the pocket on his vest, Reaper walked over and handed Brewer the leather book. The cover was faded, but he knew the words scribbled on the pages. It was Macha's code and duties. He'd read the book more times than he could recall.

"Don't let your fear govern your future." Reaper clasped the back of Brewer's neck, blue eyes watery. "Your da was a great man. Your mum died protecting him. Whatever happens, you'll make them proud." He pressed a fatherly kiss to Brewer's forehead, then walked out of the room.

Brewer choked back his emotions. He'd always looked up to Reaper, and the thought of him not being around as much didn't sit well with him.

"We all grow up, big brother," Dolly said, nudging him gently. "And now we can move forward without that scumbag." She jerked a thumb over her shoulder and nodded once before she hurried out of the room. She'd need time to grieve but would leave the rest of Shovelhead's fate to the club.

Brewer stood there, staring at Shovelhead for a moment longer before he turned on his heels and left the bastard behind. He didn't need to see what happened to Shovelhead. The club wouldn't kill him. They would make him eat his burned patch and beat him to the brink of death's embrace, but then they'd turn him over to the law. He could live with that. He didn't need to be part of the ritual, though. He had a new reason to live, and she was snuggled in his bed.

CHAPTER 36
DELPHI

The days passed in a blur. Between fixing up her restaurant and spending time with Brewer at Macha's clubhouse, Delphi almost forgot about the tiny little DNA detail. Almost.

She cracked her knuckles and stared at the television. The cooking competition usually kept her attention, but not after Brewer called, saying he had the paternity results. She sat on the edge of the couch, knees bouncing up and down. The drive from the clubhouse wasn't long, but to her, it felt like hours. She'd unlocked the door in anticipation of Brewer's arrival, and even her favorite cuddle bug couldn't ease her anxiety.

Fiona purred happily on her lap. Having the old feline around kept her company all through her adulthood thus far, and she couldn't imagine life without a cat.

"Delphi, you really should lock the door. You never know who might drop by to visit."

The blood in Delphi's veins cooled at the sound of the familiar yet unwelcome male voice. She turned her head and held in a gasp at sight of the biker standing mere feet away. "Grant, what the hell are you doing here?"

The Cutthroat with bleach-blond hair waved his three brothers into the room. "I'm here for you, baby." He grinned, but it was anything but friendly. "You've had those pesky Macha bikers swarming around you lately. I almost thought you converted to the good boy side of the MC." His brown eyes dipped to her robe, and she rushed to cover up her silky pajamas underneath. "Either you knew I was coming, or you were hoping that redhead was on his way."

Delphi swallowed the bile in her throat. "Fuck off, Grant. You and I are not together. Why can't you leave me alone?"

He sauntered toward her, his leather pants creaking with his movements. "Because I know someone you don't." He stood in front of her now. "It's about your daddy issues."

Her eyes whipped to his face. "What are you talking about?"

"I know who your bastard dad is."

"Grant—"

He flipped her coffee table over, glass shattering on the floor. "For fuck's sake, Delphi, you know my name's Granite."

She bit the inside of her cheek. His temper wasn't something she'd forgotten. It was ingrained in her memory. If she sassed him too much, she wasn't so certain what he'd do. The Grant she knew in high school was gone. This biker had replaced him. From their last run-in, she definitely didn't want to know the new Grant.

"I'm sorry. I forgot."

The anger on his face waned, and he nodded. "Good. Now, let's go." He grabbed her by the arm, and she cried out at the strength in his grip. "My club has information you want."

"Macha has the same information," she stonewalled. When that didn't entice a response from him, she added, "Brewer is on his way here right now."

Granite clenched his jaw and pulled her to his chest. Cigarette smoke and tequila lingered on his breath, and she tried not to gag. "Are you his old lady?"

She worried her lips together, uncertain how to answer. Technically, she wasn't, but Brewer claimed her as his every chance he got. "Um—"

"That's a no." Granite sneered. "Let's get out of here before your Macha boy tries to save you."

"I'm wearing pajamas."

Granite narrowed his gaze. "Stop stalling. I don't give a shit what you're wearing. You can borrow one of my shirts when we get back to Waverley." He pinched her ass. "Now, get going before I change my mind and make you get dressed in front of my brothers here."

Delphi's eyes darted to the other men in the room. Each one wore a crude smile. She immediately wished she could transport herself somewhere else. "I'll wait."

"Good girl." He kissed the top of her head. "Smells like sunshine and French food."

"Can I at least grab some shoes?"

The rumble of a bike outside snapped Granite out of whatever patience he had left. "Not today." He hoisted her over his shoulder, and Delphi noticed a gleam of metal in his open hand. "Don't squirm too much, or you might get shot."

Delphi punched Granite in the back, and he chuckled darkly. "Girl, keep it up, and I'll set the club on your plump ass. More than one would like to sample a piece of you."

Shivers ran down her spine at the threat. As bad as she wanted to escape, she couldn't.

When they stepped outside, a cool drizzle met her exposed legs. She craned her neck, trying to see if Brewer was there yet. Granite hurried across the lawn, bouncing her uncomfortably as he did. It wasn't until she was strapped to him on the back of his bike that Brewer's worried face caught her attention.

He stood at the restaurant entrance, scouring the surroundings for her.

"Brewer!" she screamed before Granite reared back and smacked her across the face. "Shut up, you bitch."

"Delphi!"

She opened her mouth to yell again, but Granite revved his engine, and the Cutthroats zoomed passed Brewer before he could hop on his bike. She couldn't ignore the three shots fired at him, but when she looked over her shoulder, Delphi sighed when she spotted Brewer fully intact.

"Why couldn't you just tell me about my dad?" she yelled over the hum of the bike.

"Because your daddy wants to meet you, and I want to fuck you."

The blood drained from her face, and she felt her breakfast rise in her throat. She couldn't go down that road again with Grant, but she needed to find out who her biological father was. She was on her way to the Cutthroat den where she'd face more than one beast. She only hoped she'd survive what would happen next.

CHAPTER 37

BREWER

"This isn't about the goddamn election!" Brewer slammed his fists on the table. Every patched member went silent. "The Cutthroats took Delphi."

"How do you know she didn't want to go with them?" Hawk asked. "You said she used to date one."

"Years ago," he growled. "She was wearing a robe. I don't think she wanted to go. They forced her."

Reaper nodded. "I agree. It doesn't sound like she had a choice. Rubble, what strategy will work best here?"

Rubble finished his sip of water. "We just wiped our asses with the Cutthroats, so they're down several members."

"Doesn't that make them more dangerous?" Doc piped up.

"Most likely, yeah." Rubble pulled out his phone and scanned it. "My contact at the Rusty Cantina said your girl's there. We can't crash into the place and turn it upside down, but we can go and try to settle this with minimal violence."

"Fuck minimal violence." Brewer shook his head. "Delphi doesn't have a gun. She wasn't trained to fight. She's a chef." His stomach turned at the thought of his woman being touched by another man, let alone a Cutthroat who had no decency whatsoever.

"Shovelhead isn't her dad." He held up the piece of paper Nikita gave to him moments before he hopped on his bike to meet Delphi. "I think one of the Cutthroats is, which is why they took her."

"Delphi deserves to know who her father is," Boulder added. "Thank the goddess it wasn't Shovelhead."

A round of grunts echoed in the room. He was grateful for that fact as well.

"Does Nikita know any of the dolls there?"

Kevlar sat up a little straighter. "Yeah, I think Kita still has a few contacts within the dollhouse. The women who stayed like having her as a resource."

"Good. I think that's the easiest way to infiltrate

without causing too much attention." He looked at Rubble. "What do you think?"

Rubble seemed to mull it over for a moment, then nodded. "I agree. The cantina can be a decoy."

"Great. They've had Delphi for longer than I care to accept, so the sooner we're there, the sooner she's safe." Brewer glanced at Reaper, who sat quietly in his spot at the head of the table. "With your permission, of course."

Reaper held up his palms. "The club will vote."

A chorus of "Ayes" met Brewer's ears, and he felt a sudden bubbling in his stomach. He should've known the Cutthroats were at the helm of this all. Shovelhead warned them that a club would come for him, but clearly the man wasn't as significant as he thought himself to be. Delphi was ten times more important to everyone involved, but especially to Brewer. She could bake madeleines like a pro, but she couldn't handle a room full of bikers who didn't give a shit about her safety. He'd save her or die trying.

CHAPTER 38
DELPHI

"You've got to be kidding me." Delphi held up the slinky see-through shirt and the skirt short enough to show off every asset from the waist down. The pair of flip-flops was better than nothing but not optimal for a rainy day.

Granite shook his head. "Put it on. Daddy wants to meet you."

"Looking like a whore?"

"Nah, that's how I want you. He doesn't care." Granite clicked the safety on his gun, then shoved it into the small of his back.

"Are you going to watch me change?"

"Yep."

Delphi flipped him her middle finger, then turned around and shed her robe and silk pajamas. She held her breath when Granite reached over and grabbed a handful of her ass before she could pull the skirt on. Once the low-cut shirt was in place, she turned around to face him. "Done."

"Great. Let's go." He tugged on her hand, leading her down the hallway. The Rusty Cantina smelled the same as it had when she was with Granite. The musty scent of sex and cigarettes could never be cleaned out of the carpet.

They made it to the back exit, and he nodded to the dollhouse in the distance. "After you meet Daddy, you and I are gonna shake the walls over there." He wiggled his brows up and down. "Don't worry. I remember how you like it."

"If you even try, you'll regret it." She struggled at his hold, but he simply laughed.

"I don't think so." He opened a door to the left of the exit and shoved her in first. The door slammed behind him, closing off whatever hopes of an escape she could think up.

It took Delphi's eyes a moment to adjust to the murky lighting and smoke-filled room. "So, you're Delphi Windsor?"

She blinked several times. "Who's asking?"

A light flipped on overhead, and she finally could see the desk in the corner. A large man was sitting behind it. A cigarette hung in his left hand, his face obscured by the smoke swirling around him.

Delphi waved her hand, hoping to cut through it. It barely helped. The air itself hurt to breathe.

"I believe I'm your father." The man stood up and zipped his pants. Delphi rolled her eyes at the flash of brown hair from a doll beneath the desk. He took a step closer, his face finally cutting through the haze. He wasn't horrible looking. His hair was dark brown, almost black, and his eyes were the same hue. He wasn't short or tall, but of average height. He didn't look familiar, but then again, she didn't know all the Cutthroat members.

Delphi narrowed her eyes. "Why do you say that?"

"I'm Sully, by the way. The club treasurer." He walked closer but didn't extend his hand. Sitting on the edge of the desk, he continued. "I spent a lot of time with your mom back in the day." He took a hit from the cigarette. "I remember when she told me she was pregnant."

"And you thought I wasn't yours?"

Sully shook his head. "No, I knew you were mine. Your mom was more careful than most the club hoppers. She and I had a relationship of sorts. There was only one time we didn't use protection."

Delphi looked the man over and couldn't help but find a few similarities. She had the same curl to her hair, albeit a different color, and they shared the same nose. "Are you sure?"

"We did a paternity test back when you were born." He crushed the cigarette into an ashtray. "You're my daughter."

A swirl of emotions flooded through her. "You knew I was your daughter and you abandoned me?" She stepped forward and slapped him across the face.

"I didn't have a choice." He rubbed his chin but didn't seem put off by her reaction. "Your mom wanted a good man to be your father, and I wouldn't leave the club."

"Then you chose the club over your daughter."

He sighed. "I guess I did."

Delphi's hands shook, and she fought back the urge to cry and smack him again. "Why now? Why'd you wait until now to tell me the truth?"

Sully's head drooped, and he crossed his arms over his chest. "Because I'm dying. Lung cancer." He chuckled. "Can't say I'm surprised. Years of smoking will do that to a man. The doctors say I have a few months left."

She didn't know how to process this information. Her biological dad decided to make himself known, and within the year he'd be gone once again. "Why did you even bother to tell me? I could've lived my whole life and never met you." She snorted. "It probably would've been better too."

"I'm sorry. I know it's selfish, but...." He stopped and coughed. The sickening sound vibrated through Delphi's body. "I wanted to know you."

Straightening her shoulders, she thought over her options. This man may have aided in bringing her to life, but she didn't owe him anything other than gratitude for being a sperm donor.

"I don't think I want to know you." She watched Sully's face, but he didn't react. "You chose the club over me. You've had almost thirty-five years to meet me and get to know me. I'm sorry you're dying. If we had more time, maybe I could forgive you, but as things stand, I can't."

Delphi turned on her heels, but Granite stopped her hasty exit.

"I understand," Sully said from behind her. "I don't blame you either. I'm a shitty dad, but I got to meet you. If that's all I get, then I'll die with that memory. Your mom raised you right. I'm glad you didn't know me when you were a kid. You had a real dad, and he treated you much better than I ever would've."

The door opened, and she found herself scowling at a group of Cutthroats with guns in their hands.

"Granite, we got trouble," a man with stringy hair clinging to his face said. "Bikers headed this way."

"Is it who I think?"

"Yep."

Nodding to Sully, Granite pulled Delphi out of the room and into the hallway. She took a deep lungful of air, glad for the change in environment. Her pulse quickened at the sound of motorcycles pulling up in the parking lot. Even if they weren't Macha, she had a chance to escape if Granite had club business to attend to for a while.

"Let's get you to the dollhouse," Granite said, picking her up again.

"Dammit, man, I know how to walk."

"Yeah, but you're too slow. I gotta deal with some shitheads."

Delphi didn't say another word while Granite hurried them to the dollhouse not far away. The rain had picked up, drenching her by the time he deposited her on one of the beds and locked the door, leaving her alone.

Pacing the stingy room, she wracked her brain. She couldn't remember seeing Sully at the Cutthroat's clubhouse, but that didn't mean he wasn't there. She'd been so concerned with Shovel-head that she ignored the other men in the club.

Delphi crossed to the barred window and opened it. She needed fresh air if she was going to survive in the room for much longer. A throbbing ache crept into her head, and she rubbed her temples, hoping to make it disappear.

A slew of curse words escaped from the hallway, and she bit her bottom lip. If Macha was there like Granite said, surely, they'd come to rescue her. The sound of guns firing made her shrink further away from the door. If she had to, she'd hold her own. She could bite, kick, and claw at any Cutthroat who came to get her. She'd survive. She always had.

Letting out a shaky breath, Delphi couldn't wrap her mind around the last few hours. Her childhood was full of lies and deceit. Of course, she didn't find any fault with her mother for keeping her parentage a secret. Not when the sperm donor didn't give a damn.

Delphi's body begged for a nap, but the bed looked far from clean. She leaned against the wall with her face toward the open window. Stray rain-drops pelted her face, and she welcomed the refreshment.

The sounds of men yelling drifted down the hallway accompanied by gunfire echoing in every direction. She couldn't think about what was happening outside. It'd only make her feel worse about the situation. She should've stayed with Brewer, tucked safely in his arms until this whole mess was sorted out.

Thinking back to Sully's revelation, she shook her head. It didn't matter which man's blood coursed through her veins. Her father died last year. He wasn't biologically hers, but he treated her as such and never faltered when it came to loving her.

"I don't know why I cared so much about finding out," she said to the empty room.

"Because knowing your past helps form your future."

Delphi whirled around and didn't hold back her relieved cry at seeing Brewer in the doorway. His lip was bruised, and a trickle of blood pooled at the corner of his eye, but he was there. He'd come for her. She rushed over to him and jumped into his arms. He tightened them around her in the best vice grip she could imagine.

Brewer kissed the nape of her neck, then pulled her back. "Are you hurt?" His blue eyes scanned her while his hands did the same. "Did he touch you?"

"No, I'm fine." She gently wiped away the blood on his brow. "Are you all right?"

"I'm just dandy, sweet cheeks." He smirked, then

winced when it opened a cut on his bottom lip. "You should see the other guy."

Her brow furrowed in the cutest way. "How many did you take on?"

Brewer tucked her hair behind her ears. "As many as I needed to get to you."

Her cheeks flamed and then alarm flashed on her face when Hawk and Kevlar walked in. She quickly tried to hide her exposed flesh. Being naked in front of Brewer was one thing. She had no desire for his brothers to see her state of undress.

Seeing her dilemma, Brewer yanked her to him and pulled his jacket over them both. "Hawk, give me your sweatshirt."

The other man begrudgingly handed over his hooded sweatshirt, leaving him in only his cut.

Brewer gently slid the warm fabric over her shoulders. "Best I can do at the moment." He kissed her forehead. "Are you sure you're okay?"

Delphi nodded against him. "I met my dad. Well, the sperm donor, I should say."

"He's a Cutthroat?"

"The treasurer, Sully."

Cursing, Brewer hugged her again. "I'm sorry I wasn't here to protect you."

"You're here now. That's all that matters."

Brewer cupped the side of her face and kissed the tip of her nose. "Let's get you home."

"I couldn't agree more."

She wrapped her arm around his waist and leaned against him. They might not be out of danger yet, but with her Macha man by her side, Delphi would be perfectly safe.

CHAPTER 39
BREWER

Distracting the Greenback Cutthroats was easy. *It should be, at least.* Brewer glanced over his shoulder at the Macha bikers following him to the cantina. The plan was simple enough. There was no way they could sneak into the cantina without the Cutthroats seeing them. Hell, he'd bet the Cutthroats already knew they were on the way. They weren't exactly inconspicuous. Not with the way they were revving engines while dressed in full Macha MC gear.

When they reached the cantina, the bikers split into three groups, two of which immediately pulled the Cutthroats into a fight at the cantina while his group went to find Delphi. Thanks to their informant within the dollhouse, Brewer knew where they were keeping Delphi. *Thank the goddess for small favors.*

He'd have to pay his sister back for this one, but it was worth it. Delphi was worth all this and more.

They parked their bikes behind the dollhouse and hurried toward the side entrance. Brewer waited until Hawk and Kevlar made it safely before opening the door. It wasn't locked, thanks to Dolly's contact. Gunshots rang out and Brewer paused to look toward the cantina. His brothers would buy them as much time as they could.

Racing up the stairs, Brewer opened the door to the third floor and a fist greeted him. He staggered back, his eye pulsing from the blow. Hawk and Kevlar caught him before he toppled down the stairs.

"You get this guy," Hawk said, pushing him back up. "I'll sneak by and distract the next one."

Brewer nodded and opened the door again, this time ducking before the Cutthroat's fist connected. Hawk rushed out of the stairwell and down the hall. Two Cutthroats came out of rooms to chase him. If he hadn't been busy dodging blows, Brewer would have chuckled at the sight of Hawk running away from the hulking Cutthroats.

"Macha scum isn't allowed here," the Cutthroat biker said, throwing a wild punch.

Brewer jabbed the man in the gut and hook punched his jaw in response. The biker fell to his knees, and Kevlar took over by kneeing the man in the face.

"Hurry and find Delphi. I have a feeling the Cutthroats won't let us stay long," Kevlar said, pulling a gun from his waistband at the small of his back.

Nodding, Brewer raced down the hallway in the opposite direction Hawk had gone. He poked his head into a few rooms, coming up empty each time. More gunfire caught his attention and his pulse skyrocketed. These shots were from inside the building. He had to find Delphi.

Rounding a corner, he spied two Cutthroats outside a door at the end of the hallway. She was in there—he just knew it. Cracking his neck, he stepped out of the shadows and braced himself for the onslaught of Cutthroat fists. He wasn't worried. Hell, he trained with an ex-MMA fighter. He could hold his own long enough for help to arrive. One thing was certain: Brewer wasn't about the let anything else happen to Delphi. Not while he still breathed.

Seeing Delphi holed up in that room sent off a primal desire in Brewer's gut. She was his. He'd make it as official as she wanted, but his word was enough. Once they made it outside the dollhouse, Brewer loaded Delphi into the truck with Doc, shutting the door behind her.

Delphi rolled down the window, her cute nose wrinkled. "Wait, where are you going?"

"I drove my bike."

"Then I'll ride with you." She reached for the handle.

He shook his head. "Nah, you're not dressed for it." He kissed her quickly, then patted the side of the truck. "I'm right behind you."

She seemed to accept this, but he didn't bother adding the last part out loud. *And I have somebody's ass to kick.*

Brewer waited until the truck pulled onto the road before he turned toward the cantina. Setting his jaw, he made quick work of the distance and strode into the bar. The upbeat mariachi music did little to soothe his fiery temper. The walls held recently peppered bullets, reminding Brewer that he was walking into trouble. Thankfully, Rubble, Cueball, and Snoopy had his back, guns drawn and ready for more action. From the looks of it, the Cutthroats had waved the white flag moments earlier, their guns in the middle of the cantina protected by armed Macha bikers.

"I need to settle up with Granite," Brewer said, searching the bar for the man.

"Somebody lookin' for me?"

Turning, Brewer met Granite's gaze and didn't think—he just swung. The other man stumbled backward, but Brewer didn't let him fall. He followed him and grabbed his vest, punching him again and again. Blood spurted from Granite's nose and mouth, landing on Brewer's jacket. He didn't give Granite a chance to even get a return blow in. The other man collapsed into a booth, his face battered.

Pulling Granite up by his shirt, Brewer lowered his voice. "Stay the fuck away from my old lady, or I swear to the goddess you'll never use your dick again." He dropped his hold and let the other man fall limp into the booth.

Stumbling backward, Brewer fixed his jacket and wiped the blood from his fist. He glanced around the cantina and noticed the Cutthroats grew more agitated. They needed to get out of there before another fight broke out. Sully stepped forward and Brewer held back throwing a punch at the bastard.

"I suggest you leave, son," he said, the warning evident in his tone.

Brewer grabbed a mug of beer and downed it before he smashed the glass on the floor. "Happy to oblige."

The rest of Macha's crew followed him out the double doors. When the rain hit Brewer's face, he finally felt his fear and anger dissolve. *The Cutthroats won't fuck with Macha anytime soon.*

He found his bike and pulled on his helmet. There was one more thing he had to do today, and he sure as hell wasn't gonna miss it.

CHAPTER 40
DELPHI

Blood mixed with water dripped down Brewer's body and circled the shower drain. Delphi knew she should've let him shower alone, but the moment he stepped foot in the clubhouse, she spotted the blood all over his face and clothes.

His muscular body was tense despite the warm water. He scrubbed his face roughly, more red tinting the water. With his back to her, Delphi couldn't help but admire his perfection. The goddess sculpted this man with her in mind. He was everything she needed and more. Tattoos intertwined along his spine and nearly covered his back. His arms were fully sleeved. Hours of intense and brilliant work had been done to show off his dedication to the club.

Sliding the clothes from her body, Delphi opened the glass door and stepped inside. She wrapped her arms around his chest, hugging him from behind. "What happened?"

He placed a hand over hers. "I'm fine."

"I know that, but what happened?" She kissed the Macha tattoo on his shoulder, her hand snaking to his stomach.

Brewer turned to face her, the water spraying his hair and turning it darker than his usual red. "I got into a fight."

Delphi lifted her brow. "About what?"

He lifted his hand and gently brushed his knuckles across the top of her breasts. "You, Delphi. Since the moment I met you, everything I've done is for you."

"But why'd you get in a fight?"

Brewer's eyes flashed. "Because that mother-fucker took you against your will and would've...." He stopped and looked away, clearly unable to complete the horrible thought.

Pushing back his wet curls, she tilted his chin toward her. His blue eyes were so full of emotion that it scared her to keep staring into them. "He didn't. You saved me."

"Will you at least triple lock your door from now on? Please." He reached around and cupped her ass.

She chuckled. "No."

"Delphi."

She hugged him, adoring the way his brows furrowed at her. "No. Because you're going to be with me to make sure it never happens again."

The worry washed away from his face, and he beamed at her. "I love you so fucking much, it shouldn't be legal."

Delphi laced her fingers in his hair and pulled his mouth closer. "I love you, Brewer Stapleton, and I promise I'll always deadbolt the door from this day forward."

His mouth closed over hers, and Delphi moaned at the sensation. Never had a man moved her so much by a single kiss. *He isn't a mere man. He's a Macha man.*

Delphi's tongue tangled with his, and she gasped when he pinched her nipple. She replied by grabbing his hardening cock and stroking it gently.

"You sure you wanna do this here, sweet cheeks?" He pointed to the transparent door. "Anybody could see. And I don't exactly keep condoms in the shower."

"I don't care." She knelt and his dick bobbed appreciatively. "You're my man. I don't want anything between us anymore."

"What about—"

She swallowed his cock, silencing his question. She didn't need protection from him.

"Fuck, Delphi." He groaned when she swirled her tongue along the top of his length.

"Damn, that's good." He placed a hand on the top of her head. He didn't push forward to make her gag. She did that on her own, sliding his length to the back of her throat until tears dripped down her cheeks.

"I wanna come down your throat, but I wanna fuck that pussy more." Brewer helped her to her feet and kissed her hard.

His kiss instantly made her light-headed and she clung to Brewer. Her back hit the shower wall, his fingers sliding in and out of her drenched pussy. "Fuck, I'll never get tired of this," he said.

Moaning, she wrapped her legs around his waist. "Please, Brewer. I need to feel you."

He smiled and rubbed his cock against her entrance. "You have no idea how bad I need to feel you too."

Before Delphi could reply, he entered her with one forceful thrust. She cried out and Brewer was there to swallow her sounds. He withdrew and thrust in again and again. While his cock pleasured her pussy, his fingers danced along her clit, encouraging her to break free and shatter around him. She rocked her hips to meet his thrusts, and suddenly, she couldn't move. Her orgasm ripped through her body, paralyzing her with pleasure.

"You're mine, Delphi. Don't you fucking forget it," he said breathlessly, his strokes faster while she rode out the delicious wave he created within her pussy.

Just before he let himself go, Brewer pulled out and sprayed her breasts with his seed. The white drizzled down her stomach, the sight too beautiful to be wrong.

Legs weakened, Delphi leaned on Brewer until they both caught their breath. "Think anybody heard us?"

Brewer's laughter filled the bathroom. He cupped her face and tenderly kissed her. "Frankly, sweet cheeks, I don't give a shit. As long as you're mine, I'm a happy man."

"How do you feel about Sully?"

Delphi fluffed her pillow and didn't bother to give the clock another glance. It was three in the morning, but time seemed to stand still when she was with Brewer. They'd napped a bit after their second round in the bedroom and neither seemed to mind losing sleep.

"I don't feel anything." She rested her head on Brewer's chest, her left leg draped over his. "He didn't care about me until his life was about to end. I think that says enough about how he feels."

Brewer traced lazy circles on her arm. "He's a dumbass, that's for damn sure. You're the best thing since, well…. You're just the best thing."

She looked up at him and grinned. "Kiss ass."

He wiggled his brows. "Yeah, I'll be kissing that ass of yours soon enough."

Rolling her eyes, Delphi snuggled in closer. She didn't need a blanket. He emitted enough heat to warm them both.

"Well, if you ever wanna talk about Sully or your parents, I'm all ears."

She leaned up on her elbow. "I know. I just hate dwelling on the past. My parents were amazing. They gave me the best life they could and protected me. I can't ask for anything better than that."

"It sounds like you're content, then."

Kissing his nipple, she nodded. "Very content."

"Girl, don't go starting something again. We do have to get up in a few hours. Some people have work." He poked her stomach. "You, not me."

Delphi laughed. She was looking forward to getting back into the swing of things with her restaurant. Thanks to Macha, all the windows had been repaired and it was time to return to work. It'd been her only focus for so long, but now she knew she could have more than one.

"How's this? If you tell me the truth about the election, I won't do anything sexy to you. But if you lie, I'll do very naughty things."

"Delphi, I don't care about that stuff."

Lifting her brows, she stuck her tongue out and slowly traced his right nipple, then the left.

"I swear."

Her tongue wiggled down his chest to his stomach.

"Delphi, I'm not one for politics."

She slid down his boxers, his cock already bouncing approvingly at her actions. "Don't lie to me." She licked his balls and grinned at his immediate reaction.

"I can't be president or VP. It wouldn't be right."

Opening her mouth, Delphi kept his gaze as she slowly put his dick in her mouth. She sucked on it slowly, working up and down his shaft. Brewer's face pinched when she increased pressure, her cheeks hollowing as her head bobbed.

"All right, all right," Brewer gasped, legs tense from holding in his release. "I'd like to be in the cabinet, but I don't think I can handle either role. They're both very important to the club."

Delphi paused and his cock popped out of her mouth. "You might've never had the chance to be a leader, but you are one, Brewer. I've known it from the day I met you. Everyone listens to you. They respect you." She pumped his dick in her hand. "If they're not smart enough to elect you, that's their fault. But you're worthy, Brewer." She placed a small kiss on his cock. "Very worthy."

Crooking his finger to beckon her closer, Brewer watched while she unhurriedly crawled up the bed. She brushed his thighs with her breasts, teasing him. It was too much fun to see the lust take over his face.

"Dammit, woman, get up here. I need you now." He grabbed Delphi's hips, making her squeal when his long erection poked her ass. She wasn't worried. No matter what they did, Brewer would always keep her safe. "You are my goddess, Delphi. I don't deserve you, but I'm damned glad you're here with me."

She stroked his beard, the wiry curls reminding her of what they felt like against her pussy. "I think we're both pretty lucky."

He kissed down the side of her neck, flaring her desire. Her breasts ached to be touched. "Last time, then you have to get some sleep. I don't want the owner to fall asleep in the soup."

Delphi giggled but stopped when he guided his

hard cock toward her entrance. Her mouth watered just thinking about the sensations he'd elicit in mere seconds. Her pussy quivered in excitement.

Lifting herself up, she grabbed his cock and sank down on him with a satisfied moan. Riding him was one of her favorite positions. There was just something about a warm, hard man between her legs that sent her heart racing. She rocked her hips and knew without a doubt, she'd never love anyone but Brewer.

CHAPTER 41
BREWER

Brewer swore it was the best spring day in years. Of course, that could've been partially due to the woman glued to his arm. She'd just finished up the dinner rush at the restaurant and hauled her sweet ass over to the clubhouse for the final tallies.

He fidgeted in his seat, the bottle of Guinness warming in his hands. Delphi squeezed his free hand three times, silently encouraging him. So far, he'd received a few head nods from the retired Macha bikers, Guz and Tiny Tim. They were the ones who'd announce the new cabinet. It was a Macha tradition, and one he both admired and feared.

"The last votes have been cast and counted," Reaper said above the hum of the clubhouse. It was filled to the brim with bikers and their families. "I'd like to thank all of you for giving me the chance to be your president." He motioned for his old lady, and Queenie parted the crowd to be next to him. "Queenie and I will tinker around the clubhouse until the new cabinet is in order, but we have plans to travel, so everybody behave."

Laughter filled the air and momentarily lifted the tension. It wasn't a populous race, but Brewer knew it was a close one.

Reaper pulled off his president patch and handed it to Guz. "It's been my honor. May the goddess ride with you."

Tears pricked Brewer's eyes as he repeated the phrase. Looking over at Delphi, he noticed her wiping at her eyes along with many others women in attendance.

Guz unfolded a piece of paper and cleared his throat. "For the role of secretary and treasurer: Kevlar."

The crowd remained silent. Only after the new president's name would they react.

"For the role of sergeant at arms: Rubble." Guz looked across the crowd. "For the role of vice president: Doc."

Brewer's stomach flipped and sweat formed on his brow. He couldn't look at Delphi but felt her gaze on him.

"And for the role of president: Brewer."

Macha's clubhouse roared with cheers. A keg of beer flowed to Brewer's left, and his brothers congratulated him, but he couldn't move. He was too dumbfounded to know if he heard correctly or if his ears were playing tricks on him.

"Brewer!" Delphi tugged on his arm, snapping him back to reality. "You won, you beautiful man." She kissed him passionately, whoops and catcalls directed their way.

Coming up for air, he grinned. It was all hitting him hard. He was Macha's president. His heart fluttered like it had the first time he rode a Harley.

Reaper walked over to him and hugged him tight. "Well done, boyo. Your parents would be so proud. I can't wait to see what you do with Macha."

Brewer fought back tears and smiled. "Thank you, Reaper." He hugged him tight. Even if he wasn't ready for this kind of leadership, his club thought he could do the job and do it well.

Reaper let go and his brothers huddled around him, laughing and passing drinks around. Brewer managed to shake the hands of his fellow cabinet members between rounds.

"You're the best choice for president," Doc said above the crowd. "Being your second-in-command will be an honor."

"So, you're not disappointed?"

Doc laughed. "Nah, brother. Isa and our baby girl keep me on my toes. I have a feeling Isa's going to surprise me with another kid soon. I'm happy to be second."

Relief coursed through Brewer. He'd always thought the presidency was Doc's birthright. As it turned out, it was his instead.

Rubble and Kevlar were equally pleased to be among the cabinet.

"We all knew Rubble would get it. Until another badass comes along, you'll always be sergeant," Kevlar said good-naturedly.

Rubble clapped Kevlar on the back. "And you get to manage the money. I'm not sure if I should cry or laugh."

Kevlar flipped off Rubble, but the men were too excited to fight. Brewer was happy to let them. This was what he'd always wanted. A place within Macha not just for bragging rights, but to make a difference. With his brothers at his side, Brewer knew their future was bright.

Dolly's smiling face greeted him after the new cabinet took shots of whiskey.

"You did it, big brother." She lightly punched him. "I'm proud of you."

He kissed the top of her head. "And I'm going to

be reviewing those bylaws about women in the club I can't lose you, sis."

She hugged him. "You won't. My girl's kinda stuck on Snowshoe, so I'll be around town somewhere."

Brewer smiled over at Yasmina, grateful that his sister found happiness through the club. *Macha always provides.* It's what his dad used to say, and Brewer finally realized what it meant.

Making his way through the loud crowd, Brewer found Delphi chatting with Isa and Nikita. The sight of her holding Isa's baby made his heart swell. Someday, they'd have their very own Macha brood, but not yet. He wanted her all to himself for a few years. He'd waited his whole life to find someone as sweet, stunning, and sassy as Delphi. He could wait to share her.

"Hey, there you are, Mr. President." Delphi beamed at him and handed off the baby to Isa. "Want me to reenact that Marilyn Monroe bit?"

Brewer chuckled, tucking her under his arm. "Not tonight, but plan on it for my birthday. For now, I wanna show you something."

Delphi's left brow cocked. "Oh, yeah? What's that?"

Guiding her away from the hubbub of celebration and music, Brewer waited until they were outside to pull a sheet of paper from his pocket. "Open it."

Taking the paper, she slowly unfurled it, a smile never leaving her cute face. Reading the contents, she looked up at him. "I don't understand. What is this?"

"I thought it was pretty obvious. All in black-and-white, spelled out."

"It says you bought a piece of land." Her eyes darted to the words, then back to him. "Right next to my restaurant."

Taking her hand in his, Brewer knelt, and Delphi's eyes bugged. "Calm down, I'm not asking that question." She seemed somewhat relieved until he added, "Yet."

Meeting her gorgeous eyes, Brewer kissed the top of her hand. "Delphi, I wanna build a life with you. Since I'm president now, there's gonna be a ton of time spent at the clubhouse, and of course you have your restaurant, and I don't want you to feel like you have to choose one over the other." He cleared his throat. "So, I bought a piece of land for us. You can design the house however you want, and it'll be our spot. Not the club's, not the restaurant's, but ours. And maybe in a few years, we'll start a family, and they can grow up there, in between our two passions."

Tears raced down Delphi's cheeks. "Are you serious?"

"Always with you, sweet cheeks."

Delphi knelt and kissed him so hard he almost lost his balance. "I'll take that as a yes."

"I love you, Brewer."

He pushed back the hair from her face, this woman more important to him than life itself. "I love you, Delphi. Now, let's go make this night one to remember."

Pulling her to her feet, Brewer didn't mind one bit when his lady led him in the direction of his room instead of the bustling party in the clubhouse. With her, every day was a celebration.

EPILOGUE

BREWER

The bright Colorado sun dipped behind the Rocky Mountains just as Brewer shut off his Harley. He patted the beast of a machine for good measure. After a somewhat successful meeting with the Greenback Cutthroats, he and his men were in dire need of sustenance.

Hawk whistled at a nymph who was walking across the parking lot. The short girl with blonde hair winked and Hawk hurried after her.

Chuckling, Brewer knew every man in Macha deserved a bit of sexual attention after the day they had. Coming to a peace agreement with the Cutthroats hadn't been easy. It took most of the day, and no one came out the clear victor. With Shovelhead officially out of both clubs, it was easy to hand the man off to the Feds for prosecution. The traitor wouldn't see the light of day without bars in front of him for the rest of his life. It didn't satisfy every man's need for blood, but Macha agreed it was the best route.

Thinking back to the agreement, he sighed. Each club would mind their own, like before, except now, Macha would keep closer tabs on the neighboring MC. The enforceability was shaky, but the truce would hold up for a year or two. *Or until they elect a new president.*

The clubhouse was loud and rambunctious, but he wouldn't want it any other way. This was what he'd grown up in and what he inherited. He'd make his parents proud, but more importantly, he'd make himself proud.

"Hey, Prez, you want next game?" Cueball asked from the pool table where it looked like he and Snoopy were losing to Kevlar and Nikita.

Grabbing a cold beer from one of the nymphs, Brewer nodded. "Sure. It'll give Delphi some easy practice."

Kevlar smirked, but Cueball was less than amused. Still, the other man didn't argue or snap back. Not any longer. Not when Macha's members looked to Brewer for leadership. Only three months into his presidency, and he wasn't used to the responsibilities and perks associated with the gig.

Leaning against the far wall, he watched the members mill about. Each one had a jovial attitude even if they were losing at a game. Children ran among the bikers, the sight truly one ripped from his childhood.

Doc and Isa were chatting in the kitchen, and Brewer noticed the two canoodling. Her Irish lilt was too familiar to be foreign anymore. Brewer smiled behind the bottle of beer. Even if she was only his distant cousin, he wanted the best for her. And it appeared Doc was it.

During her short time in Macha, Isa had completely transformed their clothing store and made a killing at it. He couldn't be happier. Especially since he now had the inside track on all the club's doings. It wouldn't be long before Doc and Isa announced that another baby was soon to be added to Macha.

From the corner of his eye, Brewer noticed Nikita dancing around the pool table. Glancing over, he grinned at the sight of the FBI agent turned old lady bragging about her recent victory. Kevlar stood beside her with a knowing look on his face. He was lucky to end up with the badass woman.

Brewer finished his drink and headed toward the kitchen. The hallway bustled with the activity of both members and the nymphs they were chasing down the stairs. He didn't miss that part of the club. Some men might, but Brewer was perfectly happy with one woman warming his bed every night.

A gust of warm air met him before he reached the kitchen. Rubble's big form filled the doorway without even trying. The club's sergeant at arms nodded once, not bothering to address the bassinet filled with pink and blue baby clothes in his arms. His old lady, Jupiter, wasn't far behind him. Though her belly wasn't overly obtrusive, she'd already started to waddle a bit when she walked. Out of all his brothers, Rubble was the one Brewer never imagined would be tamed by a woman.

Brewer let them pass without a word, a secret smile on his face. All his brothers were knocking up these beautiful women and adding to Macha's lineage. It filled him with hope for the future of the club.

"Either of you seen Delphi yet?" he asked, interrupting Doc talking to Isa's flat stomach.

Doc jumped to his feet. "Uh, no, not recently."

"Last I knew she was at the bakery," Isa said with a shrug. "Which reminds me, Doc, Queenie's dropping off Cliodhna in a few minutes, so if you want to do that thing, we'd better hurry."

In one smooth move, Doc lifted Isa off her feet

and over his shoulder. "Gotta go, Prez. Time without the baby is minimal. Chat with you later."

Brewer waved them off and shook his head. He never thought Doc would settle down, but Isa was just the woman for the job.

"Yo, Prez, your old lady's out front, asking for you," Klink called from the door.

Not bothering to grab another drink, Brewer made his way through the clubhouse and out to the lot. Sure enough, Delphi was sitting astride his bike, her hair flowing in the breeze. She hadn't seen him yet, so he took a moment to merely soak in her beauty. The cut on her shirt hinted at her breasts instead of flaunting them. *But those jeans.* He let out his breath. They hugged her thick thighs and equally lavish ass.

As if sensing his gaze, Delphi looked over and a shy smile crossed her lips. "Hey, you. Got time for a short ride?"

Brewer made quick work of the distance between them and handed her a helmet. "For you, always. Where to?"

"Our place."

Knowing the spot, he hopped on and donned a helmet. Delphi settled in behind him, her arms loose around his waist. The engine roared beneath them, and Brewer took off down the street, shifting gears quickly. He wasn't sure why she wanted to see the barren land, but he'd be damned if he didn't oblige. He'd do anything for his old lady. A truth they both knew well.

***

DELPHI

A shiver tickled through Delphi the closer they got to the spot of land directly next to her restaurant. It'd taken a bit of work and haggling between the two of them to decide on the layout of the house. So far, no construction had started, since they hadn't come to a full agreement. *Yet.* She hugged Brewer a little tighter. For as long as she could remember, having a home filled with babies and friends was all she'd wanted. *Dreams change and I along with them.*

The bike rolled to a stop and Brewer cut the engine. "What's all this?"

Instead of answering, she jumped off and rested the helmet on the back of the Harley. "Come on. I want to show you something."

She turned to see his apprehensive face, but he followed her nonetheless. A giddy laugh bubbled inside her and she tamped it down. The entire lot was filled with lit tea candles. A lone table sat in the middle with two chairs accompanying it.

"Delphi?" Brewer's brows rose. "Did I forget an anniversary?"

"Nope." She chuckled and led him to the table. Pastries filled the center along with two plates and glasses ready for use. "But I'd like to make an anniversary starting tonight."

"For what?"

They both sat down, and Delphi felt the flutter of butterflies in her stomach. "I'd like to officially move in with you. I understand your role in the club is more important now, but I'd like to be there when you fall asleep and wake up."

Brewer leaned forward in his chair, blue eyes twinkling with mischief. "That is a good idea, but—"

"But?"

He grabbed her hands and kissed the tops. "But I want something more permanent." He looked around the grass, the candles flickering in the wind. "And damn if you didn't set it up perfectly."

Delphi's palms started to sweat. She suddenly needed a drink to calm her nerves.

Brewer fished something out of his pants and stood up, taking her with him. "Delphi Windsor, you're the only woman for me. From the first time I set eyes on you, I knew it too." His gaze searched hers. "And I don't want to lose you—ever. Marry me, Delphi, because I want to have babies with you and get old and cranky together someday."

She laughed, and tears filled her eyes. "Did you seriously just say you wanted to be cranky with me?"

He kissed her forehead. "Fuck yeah. There's nothing more romantic than two old people yelling at kids to get off their lawn."

He did have a point. It wasn't the best or most romantic of proposals for some people, but it was perfect and honest, and one she couldn't say no to even if she wanted to.

Brewer chuckled and knelt. "All right, fine. I'll do it the club way." He held up a diamond ring. "Be my old lady, Delphi. I swear I'll do everything in my power to keep you safe. You'll always be loved by me."

The tears she'd been holding back rushed forth and she nodded. "Yes. Yes, to both."

Standing back up, Brewer kissed her until the sounds of the night air became mere background noise. When he pulled back, Delphi swore under her breath.

"Get used to more kisses like that, old lady," Brewer said, pinching her ass. "I save the best for last."

Giggling, she wrapped her arms around his neck. "Then kiss me again, Brewer."

"Whatever you say, sweet cheeks."

Delphi sighed into his embrace. He wasn't the man she expected to settle down with, but he was the man who had stolen her heart and challenged her every step of the way. Brewer slowly lowered them onto the grass, his lips never leaving her skin. If this was the standard for all Macha men, she was damned lucky to be part of the club.

Brewer nipped her bottom lip, making her gasp. She could get used to being worshipped on the daily. Macha was to thank for many things that went right in Snowshoe, but Delphi would forever be grateful to the goddess for the gift of Brewer. *Maybe being a president's wife won't be so bad after all.*

I hope you've loved getting to know my bikers. Looking for more bad boys? I can't wait for you to meet Cameron in Appointed by Fate.

ACKNOWLEDGMENTS

Thank you so very much to my readers. I'm blown away by the support and hunger from all of you. It's sad to say goodbye to Macha MC, but don't worry, there's more MC on the way. A huge shout-out to my publisher, editors, beta readers, and everyone involved in making this story a book. You consistently push me forward, and I'm forever grateful.

ABOUT THE AUTHOR

Skye McNeil began writing at the age of seventeen and has been lost in a love affair ever since. During the day, she moonlights as a paralegal at a law firm favoring criminal law.

Skye enjoys writing romantic comedies and cozy mysteries novels that leave readers wanting more and falling in love over and over. She writes contemporary and historical novels ranging from sweet and sassy to steamy and sultry.

Her constant writing companions are two cats and Australian Shepherd. When she's not writing, Skye enjoys spending time with family, photography, volleyball, traveling, and curling up with a cup of coffee and reading.

WEBSITE: WWW.SKYEMCNEIL.COM

FACEBOOK READERS GROUP: HTTPS://BIT.LY/2WE93R3

ABOUT THE PUBLISHER

Hot Tree Publishing loves love. Publishing adult romantic fiction, HTPubs are all about diverse reads featuring heroes and heroines to swoon over. Since opening in 2015, HTPubs have published more than 300 titles across the wide and diverse range of romantic genres. If you're chasing a happily ever after in your favourite subgenre, HTPubs have you covered.

Interested in discovering more amazing reads brought to you by Hot Tree Publishing? Head over to the website for information:

WWW.HOTTREEPUBLISHING.COM

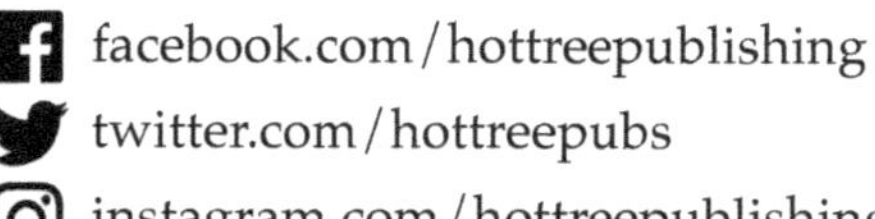

facebook.com/hottreepublishing
twitter.com/hottreepubs
instagram.com/hottreepublishing

www.ingramcontent.com/pod-product-compliance
Lightning Source LLC
Chambersburg PA
CBHW060731190726
48285CB00001B/152